A GOOD PLACE FOR THE NIGHT

STORIES BY
SAVYON LIEBRECHT

Translated from the Hebrew by Sondra Silverston

A Karen and Michael Braziller Book
PERSEA BOOKS / NEW YORK

First published in the original Hebrew in 2002 by Keter (Jerusalem). Published in the English language in 2005 by Persea Books, Inc. (New York) by arrangement with Savyon Liebrecht and The Institute for the Translation of Hebrew Literature.

Persea Books, Inc.
853 Broadway
New York, New York 10003

Library of Congress Cataloging-in-Publication Data
Liebrecht, Savyon, 1948–
A good place for the night : stories / Savyon Liebrecht ; translated from the Hebrew by Sondra Silverston.—1st American
p. cm.
"A Karen and Michael Braziller book."
ISBN 0-89255-320-0 (original trade pbk. : alk. paper)
1. Liebrecht, Savyon, 1948—Translations into English. I.
Silverston, Sondra. II. Title.
PJ5054.L444A27 2006
892.4'36—dc22   2005021802
Designed by Rita Lascaro. Typeset in Garamond.
Printed on recycled, acid-free paper.
Manufactured in the United States of America.
First Printing

PRAISE FOR SAVYON LIEBRECHT

A Man and A Woman and A Man

"A finely wrought novel. . . . strikes an original note."
—*Washington Post Book World*

"Insightful and compelling."   —*Bloomsbury Review*

"A major voice in Israeli fiction is emerging here.
—*Kirkus* (starred review)

"Exquisite reading."   —*Midwest Book Review*

"Liebrecht is a powerful and intelligent writer... Having loved her stories, I am happy to love her novel."   —Grace Paley

"[This novel] reveals the light within darkness and old age... Liebrecht plucks the raw nerves of love and of the forbidden that becomes allowed."   —Yoram Kaniuk

"Universal and yet intensely Israeli... [her work] displays great originality, and Liebrecht's simple style . . . makes her accessible to the general reader."   —*Jewish Book World*

"Compelling, intelligent."   —*Forward*

"Liebrecht mines her material to great and rewarding psychological depth. . . . a true and resonant and meaningful story... [She] knows how to snag a reader and maintain interest with a sure storyteller's skill."   —*Jerusalem Post*

"Radiant and pristine—ready to be read, absorbed, and discussed."
—*Hadassah Magazine*

Apples from the Desert

"Liebrecht has perfect pitch. . . . She takes you places you have never been before."   —*New York Times Book Review*

"Rich, exciting, believable stories. . . . that take you through the lives of real people to the heart of their emotional and moral being."
—*Washington Post Book World*

Contents

A GOOD PLACE FOR THE NIGHT

America

Here is my truth, and as of now, my only one; your truth and even you yourself don't exist yet. My mother is sitting up straight beside the board my father fastened to the table for her, smoothing a piece of black and white checked cloth over it and declaring smugly, "They say that checks are in style now, so let them have checks," as if, unwillingly, she were accepting the taste of the masses. In the first five lessons of a sewing class, she's learned to move her hands over the cloth like a skilled dressmaker. My father and I watch her reverently as she picks up the cloth, a disapproving expression on her face, and narrows her eyes to examine a single rebellious thread, ready to denounce the negligent weaver.

"There's this woman from Bialystok in our class——" She grants the weaver a reprieve and goes back to stretching the fabric on the board. We're standing behind her, but she doesn't deign to turn her head. Accustomed to our total admiration, she knows we always listen to her, standing behind her like two servants, and she doesn't even bother to raise her voice for us. "She's in her fifth month and comes specifically to make a maternity dress because all of a sudden her clothes are too small. She thought her stomach would stay flat till the ninth month because in the ghetto her sister didn't have a stomach even when she gave birth. That Bialystok talks a lot of nonsense. She dreamed she was carrying a girl and when she woke up, she wanted gum, so she believes someone's sitting up in heaven and sending her signs, and she already has a name for the girl— " She burst out laughing and turned to us, an actress about to check out her audience's loyalty. "Like the name on that yellow chewing gum wrapper with the picture of a girl's profile on it, Talma, or something like that. Not Talma—Alma."

And that's how you, Alma Roth, appear in my life, four months before you're born, thirty-four months before everything falls apart. But meanwhile, all of us, two families—two couples and two little girls—are living through their last months of peace and quiet. You are still hidden in the depths of a swelling body; your father is tending to your mother like a devoted nurse. My mother is happy with her piece of checked cloth and another piece she'll soon find in navy blue; I learn to ride a bike in a matter of minutes and my father is bursting with pride: five years old and already so accomplished.

*   *   *

The nameplate in front of you on the lectern says "Alma Roth," and you bend over it, casting a shadow on it, shade your eyes from the dazzling spotlight, and examine your audience intently. The last time we saw each other, you were almost blind with tears. For a minute, I think your eyes pass over me. Even if they linger on me, I doubt that you'll recognize me. My hair's a different color from what it was then. Even my name's different. Only the memories stay as they were, frozen like the last photograph of a young man who's been killed.

For years I've been taking an interest in various aspects of survival, attracted mainly to studies of the mechanism of repression. I occasionally go to a periodicals library to look for material. A young librarian who already knows me compiles short lists for me. The last time, he promised to show me how to find articles on the Internet. The clean, convenient, professional jargon defines things the way strong iron cages confine wild animals. But sometimes—always when exhausted or dreaming—I'm trapped by memories rising within me like a silent but sudden and dangerous tide that overflows the barriers of organized words and floods the chaos my life became. They are memories of that time when my mother and your father left my father and your mother, packed their bags and in an instant, as if they'd decided by the flip of a coin, divided the girls, who are us, between them. I was seven and a half, and you were two. Still feeling our way in our new world, we were already starting to construct for ourselves the separate truths of our life stories.

Thirteen years later, we'd hurl those truths at one another, beginning with the very first moment of our parents' story, the moment that dragged both of us into it the way a bucking horse drags its rider: the meeting between my mother and your father.

In my version, he comes to the sewing class one evening to take his wife home. The days have grown shorter and night falls quickly, and he's afraid your mother, whose stomach has already begun to make your presence known, might trip and fall in the dark. But he doesn't hurry your mother to collect her things and, to tell the truth, he forgets what brought him to that place because, over the row of heads—as if struck by lightning—he sees my mother, already wearing the new checked dress that fits her as perfectly as if she were a mannequin. She's bending over the sewing table, diligently basting a piece of navy blue cloth. In my version, the room and the twelve women holding pins between lips pursed as if for a kiss, vanish for him at that moment, as do the two hard-working instructors, walking from table to table, bending over to check stitches. Your mother vanishes too, and you in her stomach. Only my mother is left. As she focuses on the rebellious piece of cloth that will thwart her plan to turn it into a dress and force her to make do with a skirt, even before she raises her head and sees him, she becomes a part of his life. But at the time, biting the tip of her tongue in concentration, she still doesn't know that the man about to turn her life and the lives of her husband and five-year-old daughter upside down is standing there and staring at her, bewitched.

In your version, your father comes to the sewing class around the time it is ending to take your mother home. She shows him the paper pattern she cut for the maternity blouse she's going to make, and he's impressed. On the other side of the table, my mother glances at the handsome man, watches with a heart bursting with envy as he drapes a shawl around his wife and together they turn to go down to the dark street. All week her mind is feverish with plans. At the next class, my mother, who has ignored your mother's existence until then, suddenly begins treating her graciously. Your mother, grateful for the friendship, invites my mother, her husband, and her young daughter, who is me, to her house. And there, sitting prettily with her legs crossed, showing her thigh through the slit in her navy blue skirt, my mother goes to war for your father, pursuing him shamelessly, embarrassing everyone with her seductiveness. She won't leave him alone until she can carry out her plan, conquer him and come between him and his wife. After you are born, she'll go to tend to the weak new mother, to fill the head of the young father, exhausted from sleepless nights because of the baby's crying, with stories about her America. Without any pangs of conscience, she'll watch your mother clutching your father and she'll see how, as he slips out of her grasp, your mother gradually sinks into despair, loses the spark of life, and starts neglecting her baby girl. But my mother won't be able to come between him and his child, and after she leaves her husband and her own daughter, she'll have to take the child she doesn't know, who is you, as punishment, an eternal reminder of her sin.

Beyond the two truths, both equally possible, there exists one fact: two and a half years after that meeting at the sewing class, my mother is standing on the sidewalk in front of our building, suitcases and many packages at her feet. My father, very pale, helps the driver strap them onto the top of the taxi, ignores the hand my mother holds out to him in farewell, and turns toward the house. I keep calling silently to God, enlisting His help, aware the entire time that curious children are gathering around us, that heads keep appearing in windows, and I can't stop myself from holding onto her, my arms gripping her waist as if I'm trying to solder myself to her body. Her face covered with tears, she hugs me, too. I sob, "When will you come back, Mama?" and she says, "As soon as I can," and still crying, she tries to tear herself from my clutching arms.

At that moment, there is a sharp burst of explosions. I'm sure that God, answering my prayers, is now destroying the entire street, the taxi, the suitcases and bundles, and I close my eyes tightly, bracing myself for the blow. A very long time later, I open them and find, to my surprise, that everything is still standing where it was. A minute later, there's the sound of another explosion, this time from inside my body, as if my bones are being crushed and the fragments piling up under my skin. My mother must have gotten loose from me, because my hands are free, moving on their own over my body and finding it whole. The expected pain does not come either. I feel as if a long time has passed, but it turns out to be only a few seconds, because my mother is now sliding into the back seat, her head almost touching the roof on top of which her life has been loaded. Through a haze, I watch the taxi move away like a giant insect fleeing for its life, and I run a little way after it, fall and scream, "M-a-m-a," my voice a shrill solo over the chorus of cries coming from the children and the people at their windows. I get up and stare at the place where the taxi had stood and, almost blind, cross the circle of children crowding around me and run home, both knees bleeding. At the bare kitchen table—the cloth has been taken off, folded, and packed into one of the suitcases—sits my father, his back to the door, his shoulders shaking with silent weeping.

I stand behind him and reach out to touch his shoulder, but at that moment, my hand still in the air, I again hear the sounds of destruction bursting from inside my body. Because it isn't painful, I pay attention this time, curious, fascinated by the unfamiliar thing happening to me: my body is splitting open like a nut whose shell is cracked. The two halves separate, exposing raw flesh. Frightened, I watch as my body splits away and becomes completely alien to me. I know I have to get myself back inside quickly before my father turns around and sees that his daughter too has disappeared and standing in her place is a cracked creature whose innards are exposed to the world, as helpless as the turtle we once found in the sand, separated from its shell after some children had tortured it. The raw flesh suddenly moves and something rising from within it takes shape. Stunned, I look at my double, my identical twin, as it rises and stands beside me, raging, wild, red-eyed. There is an air of resolve about her that I don't have, a power I don't have, but, looking into each other's eyes, we both know that she is completely under my control. I examine her in astonishment, wondering whether she's an enemy or an ally. My father lets out a sob. I raise my hand, a queen commanding, and she passes obediently back into me. Then, strengthened and standing tall, I put my hand on my father's shoulder.

I cried in the darkness all that night, rubbing the knees my father had bandaged, confused by the events of the day, hardly believing they had really happened. I was frightened by the unfamiliar sensations flooding me, as if I'd lost my old place and still didn't have a new one, remembering over and over again how my mother had struggled to get away from me, how the children had crowded around me, how my father had cried, how my own image had emerged from inside me and had split away and become a very constant presence since then, still not revealing whether she was an enemy or an ally. Even though I was aware, like a wild animal trainer, of the danger of her fury, I also knew that she'd always stand beside me, loyal and decisive, hinting that, if I wanted her to, she would take me places where I could be calm, perform magic, make anything I wanted disappear with a wave of my hand, escape from what I was seeing and choose to see something else. That knowledge, I understand many years later, became the source of my strength. Meanwhile, on that night, curled up like a fetus on my bed that was pushed up against the wall of the closed-off balcony, both of us witnessed the moment of birth of the small whirlpool that would grow and strengthen, diminish and weaken, but would never disappear for a minute during all the years that would follow. It began to form in my belly soon after the clock struck midnight, growing inside a small seed like the eye of a storm, showing me that the focus of my longing for my mother

was not in my heart or my mind, but in the depths of my stomach, directly behind my navel, in a very specific place I once
pointed to for my father. I must have fallen asleep in the early
morning, knowing that I would have to get used to the permanent, drilling motion deep in my belly that would become completely natural, and although all the good things that would
happen in my life might dim its echoes, they would never be able
to remove it from my body, just as they would never be able to
remove it from my memory. Sometimes, in the flickering
moments of later happiness, I'd be tempted to test its existence. I'd
listen, imagine it had disappeared, but always, as if there were an
ancient landmine buried directly behind my navel, I'd feel a faint
tapping in the depths of my body, as constant as a heart beat.

The next day, uncharacteristically, I woke up on my own from
the light pouring in through the window and jumped out of bed
in a panic, afraid I'd be late for school. I ran to the kitchen to look
for my mother and found my father sitting at the table, an empty
cup of tea between his hands, his face gray. I asked in a whimper
why Mama hadn't woken me up. Only when I remembered that
I'd seen him sitting that way the day before did I realize that my
mother's leaving hadn't been a dream, and I fell silent.

He raised his face to me, trying to understand what I was so
upset about, and I could see his dead eyes slowly igniting like the
lights being turned on in the houses of the city as darkness fell. I
think it was only then that he realized that part of his life had
remained alive, that he still had a little girl he had to wake up in
the morning, make a sandwich for, and send off to school, and
that he couldn't sit at the table all day and cry. He got up, separated from the weeping man, and in an almost cheerful voice,
said, "We're staying home today," as if he'd decided to give us
both a prize.

We spent that day getting to know the house again. Its old
objects looked suddenly different, a sign that everything we had
known and were used to would never be the same: the three-
doored wardrobe, with half its contents on its way to America and
whole shelves that were bare, the drawer of beautiful lingerie that

was empty and the rod for hangers that was exposed. We saw a
forgotten handkerchief thrust far back on one of the shelves. My
father pulled it out with two fingers as if the power of the blow
my mother had inflicted was still present in what she had left
behind. He cupped it in his hand emotionally, then, remembering I was there, hesitated about what to do with it. When he
finally decided to put it back where it had been, he said in a trembling voice, "It's hers," and I added quickly, "We'll save it for her
until she comes back."

Later, like heirs examining their new property, we went through
her domain. We organized the pile of linens, folded and returned
the new ones to the bottom of the closet and tossed the rest into
the corner of the room to be washed the way she used to do on
cleaning days; we pulled out the drawers of the wardrobe where
she'd kept her panties, her bras, her jewelry, her lipsticks, her
beautiful boxes of face powder that opened with a click, her secrets
buried among them in the form of folded letters or rolled up bills
I once found shoved into the back of the drawer; we emptied the
kitchen cabinets, whose contents hadn't changed except for the
absence of the cookbook which, until the day before, had stood
between the wall and the tall cake pan with the hole in the center;
we looked through the cutlery drawer that was divided into six
compartments and found that the fancy silver cake cutters and the
six silver teaspoons with carved handles had disappeared, leaving
one compartment empty; we looked in the bathroom medicine
cabinet, its bottom shelf red from iodine stains; we also looked in
the sewing nook she'd made for herself on the balcony off the
kitchen that now contained only remnants of fabric and bits of
thread. And so, together, we went through my mother's territory.
I opened the wardrobe doors and pulled out their drawers, and my
father stood and watched, his glance moving slowly from one
object to another as if he were telling himself their histories, and I
could see how he was collapsing under the weight of memories,
shifting back and forth between intense longing and dejection.

About the time I usually came home from school, as we stood
in front of the sewing nook on the balcony and he looked disap-

pointedly at the bits of thread, I said, "She'll come back, Papa. As soon as she can." And when he didn't reply, his eyes still fixed on the same spot as if he were looking at what was left of his life, I added, "Let's take a break and do the rest of the organizing later."

"So what'll we do?" he asked, lost, unused to being home at that hour.

"Now it's time for lunch, Papa," I said in a brave voice.

And he said, "Let's go see what there is to eat."

We ate soup and a tasteless beet dish we found in pots. For dessert, we split the last slice of the cake she'd baked a week earlier for Succoth. My father had difficulty swallowing, bent his head over the plate and complained that he had a headache. When we finished eating, we stood together at the sink and washed the dishes. Right after that, my father said he wanted to rest, so I decided to go to a classmate's house and copy the homework.

At the entrance to the building, facing the street, I stopped, paralyzed at the sight of the place on the sidewalk where she had stood with all her bundles and suitcases the day before. I stayed there for a few minutes, looking at the empty spot feigning innocence, as if it hadn't been a witness to the "When will you come back, Mama?" and the "As soon as I can." Only then did I realize that my mother had left signs, not just inside the house, but outside it too. The children had seen how she tore herself from my arms and they must have told their friends, their schoolmates, their teachers, whispering the story of my father's humiliation.

I was afraid that the classmate I was planning to visit, and maybe the whole class, even the whole school, already knew the story and were passing it on to others. I retreated back up the staircase before anyone could see me, tiptoed past the door to our apartment, climbed to the top floor where there were no neighbors, and sat down on the top step. Eventually, realizing that I had no answers to the questions people might ask me, I decided to go home.

I found my father's cousin from Kiryat Motzkin sitting at the kitchen table with him. As soon as she saw me, she pulled me to her, pressing me into her soft stomach with bear hugs, as if I'd been saved from some great disaster. I could tell from her red eyes that she'd been crying, but the minute she let me go and I went out onto the closed-off balcony that was my room, I heard her dry voice reviling my mother, wishing her in Hebrew and in other languages all sorts of cruel deaths. I was shocked by the fury in her voice and the vulgarity of her violent words, some of which I didn't know. My father's cousin was a heavyset, good-humored woman known for her excellent chicken soup and her smile that was reminiscent of the fat man's smile from "Abbott and Costello." It was hard to connect those raging, insulting curses to the wonderful aroma of that chicken soup and the warmth of her body. I waited for my father's response, but he didn't shush her or argue with her, maybe because he was too stunned or exhausted, or maybe because he agreed with her.

In the evening, when we were alone again, my father said that the next day he'd go to work and I'd go to school, and he added a comment that was surprising, coming from him, or maybe he was repeating something his cousin had said to him, "Life must go on."

"On to where, Papa?"

"Onward," he waved his hand as if he knew exactly where and I shouldn't worry.

"What if people ask questions," I said out loud what had been bothering me for hours.

"What questions?"

"What happened with Mama."

"No one will ask."

"But what if?"

"Say that you don't know."

"The kids saw me crying."

"That doesn't mean you know."

"They saw the taxi and everything."

"So what does that mean?"

"That she went away with all her suitcases."

"So if someone asks, this is what you say: She went away."

"And if they ask me until when?"

"Tell them you don't know."

I looked at my father. Only a day had passed since my mother left, and he seemed more stooped. He read my look and suddenly smiled at me, but the smile only deepened the wrinkles in his cheeks and didn't remove the worry from his eyes.

"And you do know, Papa?"

"No," he said quickly.

"You don't know where she went?"

"She went far away."

"When will she come back?"

"I told you, I don't know."

"So who does?"

"No one," he said, abandoning me to a helplessness I would never be free of. "She doesn't know either."

The director of the Cinemathèque, sitting next to you behind the table that's covered with a green cloth, gets up and announces formally, "We are delighted to welcome the director and producer, Ms. Alma Roth. Time is too short to list all the awards she has won, but you are invited to read the special program, where you will see that she was even nominated for an Oscar. As part of the American Festival being held this year, we'll be showing three films Alma Roth directed and produced, beginning today with the one that has real historical value, her first film, made when she was a student at the Los Angeles Film School where she now teaches. It's called 'Dice.' If you'd like to talk with the director, you can do so in Hebrew because her Hebrew is excellent."

I remember our first meeting very well: you were lying in your rickety baby carriage, crying constantly. You were a blue-faced baby with squashed features, and your crying was earsplitting, as if you knew just how much destruction would come of that meeting of the people encircling your carriage and looking pityingly at your blue face. From where you were lying in the depths of your carriage, even if your little eyes, glittering with tears, could see, they would not have been able to take in the three of us at the apartment door. They wouldn't have been able to see me holding a bouquet of gladioli with their long, sword-sharp leaves, then the

polite handshake between my father and your mother, the emotional handshake between your father and my mother, and later
still, the sudden tension when he handed her a glass of tea and she
dropped it, as if she'd received an electric shock when their fingers
touched. Your mother quickly gathered the fragments of broken
glass and her pleasant, soothing words dispelled the tension for a
while. When they sat down to talk, they offered me a piece of
candy and sent me to the balcony to look at the people outside.
But I occupied myself smoothing out the candy wrapper so I could
add it to my collection, and I couldn't help looking into the room,
proud of my mother, glamorous in her navy blue skirt and white
silk blouse. Your mother, in contrast, looked faded and worried,
bent over the floor, trying to catch sight of splinters of the broken
glass, every once in a while seeing one and scooping it up. At
either end of the table were my father and your father, their glances
intersecting on my mother.

Your crying sent us away earlier than the adults had planned.
On the way back home, I walked between my parents, holding
their hands, hearing them talk about you and your parents above
my head. My mother said that you were an ugly baby. My father
said that all babies are ugly. My mother said that she hadn't been
an ugly baby, and that I looked like her and I hadn't been an ugly
baby either. My father said that, except for me, all babies are ugly.
My mother said that your mother—she still called her the
Bialystok—didn't know how to fix up the house so it would be a
nice place to live in. My father said it wasn't fair to ask that of a
woman who just had a baby a month ago. My mother asked my
father what he thought of your father. My father said that he
seemed like a decent person. My mother laughed. My father asked
her why she was laughing. My mother said that you say a person's
decent when you don't have anything more interesting to say
about him. My mother offered a quick list of compliments: educated, smart, handsome, and charming. My father said that he was-
n't educated or smart or handsome or charming—he was decent.
My mother said that she didn't want to argue and, in defiance of
my father, as if I were the link between them, pulled her fingers

from my hand. My father said that was the best he could say and immediately clutched my fingers pressing into his hand. We were silent all the way home.

Both our truths collapse in the face of the photos of my birthday party. Does it matter which of them saw the other first? Can we look at them with an unprejudiced eye and honestly claim that those two people, as beautiful as movie stars, so comfortable together, were not meant for each other? Can we be sure that Fate itself didn't arrange for them to meet in the sewing class and from the moment their eyes met, like in the movies, they could do nothing but walk blindly toward each other, obeying a force stronger than themselves? Now, after life has taught us how rare it is for a man and a woman who are so right for each other to meet, can we condemn them for abandoning everything that had come before? Here in these pictures, still married to other people, they already look like a perfect couple.

We celebrated my sixth birthday with two couples from our building, with you and your parents, and with our family represented by my father's cousin who, despite a headache, had come from Kiryat Motzkin with her son, Eliyahu. In the snapshot, apparently taken by one of the neighbors, the other three neighbors are in the background, my father's cousin has her hands on her temples and looks as if she's suffering, and Eliyahu, his mouth full of food, is looking covetously at the still uncut birthday cake. You are only eight months old but already full of determination, looking as if you're plotting to leap out of your mother's arms. I'm standing in anticipation next to the lit candles. My mother is at my side, leaning over the candles with me, her throat arched like that of a ballerina taking a bow, her lips poised to help me defeat the flames, her eyes on your father. My father on the right and yours on the left are looking at her, entranced.

On my seventh birthday, my parents had already decided to do without the neighbors and the sickly cousin. The puzzle of who took the picture would never be solved, but the photographer captured perfectly the moment my father straightened the crown of prickly green stems on my head. You are still in your mother's arms, the upper part of your body leaning sideways as if, ever since the previous birthday, you've been looking for a way to get out of her embrace. Your father and my mother are talking, serious, their shoulders almost touching.

What were they talking about, standing so close together, on my seventh birthday? Had they already begun devising their plan? Or maybe the plan was already made, a secret birthday gift? Maybe the tickets to America were in the inside pocket of your father's dark, pinstripe suit? Were they thinking about the landslide they'd cause in the lives of the people left behind? Did my mother imagine how my heart would pound in my breast every time I went out into the street after she left?

Obviously, her leaving was a topic of conversation in the neighborhood. Neighbors who had never spoken to me before would stop and ask how my father and I were. Others would stare at me and whisper to each other. When there was no one else in the grocery store, Moshe, the owner, looking apprehensively to the right and to the left, would ask about my mother, his most beautiful customer, he said, apparently to cheer me up, never imagining that his remark would make me forget half the list of things I'd promised my father I'd bring home. Kids from the neighborhood, including a girl who often used to come to my house to play with my mother's left-over pieces of cloth, would taunt me, shouting at me, always behind my back, that my mother ran away from my father and me. Because I stood tall as I turned to walk home, they probably couldn't guess how hurt I was. Sometimes I'd imagine people had stopped to look at me. I didn't tell my father about it. Despite the proximity of our new worlds, whose narrow borders had pushed us closer to each other, a boundary line had been drawn between us: things he knew and didn't tell me, things I was afraid to ask, things I was afraid to tell. After I stopped going out to play with the neighborhood kids, I spent the long hours home alone turning over the possibilities in my mind. In the drawn out afternoons, I stayed in the empty house, doing my homework, reading the books I took out of the public library, watching the kids playing in the street from my balcony until my father came in from work.

About three months after my mother left, the first letter arrived. His fingers trembling, my father tore open the envelope and pulled out a sheet of transparent, rustling paper. He held it as if it were made of a skin-destroying substance and moved his eyes silently and quickly over the page, probably looking for the line in which she'd written the date of her return. Then, in an increasingly steady voice, he read what she'd written about her new home: the voyage had taken two months, and this was the first chance she'd had to sit down and write a letter. She was finding it difficult to adjust, she didn't understand the language, she'd started studying English at night school and was having an especially hard time pronouncing words that had a *th* or an *r* in them. She was working long hours in a store, and she was very worried about us. Was I riding my bicycle carefully? Was I doing well in school? Had I gotten taller? Winter had probably already come. Did my wool coat still fit? And she signed the letter: With love. My father kept on looking at the page as if he were reading lines written in invisible ink, maybe checking to be sure he hadn't skipped the sentence that said when she was coming back. Then he folded the letter and put it back in the envelope, and I looked at him, puzzled, stopping my tongue from asking why her words sounded as if she'd been kidnapped from us and no longer had control over her fate.

For days afterward, we were both in a state of shock. Once, I let myself ask why she didn't come home if she was having such a hard time and missed us, but my father looked crestfallen, so I didn't ask again. Sometimes, lying in my bed on the living room balcony that had been closed off with shutters, in the moments between sleeping and waking, I'd see her bending over her sewing and humming songs with her mouth closed. Sometimes I could hear her voice, the sound of the suitcase dropping to the floor, and I'd jump out of bed, forgive her instantly for wanting to be with another girl for a while, forgive her in my father's name for wanting another man, ready to see her opening her arms to me, to be swallowed up in the folds of her body—and I'd find the room empty or the nightmarish figure of my father sitting alone in the dark. Once, when I was asleep, I felt the touch of her fingers on my cheeks, and only when it was light and I woke up did I understand that it was the edge of the curtain, fallen from the loop that held it, that had brushed across my face.

From the day she left, I started avoiding my classmates, including Dalia too, my best friend, who was now treating me as if I'd gotten sick. Every time I went to her house, her mother would look at me with pity and beg me to eat. I avoided Aliza, too. We'd started to become friends after we once exchanged brightly colored papers from our wrapping paper collections, and another time, our teacher sent me to her house to see why she hadn't come to school for two days. Her mother had opened the door a crack and said worriedly that Aliza had high fever. I asked if I could visit her and she said, as if her concern was for me, that it wasn't a good idea because her room was full of germs and that in about another week Aliza would come back to school and then we could be best friends. Aliza came back, but a few weeks later her mother died suddenly, from a dog bite. By drawing a picture on the blackboard, our teacher explained to us how a sick dog transmits its sickness to human beings. I stared at the drawing of the dog, which didn't look anything like a dog, and felt sorry for Aliza because her mother, unlike my own, would never come back. I promised myself to make friends with her when the week of mourning was over, as if that had been her mother's last wish.

Aliza returned to school stunned and sad, and she stayed apart, wandering along the fence during recess, until the teacher gave her special permission to spend recess inside. In class, from where I sat, two rows behind her, I could see her drooping shoulders and disheveled hair proclaiming: I have no mother. I immediately went back on the promise I'd made to myself when she was absent that I'd make friends with her. I had a mother. She was far away, checking out something, as my father had explained to me. No one actually told me, but I understood: the Bialystok's husband and daughter had traveled to that far-off place too.

I understood many things nobody explained to me, and that's what I told the school nurse when she took me into her office and closed the door: my mother has to check something out, she has a job in a store and she has to finish it, and meanwhile, she's studying English because only English-speaking people come into that store. The nurse said carefully: there really are people who sometimes have to check out something in their lives. Yes, I replied eagerly, my father and I know another man who had to check something out. He went too and took his little girl with him. Men who have to check things out take their children, women who have to check things out leave their children with their fathers. The nurse's eyes darkened as she leaned down and asked cautiously, "And what do you think it is, this thing she has to check out?" I replied quickly, "Maybe fabrics. They met in a sewing class."

Over the next few months, my father became grayer and more depressed. Sometimes, when he came home from his job at the printing press, he'd throw open the door and hurry to the table where I put the mail. When he saw that there was no letter from her that day either, his spirits fell immediately. A few times, maybe at the instructions of the school nurse, he'd mumble something about my mother's trip, but his sentences drifted off, unfinished. In the evening—a girl with a job to do—I tried to amuse him. I'd sit him down on the armchair which, when necessary, turned into a bed, stand in front of him and recite poems I knew by heart, or I'd imitate my teacher, Esther, talking to one of my classmates: "Solomon Diamond, because you're not only Solomon, the wisest among men, but you're also brilliant, maybe you can manage to remember who you copied that answer from?" And I'd imitate my classmate talking to the teacher: "I swear to God I did it all myself, from my own head. I was sitting next to my mother when I did my homework, ask her if I didn't say my hand hurts from so much homework." My father would look at me with shining eyes, but his mouth hardly moved, as if the muscles that pull it into a smile had atrophied.

On Saturday morning, we'd clean the house, and in the afternoon, I could sometimes convince my father to go out for a walk. But outside, our loneliness intensified among the strolling couples or groups or families. Amidst the happy, noisy crowd, I imagined us as a desert island: a man and a girl, as sad as mourners. On Saturdays, when there was a movie playing that was suitable for my age, we'd go to the movies together, entering the theater when it was already dark, because that's how I wanted it, and we got up the minute the music announced the end of the movie, pushing our way past the still seated, grumbling people, stopping at the exit door and waiting for the words "The End," hurrying to leave before the others had even stood up. At intermission, when the lights came up and people rushed out to the refreshment stand, I'd sit with my head bowed, hoping no one would see me. I was afraid that one of the kids or teachers would recognize the back of my neck and call my name, and I'd rub the muscles of my thighs, painful from so much tension, until a flickering light called in the latecomers and the blessed darkness fell.

I stopped asking my father when Mama would come back, and I didn't ask why she didn't write either. Even though my suspicions hadn't been confirmed, I now knew for sure: my mother had gone to America with the Bialystok's husband and little girl, and if she hadn't known at first what awaited her in her new home, she knew now, and even if she had planned to come back, as she'd promised me, maybe she'd changed her mind.

My eighth birthday was neither celebrated nor photographed. My father was still grieving. Our home, like the room of a beloved person who died suddenly before he could say goodbye, had corners left untouched, covered with thick dust balls. I was sitting in the kitchen reading in the Bible about the travails of the Israelites in Egypt when my father came from behind me and said, "Congratulations, Hadassa'le. Today's your birthday."

"Really?"

"Yes. Today's the day. I've been wracking my brain all week about what to buy you."

"I know what I want," I closed my Bible.

"You do?" Determination, I'd noticed recently, impressed him.

"A new tablecloth."

"A tablecloth?" He looked momentarily disappointed.

"A tablecloth." I stood up.

"Now?"

"Why not?"

"We're going together?" He suddenly gave one of his rare smiles.

"Sure."

"Okay," he said enthusiastically, "so let's get going before they close the stores."

And there, in the crowded notions store, at the long, narrow wooden counter that smelled of varnish, looking over the meager selection of tablecloths, none of which was as beautiful as the one my mother had taken with her and was now probably spread on some table in America, we met your mother, sad and frail, looking as if she were always on the verge of fainting. My father didn't notice her, but I tugged at his shirt until his ear was level with my mouth and whispered, "There's Bialystok."

What is your truth about that meeting in the notions store, and what is that truth of yours worth? You are two and half years old, on the other side of the ocean. My mother wakes you in the morning, feeds you, combs your hair, and bathes you; she buys, washes, and irons your dresses; wipes away your tears when you cry; takes you for walks in big American parks; checks to see if you brushed your teeth before she puts you to sleep; gets up on stormy nights to see if you're tucked in; sits on the side of your bed when you're sick, her hand on your forehead all night; happy when you pronounce the *th* properly. Maybe when she hugs you, she remembers me sometimes. The three of you move farther away from me, images retreating from a moving train, snatched into the background. The image of your father is completely blurred in my memory. My mother's features are starting to fade, but in my memory, her movements, their sweeping exaggeration so full of charm, are separated from her features, from the sound of her voice. I remember you as a baby lying in your carriage and screaming to high heaven. Did you calm down with my mother? Do you remember your own mother? Do you feel her from so far away? And if you do, do you know about her meeting with my father? What can you know about that meeting? I was there between the two of them, at the wooden counter smooth from so much use, the three of us fingering the fabric of the tablecloths, I curiously, my father awkwardly, your mother expertly. She chose a nylon tablecloth of embossed roses for us, and my father told the salesman to wrap it nicely because it was the birthday present I'd asked for. Your mother, looking as if she'd just awakened from her faint, asked which birthday. My father said proudly that today I was eight years old and she looked at me as if she were seeing me for the first time. Years later, she told me that that was the moment she began to love me, because if a child asks for a tablecloth for her birthday, that means her home is important to her. She mumbled, "Eight years old, what a big girl. Congratulations to you, to both of you," and stumbled out of the store.

On the way home, both of us holding the thin string that tied the wrapping around the tablecloth, I said to my father, "It was nice of her to help us."

"Yes," he said dreamily, as if I'd given him something to think about.

"She looks sad."

"Yes."

"She probably misses her little girl." I averted my eyes.

I didn't dare talk about my mother's missing us. It had been seven months since she stood with her back to the entrance to our building with her packed belongings around her, and I still wanted to believe she'd hurry back as she'd promised. I didn't know what was taking her so long. Even the last letter we got from her, in a blue, almost transparent paper envelope, didn't help me to understand.

My father, maybe to cheer me up after I told him about my conversation with the school nurse, managed—without explaining how he knew about it—to help me keep believing that Mama had gone on an urgent, necessary trip but wanted very much to come back to us. Meanwhile, he was careful not to touch her things and didn't try to improve the food he cooked, which was bland and unappetizing though I ate it without complaining.

"Of course she misses her," he echoed my words, his compassionate voice speaking of Bialystok.

"So why did she let them take her so far away?"

"Maybe she had no choice."

And of all the things I didn't understand, I dared to express this: "Maybe her little girl misses her too."

"Maybe," he said after a while.

"I'm sure she misses her," I dared even more.

"But she has her father," he said cautiously.

"But maybe she wants her mother."

He didn't object. "Maybe. But they're probably taking good care of her."

He didn't say it, and I didn't want to remind him: it was my mother who was taking good care of her.

At home, I spread the tablecloth on the table and the small kitchen seemed to brighten. My father and I were thrilled by the sight of the room that had changed so suddenly, and I said boldly, "Maybe we should invite her over. So she can see how beautiful the tablecloth is."

"Yes," he agreed, as if surrendering to the justice of it.

"Because she picked it out."

"Very true."

We didn't talk about her and the invitation again, as if we'd fulfilled our obligation to her merely by suggesting it, but I couldn't stop thinking about her stooped figure walking out into the street after she'd said in a defeated voice, "Eight years old, what a big girl."

In the weeks that followed, I'd walk to and from school more slowly, looking for your mother in the streets, going past your old house, hoping I'd accidentally bump into her. The shutters were always closed, sheltering the dark rooms.

One night, I heard my father groan. In my imagination, the whole house was a mournful creature. The walls, the dishes, the chairs, and even the handkerchief left behind by mistake groaned occasionally. But that night, I knew that the voice I was hearing came from my father's throat: he might have been crying or moaning in his sleep. The next day I saw your mother, like an omen, standing in the bakery next to the town hall, dressed in a too-large, greenish uniform, pale and weak, as if she were about to fall down and disappear in the starched jacket. Her arms were filled with challahs that she was placing, one by one, with her free hand, into a cabinet without doors. There was such sadness in her eyes, in her face, in her fingers that she might have been putting dead babies, not challahs, into the cabinet. Horrified by the thought, I stood in front of her on the other side of the bakery window and looked at her. She was engrossed in her work, moving as if she were moon-struck, and when she put down the last challah, she turned around and was swallowed up in the depths of the bakery.

I thought about her all that day, seeing again and again that dreamy motion with which she had placed the challahs. The image of dead babies was gone, and now it looked to me like the movement of a farmer sowing his field, a handful of seeds in a sack hanging from his body, scattering them in an arc over the furrows. The next day, in the middle of gym class, I suddenly began to worry: what would happen if she fell or fainted in her house behind the closed shutters? After all, she was most probably alone, and no one would even know.

In the late afternoon, on my way home from the library, feeling as if I had nothing to lose and perhaps influenced by my reading of *Anne of Green Gables*, which, at the recommendation of the librarian, I'd exchanged for *Tom Sawyer*, I suddenly felt very bold.

A woman with unkempt hair opened the door, her silhouette engulfed by the gloom of the house: your mother. She didn't recognize me and was about to close the door on me, shaking her head "No," thinking I was selling something, but at the last minute, through the narrowing crack of the door, she saw my face and stopped.

"Aren't you the daughter—?"

"Yes."

She hesitated for a minute, then opened the door.

"You want to come in?"

I went in. The room was neat, its furniture sparse. In the corner was a tall pile of books. An open volume lay face down on the table, as if she'd just been reading it. Photographs stood on the large, old-fashioned radio, one of them showing you between your parents, your head at the same height as theirs.

"Alma's not here," she said.

"I know." I wanted to say: she's in America.

"I thought maybe you came to play with her."

"No." I wanted to say: I couldn't stand her.

"Well, yes, she is younger than you . . . "

"Yes." I wanted to say: And besides, she was always crying.

She looked carefully at me, as if she could hear my thoughts too and was speculating on answers. Suddenly, she asked in a loud voice, as if proclaiming something, "You like chocolate milk?"

"Chocolate milk?"

"Yes. They sent me chocolate milk powder. I hardly ever drink it, but I could make you some." Seeing my hesitation, she added, "And it's healthy, too. Would you like some?"

"Okay."

"Wait here two minutes," she said, cheering up.

She left and I turned to the photos, hypnotized. Here were the new people who now filled my mother's life. Your good-looking father, an amused and slightly malicious laugh at the corners of his mouth, as if he were a witness to something no one else could see; you, your expression unchanged for years—complaining and suspicious, as if you'd just been deprived of something—holding onto your father's collar. Next to the both of you, your mother, light shining in her eyes, a very different woman from the one who had opened the door for me.

Your mother came in from the hallway as if she'd put on an instant disguise: her hair was combed and her face pleasant. She opened the window shutters and on the way to the kitchen asked, "You like things very sweet, right?"

I followed her into the kitchen, also neat and sparsely furnished, a row of dusty cactus plants on the sill, and watched her mix the chocolate milk.

"Do you want to drink here or on the balcony?" she asked.

"It doesn't matter," I said. I wondered when she'd ask why I'd come, but she was busy with the chocolate milk, focused on the milk rising in the saucepan.

"Do you like to read?" she asked without looking at me, and I saw that since I'd come in, I'd been clutching my library book to my chest.

"Yes."

"That's good. Books are good friends." She grabbed the pan off the flame and poured the bubbling milk into the glass.

"So," she put the glass of chocolate milk down in front of me on the kitchen table, "you didn't come to play with Alma?"

She said your name without pain, as if you'd gone and would be right back, and I wondered if my mother said my name that way too, or maybe she'd forgotten me and my name altogether, busy with her English and her *th* and her store.

"I came to say thank you very much for the tablecloth."

"Oh, does it look nice?"

"You can come to see for yourself."

That's how, in a casual voice, with a fateful directness that could be explained only with the distance of time, I invited your mother into our lives.

That evening, for my father, I imitated the custodian chasing cats from the schoolyard: "Scat, scat, go home, this place is for children, not cats," and then, as was our habit, I taught him what I'd learned that day in English class. He'd take a quick look through my other notebooks, but he asked to learn the English words, and he'd do my homework with me, making sure to check the corrections of the previous day's lesson we'd made in class. As we were doing that, I told him, as if suddenly remembering, that I'd invited the Bialystok to visit us.

"What did you do?" he asked in alarm.

"I invited her to see the tablecloth."

"Why?" His shoulders sagged.

"Because she helped us pick it out."

His distress increased. "So what. Is that a reason to invite someone? You say thank you nicely and that's that."

"I already asked her to come."

"So go and tell her we can't. That we're busy."

"You want me to lie?"

He said nothing, trapped. "And she said she'd come?"

"On Saturday."

"On Saturday? You mean for lunch?"

"No. In the afternoon. Five o'clock. She said she'd bring cake."

For three days, we cleaned and fixed up the house together. My father, constantly grumbling but still trying to make things nice for our guest, whitewashed one wall in the kitchen and changed the eroded rubber hose that was attached to the kitchen faucet. As he worked, he asked his questions, straightening up and looking at me in amazement with almost every reply.

"Where did you see her, in the street?"

"No. I went to her house."

"You mean she invited you over?"

"No."

"So what happened?"

"I went without an invitation."

"You remembered where she lives?"

"Sure. Next to school."

"And she remembered you?"

"Yes. She gave me chocolate milk."

"Really?"

"Yes. And cake. She works in a bakery. She has cakes."

"She works?"

"Yes. She said that if she'd known I was coming, she would have brought a birthday cake with candles."

"I didn't know she works."

"She told me that it's hard for her there."

"So you actually had a whole conversation."

"Until I finished the chocolate milk."

Our daily routine was already solidly established by then: every morning, already washed and dressed, my father would wake me up. While I washed my face, brushed my teeth, and got dressed, he'd make us both tea and slices of bread with cheese, and he'd make a sandwich for me, cut it into four pieces, and put it into my cloth sandwich bag. Then we'd sit down and eat together in silence, concentrating, like two soldiers having their last meal before the big battle. When we finished, at exactly seven-thirty, he'd wash the plates and I'd make my bed, which anyone could see from the front door because it was on the balcony. At noon, I'd come home from school, eat a sandwich and a hardboiled egg, do my homework, watch the kids playing outside, read my library book, and wait for my father. In the early evening, he'd come home and make us a hot meal. Sometimes he'd sit and read the newspaper he held open between us as if he were hiding from me. Sometimes he'd tell me about something he was reading in the paper, his voice emerging from behind the page. Sometimes I'd be the one to tell him something that had happened that day in school. A few times a week, I'd go to the public library to exchange books, but sometimes I could see the great sadness descend on him, and I'd decide to forgo the book and entertain him with imitations.

On Saturday afternoon at exactly five, your mother knocked on our door. She brought a poppy seed cake and a present for me: a shiny pink hair ribbon with pointed edges. Years later I tried to recreate that first moment my father and I opened the door for her together. From where she stood, she could see my mother's sewing board, as if my mother were still there with us. There must have been a moment of awkwardness, but I couldn't remember it. Nor did I remember if we shook hands or what my father said to her. I think your mother remarked that the room looked different. Maybe her heart constricted inside her at the sight of the place she had once visited with her husband and baby daughter before her world fell apart.

That afternoon is etched in my memory like a precious painting, illuminated by a soft, golden light as if it were dipped in honey. It has remained fixed in my mind as an image of a small window opening onto the world from inside a cellar. I remember how she admired the tablecloth in the kitchen, how she braided my hair with the ribbon, and my father said, "Finally I have a girl like the ones in the magazines," how, when she talked about *Don*

Quixote, which I told her I'd taken out of the library, her eyes lit up and she suddenly became beautiful. I remember how my father closed his eyes when he ate the poppy seed cake, how he went on and on telling stories about his childhood, most of which were new to me, how he suddenly noticed that it was almost nine at night and I was awake even though I had school the next day. I remember how I said good night at the door, floating with joy when he left to walk your mother home, how I tossed and turned sleeplessly in bed, not at all worried that my father still hadn't come back. And I remember how my head spun all the next day, how my teacher scolded me, surprised that I wasn't listening to her, how I could not stop thinking that if my mother was raising you, why shouldn't your mother raise me? I remember how, during the long recess, I suddenly saw your mother standing at the gate, peering in at the children, all of whom seemed to look alike to her, and how I went up to her and asked what she was looking for and it turned out that she was looking for me, and she gave me a piece of cake wrapped in brown paper, and smoothed my hair with one hand.

My father, most probably embarrassed by the meeting with your mother, didn't mention her at all, as if he hadn't gone out to walk her home, coming back at midnight. For the first three days after that Saturday when we invited your mother to see the table-cloth, I'd glance at her apartment on my way to and from school and see the shutters closed, as usual. After the day she came to give me a piece of cake, I'd hurry out into the yard at recess, but she didn't come again. On Wednesday, across from the newspaper my father was hiding behind, I finally lost patience.

"What happened with her?"

"With who?"

"With the Bialystok."

He lowered the paper and showed his face. "Her name's Dora."

"So with Dora."

We looked at each other over the newspaper, each peering with tense curiosity into the other's eyes. I myself didn't understand why I hadn't told him that she'd come to school at recess.

"So what happened with her?"

"What should have happened?"

"I don't know. I wasn't with you. Maybe she asked us to come over and you forgot."

"Why should she ask us to come over?"

"She has lots of chocolate milk."

"Is that why?"

"She has lots of chocolate milk and she hardly drinks any. She said it would be a shame if it got spoiled."

"Is that the only reason?"

"No."

"Then what?" He looked carefully at me.

"Then maybe we should ask her to go for a walk on Saturday."

"A walk?" He didn't look happy, but he didn't reject the idea either.

"Maybe to the movies?" I bargained immediately.

"Maybe." He didn't object.

I was silent for a minute, plotting.

I finally asked, "How can we give her the invitation?"

"Maybe we'll see her by accident."

"Nothing happens by accident," I said quickly.

"So, what then?"

"So I'll write to her," I decided. "I'll put an invitation in her mailbox."

"Okay."

"What should I write?"

All that afternoon, I drafted letters to your mother. I filled a whole page with attempts to put together a sentence that wouldn't be too eager or too cool, that wouldn't look as if we were inviting her casually and yet wouldn't imply that we were in the habit of inviting women to the movies either. He sat beside me as I copied the final version, his eyes glued to the special sewing board he'd fastened to the table for my mother and took up half of it.

"I've been thinking about that too," I said.

"About what?" He was alarmed.

"That if you take that off, there'd be more room."

My father took the board off the table that day, and the next day, on my way to school, I dropped the letter into your mother's mailbox.

Your mother arrived at the appointed hour on Saturday. We stood at the door, smiling hesitantly at each other. Her hand moved out automatically, and I stood without moving as she arranged my hair. Then she handed me a package and said, "Put it in the refrigerator. It's apple cake."

Then the three of us went outside. For the first time in months, neither my father nor I were alone. The light was pleasant and exactly right, and I moved in it beaming, walking between them like a bridesmaid. The whole way, apparently being careful not to talk about anything else, they talked about me. My father, swelling with pride, told her how smart I was, repeated what my teacher had said on parent-teacher night. In a voice surprisingly strong for her frail body, she talked about my visit to her and how impressed she'd been by the courage I'd shown in deciding to come.

Suddenly, I saw a girl from my class, her parents, and her baby brother in his carriage coming toward us. Deliberately, I held out my right hand to my father and my left to Dora. My father, used to this, took my hand right away, and Dora, taken aback by the unfamiliar touch, after a moment regained her composure and clasped her fingers around mine. And that's how we walked to the movies, crossing the world like Moses with the Israelites behind him, between the walls of water, my father at my right, Dora at my left, and I between them, a live electric wire.

Later, I sat between them in the movies, my knees bent, scrunching down so they could whisper above my head without any problem. For the first time since my mother left, I saw happiness on my father's face, not in a twitchy smile that would appear on his lips and vanish immediately, but in hearty laughter that wrinkled his eyes and exposed the gold fillings deep in his mouth. For the first time in my life, I wasn't completely carried away into the gripping lives of the movie heroes. From force of habit, my eyes followed the images and the subtitles, but my attention was on the small movements on either side of me. On the screen were

two almost naked children crossing a frozen river hand in hand.
Dora was moving her head on my right, signaling that she wanted
to say something, and my father responded immediately on my
left, inclining his head over mine, attentive, and she whispered in
his ear words I couldn't hear, but I guessed that she was telling
him how sorry she felt for the children. My heart warmed. My
father's heart warmed, too, I knew. And my first thought was of
you, abandoned to the mercy of my mother. Maybe the woman on
my right was thinking about you, too, wondering if you were
dressed properly, if you slept properly, ate properly. For some reason, I was seized with an urgent desire to reassure her about my
mother's maternal abilities, to tell her how clean my clothes had
always been, how my shoes had always been polished, how strict
she'd been about bathing and brushing teeth. And even though all
that was true, and even though sometimes, at the most unexpected
moments, my stomach would still hurt from missing my mother
so much, I was already aware of the deceit beyond the spotless
clothes; but before she got up and left, I'd been so proud of her, her
small admirer emulating my father, her big admirer.

During intermission, I straightened up in my seat, and with my
head held high, I looked all around me. Then I climbed onto my
seat and stood on my knees facing the noisy theater, searching for
kids from the neighborhood or from my class. So they'd look and
see how my father had found himself a woman and so they'd stop
feeling sorry for him because he was lonely. And they'd better stop
feeling sorry for me, too. There was no one in my class who ate the
best cake in town like I did.

Over the next few months, our lives settled into a new routine.
During the week, my father was at work most of the time, and
Dora worked during the day and cleaned her house and read books
in the evening. Sometimes, I'd stop in to see her on my way back
from the library, and she'd make me a mug of chocolate milk, tell
me what she was reading, and send me home with a small cactus
plant, the offspring of one of hers. Once she even went to the
library with me. And once, she invited me to go with her to the
private library where she borrowed foreign-language books from

the hunchbacked, very pale librarian who spoke German. On the street, unlike the purposeful way I held her hand on Saturdays, showing off to the world, our hands now met spontaneously. On Saturdays, in the afternoon, she'd come to our place, bringing a coffee cake, a cheesecake, or a chocolate cake. My father would make us tea, I'd slice the cake, and Dora would comb my hair and braid it with a ribbon. After we drank and ate, the three of us went out into the world, to be among the people strolling along the wide boulevard, with me always between them. Almost always we went to the movies with tickets my father had bought during the week. Sometimes a button had to be sewn on, or a piece of clothing had to be mended, or a book covered, and Dora did this while drinking her tea, so we'd go out a little later. After the movie, sometimes we'd walk her home and say goodnight to her, and my father and I would continue on home together. Sometimes they would take me home first, and Papa would walk Dora home alone. I'd start reading my library book right away, managing to get through thirty or forty pages before he came back.

The last time my father and I discussed my mother's absence was a chance occurrence that stunned us both. We were in the kitchen on one of those routine evenings of ours. He was cleaning the refrigerator and I was reading aloud verses from the Bible that I was being tested on the next day: "And when she could no longer hide him, she took for him a basket of bulrushes, and daubed it with bitumin and with pitch; and she put the child therein, and laid it among the reeds by the river's brink. And his sister stood at a distance, to know what would be done to him..." My throat suddenly dried up and I fell silent.

"At the Yarkon River, people pay money for that," my father said, his head deep inside the refrigerator. "Baby Moses got a free ride."

Silent sobbing shook my body, the kind of weeping that pours unobstructed from a dry, painful throat. It released all the sorrow, humiliation, and fear of a child abandoned willingly, not at the king's command, abandoned without love, without concern, and without appointing protectors for her. How could she have gotten into the taxi and not looked back, not seen me running after the moving car? What if my father had packed up his belongings and had gone away too?

My father, alarmed and upset, as if he had heard my thoughts, left the refrigerator open, came over to me and pressed me to his body, and I was suddenly engulfed by the heavy smell of sealed food and the pungent odor of laundry soap.

"There, there," he said, so close to me that he seemed to be speaking into my body, "the king's daughter found him in the end and he had a great time in the palace. You've cried more than he did, so enough, enough."

We didn't mention my mother that evening, as if neither of us knew why I'd burst into tears, and we didn't talk about her for years afterward. If either of us remembered her, we kept the memory in our thoughts or in our dreams. Once, after I told him about *Oliver Twist*, which I'd taken out of the library, he asked me why all the books I read were about orphans.

The less we talked about my mother, the more we talked about Dora. There are things in life that I find mysterious and I can't figure out just from hints. I don't dare ask for more than hints. My father, whose thoughts I can frequently guess, spoke circumspectly whenever Dora's name came up. He once told me that working in the bakery was hard for her, but she had to support herself and pay what she owed on her apartment, so she couldn't leave. I asked why she didn't look for a different job. My father replied that she was still a little sick, so it was hard to find something suitable. I asked what sickness she had. My father hesitated, then said she was sad. I asked him if sadness is a sickness. My father hesitated: a little sadness can grow and then sometimes it's considered a sickness, and employers don't like to give jobs to sad people. Sad people drive customers away. I said that he was sad too, but he still worked in a place that suited him. My father smiled and said that he wasn't sad because I was his girl, and we hugged to confirm his words.

Before I fell asleep that night, I had the thought that I was also Dora's a little bit, and thinking about her, I could recreate the pleasant sensation that flowed through my whole body when she held my hand.

ou'd planned so long in advance, and you had the
wanted to get away from you, afraid you might ask
nd I was aware of my attentive double inside me,
piled like a snake preparing its poison. Every once in
uard would toss a funny remark at us, but it didn't
You said that you'd been living on a kibbutz for six
your father's uncle. I didn't ask why you left your
ica. I didn't ask how my mother was, and you did-
o tell me. You didn't ask about Dora, much to my
n't ask about me either. You wanted to hear only one
: how your father met my mother. As if you were
understand the story from its first moment. I told
father started pursuing my mother from the minute
he sewing class, and you protested with a vehemence
tand. You claimed that my mother had set a trap for
d seduced him into going to America. You couldn't
d told you that. I too protested. I defended my ver-
emence I didn't understand, and I couldn't tell you
t to me.

econd Lieutenant alone, Alma. Today's Friday. Have
uard called.

I had a boyfriend. My double moved inside me. You
ave a boyfriend, I'd better hold on to him so no one
away from me. I looked hard at you, trying to fig-
ou were thinking. In our family, men get snatched,
tched, you said, your lips clenched in bitterness,
forming grooves of old age over your upper lip.
, girls, why are you sitting like camels next to the
serious? What happened? Hey Amos, get a load of
't they look like they're planning a war? What's all
s on Friday afternoon? Go home and wash your hair,
n you're boyfriend comes, he'll have something to
ues on."

uddenly and angrily. You stood up abruptly, wiped
, shaking the butterflies on the fabric, and without
f goodbye, walked to the bus stop. My bus, which

During that period, in the new calm that had come into my life
and my father's, a fear began to haunt me: that my mother would
suddenly return and toss Dora out of our lives. One day—the horrifying thought tore through my serenity—one day I'd come
home from school and see a taxi parked in front of our house, its
roof loaded with suitcases and my mother sitting in the backseat
surrounded by lots of colorful bags; or I'd open the door and the
house would be full of suitcases and packages, and there she'd be,
sitting at the table. Maybe my father had reattached the sewing
board and she was already busy sewing or occupied with some
other hobby she'd learned in America, and those quiet times with
Dora would disappear from our lives and the frenzy, the overwhelming uproar and noisy exuberance would return and my
father would be drawn back into the old admiration, would
become smaller and go back to being her Sancho Panza. My entire
body constricted, as if that weren't a passing thought, but reality,
and sirens roused that double of myself as if she were Sleeping
Beauty. She leaped up out of me to stand at my side, not at all
angry about the false alarm. She'd check out the situation, calm
down, and sink back inside me until the moment of truth, when
she'd reappear and inspire me with strength. Then the two of us
would take my mother's suitcases and packages, throw them into
the taxi, drag my mother down the steps and across the sidewalk
in front of the neighbors watching from their windows, shove her
in among her things, disheveled and crying, and slam the door
shut. And even before the taxi drove off, we'd turn around and go
back to Papa and Dora.

My mother, as if she could know on the other side of the ocean
that my father and I were starting to recover from her, suddenly
began to write letters regularly in sloppy handwriting. Sometimes
a package would arrive from America, well packed and containing
things I was used to seeing in Dora's kitchen: powdered cocoa in a
square box, small rectangles of sugar, powdered milk. Sometimes
she'd add clothes for me, very few of them in my size, and Dora
would alter them, ripping out seams, cutting, making them larger.
My father would read the letters carefully, sometimes saving them

to show to Dora. He'd point to a line and they would discuss it, sitting at the table like two students struggling to decipher a difficult sentence. When I asked what the letters said, my father tried to avoid answering, and Dora said, "Tell the girl the truth. She can understand already." And my father said, "She needs papers from some rabbi in America to separate for good."

"But she's already separated," I said. With my own eyes, I'd seen the taxi; with my own legs, I'd run after it.

"The rabbi in America is causing problems." He said the word "America" resentfully. America, the source of his misery.

A short time before my tenth birthday, I asked for a present: I wanted Dora to be my mother. Dora laughed, embarrassed but joyful. "Look, just look how you've grown up. Two years ago, a tablecloth was enough for you and now you have such big requests." And my father said, "What my girl asks for, my girl gets."

What made me dizzy with happiness when I was ten, depressed me when I was fourteen. My father was as dear to me as always and Dora closer than before, but the maturing eye saw more and more clearly how the link between them only intensified their misery, their despondency. With a constant feeling of guilt, I'd look at them sitting together at the table, walking in the street one step in front of me, and I'd see what I wouldn't understand until I fell in and out of love myself—two deserted remnants of another love affair who had come together not through passion or love or choice, but through the weakness of helplessness, devastation. Their partnership, I was surprised to discover, did not cancel out either one's sorrow, but heightened it. And in contrast to that sight —which once made me burst into tears—my mother's image rose, erect and regal, glamorous and enchanting. Her face in old snapshots blended with the faces of movie stars. She captured my imagination with her beauty and her stormy love story, the likes of which exist only in books and movies, triumphing over reality and distance. I failed to remember that my father and I and Dora had paid the price for her marvelous love story, which had carried her off to the land of great joy, America.

One Friday at noon, the
called to me from a distanc
what's happening? There's
get into the base without
the IDF*, never heard of
secrecy, landed here straigh
inside me as if by magic. S
silent as stone, and now, re
responding to a hidden cry,
the butterfly blouse? Beer
poor thing. I told her, Alr
coffee house in Tel Aviv.
Probably dried up out the
she ate a candy bar for lur
shelter, "Alma, where'd y
Lieutenant Dassie."

You got up from the bus
thin teenager, determined
to a quick calculation. In
you, I never imagined this
said in surprisingly good H
talk to you."

Your Hebrew managed
you said, "Dora's daughter.

My heart stopped. I t
There'd been ten years of
let anyone mess it up. Had
mother raised you from th
Did you think of yourself a

"Need a little help from
Want them to come in thei
sec, the whole seventh regi

We sat in the shade of tl
to the camp and the main
up like enemies on a batt
alive. You were demandin

*Israeli Defense Forces

conversation
upper hand; I
about Dora,
well hidden, o
a while, the g
make us smile
months, with
home in Ame
n't volunteer
relief. You dic
thing from m
determined to
you that your
he saw her in
I didn't under
your father, h
tell me who h
sion with a ve
who had told

"Leave the
a heart," the g

You asked
said that if I
can snatch hi
ure out what
babies get sn
almost hatred

"Go to a ca
tree? Why so
those two. Do
that seriousne
curl it, so wh
lay his baby b

We parted
off your blous
a single word

During that period, in the new calm that had come into my life and my father's, a fear began to haunt me: that my mother would suddenly return and toss Dora out of our lives. One day—the horrifying thought tore through my serenity—one day I'd come home from school and see a taxi parked in front of our house, its roof loaded with suitcases and my mother sitting in the backseat surrounded by lots of colorful bags; or I'd open the door and the house would be full of suitcases and packages, and there she'd be, sitting at the table. Maybe my father had reattached the sewing board and she was already busy sewing or occupied with some other hobby she'd learned in America, and those quiet times with Dora would disappear from our lives and the frenzy, the overwhelming uproar and noisy exuberance would return and my father would be drawn back into the old admiration, would become smaller and go back to being her Sancho Panza. My entire body constricted, as if that weren't a passing thought, but reality, and sirens roused that double of myself as if she were Sleeping Beauty. She leaped up out of me to stand at my side, not at all angry about the false alarm. She'd check out the situation, calm down, and sink back inside me until the moment of truth, when she'd reappear and inspire me with strength. Then the two of us would take my mother's suitcases and packages, throw them into the taxi, drag my mother down the steps and across the sidewalk in front of the neighbors watching from their windows, shove her in among her things, disheveled and crying, and slam the door shut. And even before the taxi drove off, we'd turn around and go back to Papa and Dora.

My mother, as if she could know on the other side of the ocean that my father and I were starting to recover from her, suddenly began to write letters regularly in sloppy handwriting. Sometimes a package would arrive from America, well packed and containing things I was used to seeing in Dora's kitchen: powdered cocoa in a square box, small rectangles of sugar, powdered milk. Sometimes she'd add clothes for me, very few of them in my size, and Dora would alter them, ripping out seams, cutting, making them larger. My father would read the letters carefully, sometimes saving them to show to Dora. He'd point to a line and they would discuss it, sitting at the table like two students struggling to decipher a difficult sentence. When I asked what the letters said, my father tried to avoid answering, and Dora said, "Tell the girl the truth. She can understand already." And my father said, "She needs papers from some rabbi in America to separate for good."

"But she's already separated," I said. With my own eyes, I'd seen the taxi; with my own legs, I'd run after it.

"The rabbi in America is causing problems." He said the word "America" resentfully. America, the source of his misery.

A short time before my tenth birthday, I asked for a present: I wanted Dora to be my mother. Dora laughed, embarrassed but joyful. "Look, just look how you've grown up. Two years ago, a tablecloth was enough for you and now you have such big requests." And my father said, "What my girl asks for, my girl gets."

What made me dizzy with happiness when I was ten, depressed me when I was fourteen. My father was as dear to me as always and Dora closer than before, but the maturing eye saw more and more clearly how the link between them only intensified their misery, their despondency. With a constant feeling of guilt, I'd look at them sitting together at the table, walking in the street one step in front of me, and I'd see what I wouldn't understand until I fell in and out of love myself—two deserted remnants of another love affair who had come together not through passion or love or choice, but through the weakness of helplessness, devastation. Their partnership, I was surprised to discover, did not cancel out either one's sorrow, but heightened it. And in contrast to that sight —which once made me burst into tears—my mother's image rose, erect and regal, glamorous and enchanting. Her face in old snapshots blended with the faces of movie stars. She captured my imagination with her beauty and her stormy love story, the likes of which exist only in books and movies, triumphing over reality and distance. I failed to remember that my father and I and Dora had paid the price for her marvelous love story, which had carried her off to the land of great joy, America.

One Friday at noon, the hour we left the army base, the guard called to me from a distance, "Hi there, Second Lieutenant Dassie, what's happening? There's some girl here named Alma, wanted to get into the base without permission, that Alma, never heard of the IDF*, never heard of field security, never heard of military secrecy, landed here straight from the moon . . ." My double rose inside me as if by magic. She'd been asleep in her place for years, silent as stone, and now, recognizing the danger even before I did, responding to a hidden cry, she too heard the guard. "See her with the butterfly blouse? Been waiting for you since this morning, poor thing. I told her, Alma, dear Alma, this is the army, not a coffee house in Tel Aviv. She's sitting over there on a bench. Probably dried up out there in the heat. I gave her a candy bar, she ate a candy bar for lunch." He shouted toward the bus stop shelter, "Alma, where'd you disappear to now—here's Second Lieutenant Dassie."

You got up from the bus stop bench and came over to me, a tall, thin teenager, determined and serious, fifteen years old according to a quick calculation. In all my fantasies about a meeting with you, I never imagined this moment when you came up to me and said in surprisingly good Hebrew, in a demanding tone, "I have to talk to you."

Your Hebrew managed to throw me, so I couldn't speak. Then you said, "Dora's daughter."

My heart stopped. I thought of myself as Dora's daughter. There'd been ten years of order in our lives, and I wasn't going to let anyone mess it up. Had you come to demand your mother? My mother raised you from the age of two, wasn't *she* your mother? Did you think of yourself as Dora's daughter?

"Need a little help from your friends, Second Lieutenant Dassie? Want them to come in their tanks? Just say the word, and in half a sec, the whole seventh regiment is behind you, left, right, hup—"

We sat in the shade of the eucalyptus tree between the entrance to the camp and the main road, talking tensely, sizing each other up like enemies on a battlefield where only one would get out alive. You were demanding and restless, confidently leading the

---
*Israeli Defense Forces

conversation you'd planned so long in advance, and you had the upper hand; I wanted to get away from you, afraid you might ask about Dora, and I was aware of my attentive double inside me, well hidden, coiled like a snake preparing its poison. Every once in a while, the guard would toss a funny remark at us, but it didn't make us smile. You said that you'd been living on a kibbutz for six months, with your father's uncle. I didn't ask why you left your home in America. I didn't ask how my mother was, and you didn't volunteer to tell me. You didn't ask about Dora, much to my relief. You didn't ask about me either. You wanted to hear only one thing from me: how your father met my mother. As if you were determined to understand the story from its first moment. I told you that your father started pursuing my mother from the minute he saw her in the sewing class, and you protested with a vehemence I didn't understand. You claimed that my mother had set a trap for your father, had seduced him into going to America. You couldn't tell me who had told you that. I too protested. I defended my version with a vehemence I didn't understand, and I couldn't tell you who had told it to me.

"Leave the Second Lieutenant alone, Alma. Today's Friday. Have a heart," the guard called.

You asked if I had a boyfriend. My double moved inside me. You said that if I have a boyfriend, I'd better hold on to him so no one can snatch him away from me. I looked hard at you, trying to figure out what you were thinking. In our family, men get snatched, babies get snatched, you said, your lips clenched in bitterness, almost hatred, forming grooves of old age over your upper lip.

"Go to a café, girls, why are you sitting like camels next to the tree? Why so serious? What happened? Hey Amos, get a load of those two. Don't they look like they're planning a war? What's all that seriousness on Friday afternoon? Go home and wash your hair, curl it, so when you're boyfriend comes, he'll have something to lay his baby blues on."

We parted suddenly and angrily. You stood up abruptly, wiped off your blouse, shaking the butterflies on the fabric, and without a single word of goodbye, walked to the bus stop. My bus, which came once every hour, was about to arrive, but I didn't want to get on the same bus as you, so I walked firmly back to the base, feeling my raging double, which had had no release, move restlessly inside me. At the gate, I turned and looked at you, trying to find an answer from a distance to a question I did not know. You were standing with your back to me, dismissing me, and I knew I wouldn't tell Dora about our meeting.

"Is that you, Second Lieutenant Dassie? God help us. You know who you look like all of a sudden? Like Menshke before he freaked out on us and started shooting up the place. You scare me, you really do. So what were all those faces you were making? Couldn't agree about the war? So make peace. Did you think about making peace? Also an option, God knows. But if you go to war anyway, and if you take her prisoner, I volunteer to be the guard at the prisoners' camp. Do we have a deal, Second Lieutenant Dassie?"

Seven years later, you burst onto the scene again. You couldn't know that you'd picked the worst possible time, because my life was too full to contain you. I was studying psychology then, in the middle of exams, working evenings in a diagnostic center for children with learning disabilities, married to Dror almost a year—and we were fighting more all the time. During that period, I was tempted to pack my things and leave, but I kept my promise to my father to hold my marriage together at least a year, because the first year tended to be rough and if we could just get through it, we'd be on the "right track." In the midst of all that, I found out I was pregnant, and I was still holding the phone receiver in my hand after the conversation with the gynecologist when I decided that if the situation with Dror didn't improve, I'd get an abortion. During the weeks that followed, I struggled against the maternal feelings that sometimes rose in me, against getting attached to the tiny creature forming inside me, for the time being making its presence known mainly through morning sickness.

Three days before Purim, I was on my way home, thinking nostalgically about how hard it had been for me, when I was a child, to fall asleep the night before the holiday and how I'd wake up every hour to run my hands over the ballerina costume or the clown costume my mother, and later Dora, had made for me. Now, all I wanted to do was sink into the darkness and sleep for two straight days. In the narrow lane leading to the house, I remembered the huge dog that had suddenly appeared in front of me a few weeks earlier, scaring me so much that I almost fainted, and I promised myself to stop coming home when it was dark.

Almost at the door, I felt exhausted but suddenly I remembered that Dror had left the house that morning, slammed the door after a fight over my refusal to go to a family party his aunt was giving. For the month since I'd found out I was pregnant, he'd been trying to make up quickly after every fight. He'd make salami sandwiches and write apologies on them with mustard: "From your idiot husband," yellow on the reddish-brown. Or he'd write on the tray with letters made of tiny candies: "Dassie, come home." At the door, I decided, if he tries to make up, I'll forgive him and go to his aunt's with him; if he ignores me when I come in, if he keeps on reading and doesn't look up, the way he's done many times before, I won't talk to him till tomorrow.

Dror opened the door looking confused, almost like a stranger. You were sitting inside, your legs crossed, your skirt hitched up, exposing your white thighs. You were very different from the furious young girl you'd been at the age of fifteen. And you didn't look like either of them: you were sturdier and surer of yourself than your mother, fairer and fuller than my mother. But there was something in the way you sat, the way you moved your head, as if you were trying to imitate my mother, when she was still my mother. The woman I'd never really known was resurrected in you. The ghostly image already blurred in my mind was now you, bent over the photo album open on the low table and looking intently at the pictures of our wedding you'd asked to see or that Dror had volunteered to show you.

My faithful double stood behind me immediately: a safety net for a circus acrobat now entering the center of the big top.

Dror said, "Your sister from America is here." He was puzzled and angry, his voice a question mark with a rebuke on its tail—as if he were a Mossad agent finding out that he's married to a spy.

"She's not my sister." I observed the two wine glasses and the overflowing ashtray on the table, and also the abrupt movement of legs uncrossing, and you stood up, waiting, looking sour as I'd seen you in pictures from your childhood.

The ancient whirlpool stirring in my stomach made the fetus dizzy. There was something of my distant childhood in the air, and my double and I moved our heads forward, clearly recognizing the smell of danger. Between us, on the table, everyone was smiling: I in my wedding dress, my father and your mother in their fancy clothes standing on either side of me, your mother straightening my veil in a familiar gesture. And there, your mother is standing beside me under the wedding canopy, wiping tears from her eyes. What did those pictures make you feel, I wondered, not really wanting to know. I was exhausted from school, from diagnostic tests, from confrontations with learning disabled children, from the tension of my fights with Dror, from the new heaviness in my stomach, and now, suddenly, from the anxiety your defiant stance was making me feel. Only the presence of my double, ready and waiting for my instructions, calmed me. One word from me, and she'd reach out and kill for me or carry me off far away.

"Hello." You extended your hand across the table, as if you'd spent seven years planning to put right that meeting near the gate of the army base.

"What do you want?" I ignored your hand, again fanning the flames of anger over that meeting, scrutinizing your stance. At the same time, I noticed Dror's shocked expression.

"I came to visit . . ."

"For that you need an invitation." My double was speaking from my throat with a rudeness that surprised Dror and, to tell the truth, it surprised me, too. Your eyes blinked rapidly. This wasn't the way you'd imagined our next encounter. You thought you'd call me sister and I'd forget that first meeting, ignore the alarms you set off, and fall into your arms. But the echoes of that

meeting in the shade of the eucalyptus tree had not yet died down
in me. And my mother was standing between us too, intensifying
my agitation.

"I wanted to see you . . . to talk . . . "

"You should have written first, or called."

"She called at noon," Dror said, coming to your defense.

"I wasn't here at noon." I raised my voice, going to war with
both of you now.

"I invited her," he argued.

"She's not your guest," I shot back, "it's not for you to invite
her."

"She's been waiting for a few hours already."

"She should have asked me if I wanted her to wait."

"I invited her—"

"I heard you," my voice soared. "But I didn't invite her. I don't
want her to wait."

"She came from Haifa. I invited her to stay overnight here."

My double's voice, thicker than the devil's, said, "She will not
sleep here."

"She can't go back now. The last bus left."

"So let her wait at the bus stop. The first bus leaves in another
few hours."

Dror gave me a hard, penetrating look, trying to figure out
what was going on inside me.

"I'll drive her to Haifa," he said, He to get his bag.

"You won't drive her anywhere."

"So what do you suggest?"

"That she get out of here."

"I'm driving her," he snapped, taking his bag.

Putting my hand on my stomach, I said, "If you drive her, don't
come back."

Slowly he put his bag down. "So I'll take her to a taxi stand."

"You won't take her anywhere."

Dror looked at me as if I'd changed into some strange creature
right in front of his eyes, and I understood right away that my
double had risen inside me.

You picked up your brightly colored backpack and headed for the door, feeling your way, almost blind with tears. You went out without a word, leaving Dror and me scorching each other with our looks.

"If anything happens to her—"

"Nothing will happen to her."

"If she gets raped, it'll be on your conscience."

"She won't get raped." I reached out to my double.

His expression changed all at once, as if he'd seen something new, and he suddenly came over to me and hugged me hard, and I began to cry hysterically.

I couldn't tell him what I'd tried so hard to keep from myself: my terrifying fantasy that one day you'd show up where I worked, or you'd call me at home, or you'd be waiting for me, sitting in the armchair in the living room when I got home, a perfect model of my mother, and that within days, you'd take away the people I love, my father and your mother too, and if I had children, maybe you'd seduce them into going with you. But he understood by himself, and before we fell asleep in each other's arms, he laughed into my hair, sweet-talking me, "Did you think she'd seduce me? My excellent redhead genes are in your womb now. I wouldn't give them up so easily." I wanted to say, you have no idea how easily my mother gave up her excellent genes. Then I suddenly remembered how I'd explained to the school nurse that fathers don't give up their children. As I began drifting off to sleep, I put my hand on his arm that encircled my stomach and thought that maybe I'd been right, that children see things that grown-ups don't. "So what is she to you?" he asked in the darkness.

"My mother raised her, and her mother raised me," I said, hardly able to believe my own words.

"Mother swapping." Dror laughed.

"Yes, more or less."

"Why didn't you tell me?"

"I was afraid you'd take off."

"Any other skeletons in the closet?"

"That one's enough."

I was afraid you'd come back again the next day, but you didn't even call. For days afterward, I'd look for signs of you in my house like the suspicious woman I once saw in a movie, careful to remember how I'd placed the pillows on the couch to see whether they'd been touched, drawing a thin pencil line to mark the level of wines in their bottles, rushing to pick up the receiver when the phone rang. On the street, I'd turn around every once in a while to make sure you weren't behind me. But you disappeared for nineteen years, during which my father and both our mothers died. I was with Dora for every one of her painful last years, and I had her buried next to my father and planted cactuses on her grave. I learned of my mother's death from the message you left in formal English on my answering machine. Our mothers died in the same year.

I'm examining you now from the thirteenth row, a distance at which details are blurred, but the overall picture is clear. In two months, you'll be forty-one. What can I learn about you from the tailored gray suit you're wearing, from the scarf wound around your neck, a tie like a hangman's noose, from your hair, as neat and smooth as a motorcycle helmet, cut in ruthless, straight lines, hanging obediently around your face? The movements of your hands are cautious, restrained. You keep your elbows under control, pressed to your body. What can your appearance tell me about the way you lived your life in the tumult that always surrounded my mother? Did she generously clear a space for you between herself and your father? Did you have to fight her for that bit of space? Were you wounded in the war for a place between them? Do you sometimes recall that strange meeting of ours at the entrance to the army base when each of us stuck stubbornly to her own version of events? Was that really why you sought me out then? Were you able to figure out my response on the day I threw you out of the house Dror and I lived in? Do you—the whirlpool in my stomach, which has been calm over the last few years, is slowly coming to life, like a slumbering volcano—do you think about me more and more frequently, as I do about you?

The hall darkens like night falling quickly: light, twilight, total darkness. The viewers immediately abandon themselves to the next minute, sinking into their seats in anticipation. Appearing on the screen are flickering letters thanking the foundations, individuals, merchants, friends who helped produce the film, and then the name of the movie, 'Dice,' and under it, across the entire screen, a quote from Albert Einstein: "God does not play dice." The first shot is of a blue sky stretched from end to end, deepening into a dark sunset-blue, gray-blue, gray-black, black, illuminated by pink-gray, kindling into peach-pink, orange-pink, red-orange, flaming sunrise red. Then there's a sky of rain clouds lightening into a spring sky in the colors of baby clothes. The camera penetrates inward and rises quickly, taking with it the sound of the viewers catching their breath, about to smash into the ceiling of the sky. But no, it swerves suddenly, dives, and stops in front of a tall, New York building. The sound of an explosion instantly pierces the silence, bundles of dynamite are ignited one after the other, spewing round fire clouds and long flames, and the building, like a tall man suddenly fainting, collapses between two new, upright edifices, imploding. The rooftop sinks, squashing floor after floor under it, and before it reaches the ground, the camera goes into slow motion, as if it's pressed up against the building that is falling from the sky, and I hold my breath in the face of the terrible, mesmerizing destruction until the rooftop hits the bottom, rises slightly from the blast, then lands quietly on the ground, and the camera goes back to regular speed, revealing an enormous landslide of smashed bricks, metal and glass. An aura of dust separates the ruins under it from the innocent sky above it, and a pillar rises from it to the sky, reminding me of the divine pillar of fire that led the Israelites from Egypt to the Land of Israel.

Now the screen is divided in half, and a naked baby appears on the left side, crawling eagerly toward a pile of blocks that have photographs of facial features on their sides. For the next twenty minutes, dozens of building are demolished on the right half of the screen, collapsing over and over again into pillars of smoke and fire among buildings left standing. Until the words "The End" flicker on the screen, the baby will play with the blocks, trying to join them so that the facial features on them form a whole picture. Cruelly, amusingly, charmingly, angrily, mischievously, curiously, the baby will roll the blocks, put one on top of the other, hurl them at each other, revealing lips blowing a kiss, clenched teeth, a serious eye, an eye crinkled in laughter, the tip of a curl, nostrils, an earlobe.

"The End" appears on the screen, the lights come up slowly, and the viewers straighten up and gaze around as if they were waking from sleep, looking at their neighbors for help, embarrassed, trying to figure out if they've seen a masterpiece or a clever trick. They applaud out of politeness, not out of overwhelming emotion, and many have already stood up, pushing to leave. I remain seated, confused and agitated, waiting for you.

You suddenly appear from the side of the stage, your rapid steps swallowing the distance to the table at the other side. The applause, which has already subsided, begins again for you. You snatch up the microphone and I hear you say, "Thank you very much. I have a request: if there's a woman in the audience by the name of Hadassa, or Dassie, née Bergenwasser, I would very much like her to come and see me." You hesitate, then add, "Or if someone knows her, I'd appreciate it if you'd ask her to get in touch with me through the Cinemathèque director."

*   *   *

Then we're sitting across from each other on the restaurant balcony among a crowd of relaxed people, pictures of the destruction in your movie constantly passing through my mind, as if a projector were sitting on my optic nerve. Through the dust clouds rising like atomic mushrooms above the landslides of bricks, I look at you. From close up, I can see the vest of your tailored gray suit, and it's wrinkled. You've taken the scarf off your neck, the spray holding your hair in place glitters in the sun, the dark lenses of your glasses are a barrier between our eyes. Through the carefully maintained outer coating, I can see clearly the girl I'd followed so enviously from a distance, the girl my mother left me for and raised, and now, to my astonishment, I see in you the abandoned child, not the chosen one. You're examining me too, probably seeing very easily the abandoned child inside me.

There's something natural and comforting in our sitting here this way, as if we always knew that somewhere, sometime, we'd seek each other out so that we could again bring together the separate versions of our truths and complete the picture that had split our childhoods apart.

We scrutinize each other in prolonged silence, until I realize that you, still faithful to the rules of the game, are granting me, the older one, the advantage of the opening shot.

"A lot of destruction," I say, careful to maintain a matter-of-fact tone, not to give away my surprise, my sadness and anxiety, which would be weapons in the hands of the enemy.

"Where?" You too are cautious. Your eyebrows, a single line with the frames of your Pierre Cardin glasses, do not even rise.

"In your film."

"Ah . . ."

"There's a lot of destruction in America." I take a deep breath and a small step forward.

"Isn't there everywhere?" Your question is either provocative or innocent, but your voice is sorrowful.

"For you, it's in America,"

"But there's a baby in it, too." You are innocent again, opening your lips like a baby.

"Babies are also destruction sometimes."

"The baby in my film is trying to build." Now your lips are tightly closed.

I have no mercy for that baby either. "How far does he get? He doesn't even manage to put two blocks together."

Surprised, you ask, "Is that how you see it?"

"See what?"

"Babies."

"That's how I see your film."

You're quiet for a minute, pausing, either to digest my answer or prepare for the next round.

"Is that your baby?" I intend to rattle her.

My question doesn't surprise you at all. "No," you say with tense lips. "And I'm not married."

"Were you ever married?"

"No. And I have no children," you say quickly, for some reason, adding cautiously, "Are you still with that redhead?"

"No."

"With a different redhead?"

Neither of us smiles.

"With a different non-redhead. And I have two boys."

"Good for you," you snap in English, your tone somewhere between disgust and impatience.

"What does that 'good for you' mean?"

"It means that I wasn't raised to live a normal life. That's what the 'good for you' means." Your eyebrows move closer together, going beyond the Pierre Cardin boundary.

The waitress, as if on cue, arrives just as our conversation shifts. We both order ice coffee. A brief silence falls when she leaves. We were close to the nerve, and we stopped. From there, it's hard to move forward and hard to retreat. I think that you too know how close we are and how alien we are to each other.

"Where did you find all those buildings?" I choose a temporary, safe distance from the exposed nerve.

"I had a friend who worked for a demolition company. I was addicted to demolition for a whole year."

"Addicted to demolition," I repeat with subtle scorn, intending to neutralize your dramatics right then and there.

"Exactly. With all the symptoms of addiction, the excitement, the shakes, everything. It's a serious business, demolition. Sometimes you have to invest as much in it as you invest in building. You have to know how to destroy."

You stop, waiting. Waiting for my response to your last sentence, which was apparently meant to hurt. I refuse to cooperate with you, shift things to the side. "Your Hebrew –"

You interrupt me sharply. "You've already said that. I've been speaking Hebrew my whole life. All my friends were Israelis."

"The one who tears down buildings too?"

"Especially him." Neither of us smile. We wait, sizing each other up.

"Demolition, is that what interests you?"

"You interest me," you respond, in a tone surprisingly soft, filled with generosity.

Your maneuver succeeds and I'm taken off guard. I choke up, but manage to say, like a person showing her willingness to examine the past, "You were completely out of your mind at that first meeting."

"You were completely out of your mind at the second one. I thought you might show up one day and hit me."

"I don't go to America."

"That's interesting."

"Is that what interests you?"

"No. How you managed to survive is what interests me. The redheads and the non-redheads, your sons—I asked myself many times what you must have gone through. I was a baby, but you understood, you were older."

"I was in second grade."

"Mom always boasted about how you learned to read on your first day in the first grade."

We look at each other unsmilingly. The word "Mom" opens an abyss in that conversation, stops us both.

"So what should we call them?"

Only now do I register the comment you made earlier. Was she proud of me then? Did she say it to put you down?

"So what shall we call them?" you repeat more loudly, almost desperately.

"Maybe by their first names."

"That would be odd." You look stressed, as if what you decide now will change the past. "Maybe we should call the one who gave birth to us 'mother.'"

"Okay." What might sound strange to a stranger was a solution of sorts to someone who'd been living with that strangeness all his life.

You think about it for a minute. "Actually, if you don't mind, the opposite is more comfortable for me. What do you say?" You insist on leaving things unresolved.

"That's okay, too." Are we allies or enemies?

"I have a question and I can't help it, I have to ask." You look into my eyes. "Mom...I mean my mother, your mother...did she ever mention me?"

I take a deep breath. You are the first to surrender. And how easily I make you do it, without a battle. According to rules that aren't completely clear to me, I know that you too think you're waving a white flag at me. Before our meeting, I memorized a cruel speech for you, but your sudden surrender has foiled my plans. I begin speaking and hear in my voice the generosity that had been in yours earlier, maybe because I'm talking to you through the sunglasses, through the elegant suit, to the trembling girl inside you. "All the time. She missed you terribly, all the time, kept pictures of you in the living room. We'd celebrate your birthdays. The best cake I ever ate was on your birthdays. She wrote letters to your father asking for pictures of you, but he didn't send any. She talked about you endlessly, waited for you to come. Her last words were about you..."

You reach quickly for your bag and forage around in it. You never imagined that the conversation with me would bring you to tears, so you didn't prepare a handkerchief in advance. From the depths of your purse, you take out a crumpled tissue and shove it under your sunglasses, making them rise onto your forehead. You wipe away the moisture that has accumulated in your eyes, leaving a gray smear of eyeliner on your lids. The two-year-old girl who'd looked out at me over the sideboard in my father's apartment for years peers out at me for an instant before you put your glasses back in place, restoring those dozens of years to yourself.

"Mom used to show me your picture." You sit up straight, taking it upon yourself to put the conversation back on track, blow your nose, dirtying it too with the remains of eyeliner.

"What picture?"

"Between two trees, riding a bike. It was the day you learned how to ride."

The bicycle seat was high and its edge dug into my bottom. From behind me, the yelling coming from my mother—my

mother then—scared me, "She'll fall, she'll fall!" But Papa whispered in my ear, serious and firm, as if he were giving me battle
orders, "Forward all the time, Hadassa'le, don't take your eyes off
what's in front of you." I said, "But Mama's making me afraid I'll
fall," and he said, as if he suddenly knew the future, "Don't pay
attention to her."

"I know that picture." My heart is suddenly spilling over. "I was
five. They were very proud of me that day." My parents were united
in their pride and I learn, my heart constricting, that among the
things she packed before she left was at least one picture of me.

"When did you know about me?"

"As soon as you were born. I went to visit your house with my
parents."

"Were my mother and father already. . . "

"She was still only my mother then."

"But they knew each other already. . . "

"They were apparently already in love."

She looks hurt. The offense taken by a two-week-old infant
spreads over her face, covered with peach-toned makeup.

"The people I told my. . . our story to. . . "

"How many people did you tell?" I am suddenly aware of the
disturbing fact that my secret life and the story of her life are
joined like Siamese twins.

"Does that bother you?"

"I like to choose for myself the people I tell about myself."

"I chose them, too. I told mainly my psychologists."

"Psychologists? In the plural?"

"Very much in the plural. And there were psychiatrists, too."

"How many did you have?"

"Loads of them. I've been in therapy most of my life. And
almost all of them said it was strange that we went with our
fathers. Usually, girls stay with the mothers."

"And without psychologists, you didn't know your story was
strange?"

"No."

"Why did they take you to a psychologist in the first place?"

"At first, because I didn't remember anything. To this day, I don't remember the first four years of my life. Not even hypnosis helped."

"What happened that was so terrible?" I remember the visions that haunted me: my mother waking you up in the morning with a hug; feeding you with love; combing your hair and bathing you; buying, washing, and ironing your dresses; wiping your tears when you cried; smiling at you when you say the *th* properly; strolling with you in big American parks; checking to see if you brushed your teeth before she put you to sleep; getting up on stormy nights to see if you're covered. Why did you want to forget?

"I suppose it was during the years that your mother was hospitalized."

"Hospitalized where?"

"In a mental hospital."

"My mother?"

"Yes."

"I didn't know."

"You were a child, so they didn't tell you. The first two years in America, she was in the hospital. For the first few months, she worked in the store with him and went to English classes twice a week and kept the house clean and was happy, but he started going out with women who came into the store or just women he knew. He liked women and they liked him. One woman told me that one Sunday, in the park, he went off with her and left my mother and me on a bench. And she just went crazy a few months after we arrived. That's what they told me."

"So who took care of you?"

"All sorts of babysitters and neighbors. When she came back, she wasn't able to look after me."

"So why didn't she come home to my father?" I was beginning to forgive the woman who, at the time, had been half the age I am now. I was beginning to forgive her even though she could easily have corrected the mistake she made and changed the fates of several people, including me.

"She had no money."

"She didn't come back because of money?" A few months after she left, my father would still wait tremblingly for her letters, and I used to dream about her at night. I recall the letters she wrote then describing how much she longed to come back, and we didn't believe it.

"Of course it was because of money. She didn't have a penny."

"And your father?"

"Neither did he. He was always in debt."

"And after those two years in the hospital . . . "

"She came home. I was four then, and it's from about that time that I remember her. Her and other things. She changed. That's what my father said. He said that in Israel, she was always laughing, carefree, charming, and full of life. In his last week, he confessed to me that all his women were full of life when he met them, and after a while, they all got depressed. I don't remember her laughing a lot. Most of the time she cried, said she had headaches."

"How awful." The ancient whirlpool came to life deep inside my body.

"Yes. She was pretty sad all those years, always had headaches, millions of treatments and painkillers. My father went off with other women. Sometimes, he'd disappear for a few days, sometimes he'd bring them home. And she went to live in the back room next to the yard, said that's where she felt the best, close to the earth on the way to the grave. She'd walk around that room, talking to herself and shouting at the trees outside."

"How . . . how did she die?"

"The way she lived. Like a dog, alone. With your picture in her pocket."

Very slowly, the woman in my imagination wearing the evening gown changes into a shadow of a woman pacing within the walls of a back room, lying on a hospital bed, covered by sheets soiled with excrement. The image of my mother is sketched in my memory with such faint lines that she switches easily from one figure to another. "It's a good thing my father didn't know. It would have destroyed him."

"What do you mean, he didn't know?" For the first time, your eyebrows rise over the straight line of your Pierre Cardins.

"He never mentioned it."

"Maybe. But he knew."

My double, which you can't see, steps away easily and stands beside me. A puzzled look comes into your eyes when I slide to the side of my chair to make room for her.

You add, "Your aunt from Kiriyat Motzkin knew, too. My father wrote to tell them that if they wanted her back, they should buy her a ticket. They didn't want her back."

"I don't believe you." It occurs to me that you are reverting to your habit of appearing every few years to disrupt my peace and quiet.

"You don't have to believe it. But it's the truth."

"My father missed her even after he met your mother."

"That's what he told you. What did you think, that he would tell you the truth?"

"Maybe your father wrote, but my father didn't get any letters."

"So how did he write back, if he didn't get them?"

"Who said he wrote back?"

"I have his letters. I can show you. He didn't want her. He wrote to my father that the person who made her crazy should take care of her. He wrote: 'I won't take care of a crazy woman who was made crazy by someone else.'"

I lean forward from the force of the pain digging into my stomach. I'm prepared to hear various versions of my mother's story from you, but I won't let you undermine the truth I know about my father. My elbows drill into my knees as I bend to stop the whirling in my stomach. My double hugs me from behind, keeps me from falling forward to your feet. Her presence fills me with strength, and I now refuse to listen to things I would have been ready to listen to before. I don't recognize the people being described here as my father and my mother, and if I were to insist on hearing the details of this tale you are spinning for me, I could easily expose the contradictions and the farfetched theories, but the stomachache is already climbing, rising to my shoulders. My double is helping me sit up straight. The real story is now completely clear to me: Alma herself went crazy and was hospitalized in some institution when she was very young, and that's why she doesn't remember anything that happened before she was four. When she came home from the institution, a crazy four-year-old girl, her sick brain had already distorted reality, and all the psychologists and psychiatrists who have treated her since then and all the drugs she must have taken over the dozens of years added to the distortion. If I sit with her and start the conversation over again, I can easily find out the meaning of the back-room-on-the-way-to-the-grave she's talking about. Maybe that's where they locked her up when she carried on. But the pain is already at the back of my neck, and the headache is coming on. And the film she presented at the Cinemathèque, if I go back over all the details, is proof of the director's definite madness.

Still immersed in my thoughts, I see you talking. Your lips move and I am borne out of my thoughts like a diver rising to the surface of the water as I hear you say, "And that's how she died, with some black practical nurse who was looking after her, and it was terribly sad."

My double gets me to my feet, and we blend into a single body. "Listen, I feel a headache coming on. I have to go."

"You get headaches, too? Too bad." You put your hand on the cigarettes and lighter, shielding them as if we were threatening to snatch them from you, "We haven't even begun to talk... I thought that now we'd be able to..."

"I'm sorry."

"What a shame. I thought we'd talk a little bit about my film too."

"I have nothing to say about your film." We open my bag and rummage around in it.

"I'm sure it affected you..."

We put a bill on the table, put a glass on it so it won't blow away, "If you want so much to talk about it, then listen: you were looking for someone to hang your mediocre film on, and you found Einstein. But that quote of his is forced onto the film, it's unclear, out of place, irrelevant, and pretentious. What did you want to say? That there *is* order in the world? That it's ironic and there's *no* order in the world? That everything's predetermined? That we have no choice? Absolute determinism? And if so—what's your position? What's your moral position about all of this? It's not a film—it's simplistic bullshit. Your aesthetic perception is unclear. The shots of the buildings are tedious. You thought it was so clever to join the beginning and the end, a baby and destruction. It's only some childish nonsense with a childish title."

"That's the whole point," you say with great generosity, with surprising gentleness in the face of our abuse. "It's a film about childhood, our childhood. The critics can't know, neither can the viewers, but I was sure you'd understand, only you can. You must have seen our faces and our parents' faces on the blocks. Of course you did. Even your face from the picture with the bike is there, on the blue block."

"I don't want to be in your film!" Your conciliatory tone is making me angry. Inside us, the whirlpool is drilling.

"But you know what Einstein meant," you say sadly, compassionately, as if Einstein himself had appointed you to give me a message and you see the painful path I will have to travel to the place you have already reached, and you take our hand in both of yours.

We'll destroy that film, we don't want to be part of it, we yank our hand out of yours, we'll delete it from our memory and it'll disappear the way a document disappears from a computer screen with the press of a key. We grab frantically at the straps of our handbag, wishing that the film would burn up, get lost or mutilated, and no one in the world would ever see it. We turn our back to you, we ourselves are planning to forget this insane meeting with you—we start walking down the stairs—and all the crazy, crazy things you said. We stick a hand into the bag, we could tell you a few truths too—walking quickly, we pull our keys out of our bag violently and it slaps against our stomach—but it's clear that you're crazy, you inherited your mother's madness and you're on the verge of hospitalization or suicide, and maybe that's why they protected you. We stop at our car parked across from the balcony you're still sitting on, from where you're watching us, but we don't look up at you. My mother died of sadness and a broken heart— we stick the key into its hole—and that's the only true thing we said—we throw open the car door—but my mother never mentioned you, never—we get into the car—she forgot you completely and it didn't take her long to put away your pictures, and the cakes I told you about were for our birthdays, ours—we start the car—if we had known that this is how the conversation would end, we would have told you the truth—we pull the car quickly out of the row—even though you're definitely upset and on the verge of suicide, we wouldn't have protected you, but you told us a pack of lies too, a pack of lies, a pack of lies about your mother, and we're very very sorry we lied to you. Blinded, we drive toward the parking lot exit, blinded, completely blinded.

Kibbutz

The fingertips appeared first, pressing against the glass, and lingered a moment as if gathering courage before slowly rising. The entire length of the fingers was exposed as they crept up the window, followed by a wrist, a forearm, and an upper arm. Then the hand stopped and the fingers spread out like a palmated leaf plastered against the outside of the window.

Devora, who was busy getting patients' files ready for the doctor's visit the next day, froze in mid-action and, mesmerized, looked at the hairy, masculine arm, its fleshy palm deeply etched with lines, and she was seized by a fierce wave of heat like the hot flashes that used to overtake her before she started stuffing her body with hormone replacements. She wondered at the power Melech had to give her a jolt, to make her heart drop as if she were in an elevator that had stopped abruptly, as if he'd managed to decipher the code buried deep within her, concealed from her husband and even from her daughters.

She looked now at the fingers spread firmly, demandingly, and remembered the first time she saw that hand climbing up the outside of the clinic window—it was the hand of a three-year-old, its fingers spread entreatingly.

She went quickly to the window and tapped on her side of the glass, one hard rap and two light taps, their private signal all those years. The head popped up immediately, the hair blue-black, like his mother's; the astonishingly light, almost transparent eyes, like his father's. Devora looked at Melech's face, frightened by what she saw: something bad, very bad.

And in an instant, they were at the door, hugging each other tightly. They were standing exactly where they had stood a thousand times, enveloped by the same heat that had streamed from her to him when he had run to her, fast as an arrow, on his way from the children's house to his parents' room and she had smothered him in her embrace. In the years that followed, he'd grown taller until, toward the end of middle school, in a single summer's growth spurt, he became the same height as she was, and they found a new way to embrace: like dancing partners changing steps, her head against her shoulder.

"What a surprise, Melech," she said now, slowly, finding it hard to believe he was here, as if she were witnessing a miracle. Proudly she straightened the epaulette that showed his second-lieutenant's stripe. She searched his eyes for the bad thing they had reflected and found his pupils contracted, sharpened, as if even his involuntary muscles were joining in a declaration of hostility. "I was beginning to think you'd forgotten I exist. And all of a sudden, you're here—what a surprise."

"A good one?"

She picked up on the provocative tone of the first words that came out of his mouth and she knew she had read his eyes correctly.

"A wonderful one." Her voice was bursting with love. She refused to let his defiant tone pull her in. "Have you eaten, Melech?"

"I'm not hungry."

"But you should eat a little something. Have some plums." She pulled him into the clinic, ignoring what she'd seen in his eyes, what she'd heard in his voice. "The orchards are exploding with plums this year. Families from the city come and pick them right off the trees, and they have no shame about loading up their SUV's with them. Yesterday, Aharon brought a whole crate of gorgeous plums that are just going to rot here, and you know what it made me think of? The plum cakes your mother used to bake. The smell drove everyone crazy; it carried all the way to the main road."

His sudden squint narrowed his eyes to cracks, as if he'd stumbled into an unexpected storm, and he now wore the defensive expression she'd known from the time he was a child, when he'd cut himself off abruptly, lower an iron curtain between himself and the world. He'd turn his vulnerability inward, gather up the heat of his anger an instant before it attacked the person who'd hurt him, or else run away to let out the pent up rage. Devora looked at his face now, troubled by the agitation that signaled the presence of the bad thing within him.

"Is something wrong, Melech?"

He took a step into the clinic and looked around with wild, searching eyes.

She forced herself to speak calmly. "What's wrong, Melech?"

"Why do you think something's wrong?"

"Because I see it in your eyes." These were the words they both knew from his childhood.

"What do you see, Devora?"

"If there's one thing I know, it's your eyes. Is it something with your girlfriend?"

"No. That's over."

"What a shame, she's a sweet girl. So what is it, the army?"

"No."

"Your health?"

"No."

"I know, your loneliness." She rejoiced at this new possibility, forcing down the tension rising within her, the bright flashes of danger. "Loneliness can be a terrible thing, I know. You have to come here more often when you're on leave, Melech. This is still home. The army isn't home."

"It isn't?"

"Of course not. I put your notice about the outstanding officer awards ceremony on the bulletin board."

"Really?" He spit out the word through curled lips.

"Yes, really."

"But you know no one'll come."

"They've already sent you lots of good wishes."

"Lots of good wishes and what else?"

"What do you mean, 'what else'?"

"I mean lots of questions about the room, too?"

"The room?" She hesitated and shot him a glance, wondering if his agitation had something to do with the room.

"The room. Yes, the room."

"You can't blame them." She stopped pretending.

"Why not?"

"Because there's a shortage of rooms and they can't stand to see one that's been empty for two years already. It was empty for years before that, that's true, but no one wanted it then. And you've hardly been here over the last year. But you can be sure that if anyone has the nerve to ask, I rise up on my haunches and they back down."

"I dreamed that I came here and found all my stuff thrown outside and your Yarden living in it."

"Is that why you came?" She tried to catch his eye.

He evaded her. "No." Then chuckling to himself, he said, "What exactly do you tell them when you rise up on your haunches?"

"I tell them that you plan to come back after the army."

"And will I come back?" A malicious spark flashed.

"I hope so."

"Devora," he said, suddenly switching gears . His voice changed, as if he'd been playing games until now and had tired of them. His familiar voice returned, the familiar eyes, and the familiar, irresistible expression. "Can I ask you for something, Devora?"

"For the moon." Out of habit, she replied with the same phrase she'd used whenever he'd asked for something from the time he was three.

"Do you remember how you used to open the photo album and tell me the story of my parents, picture by picture?"

She looked at him inquisitively. "Of course I remember," she said like someone quickly shoving the tip of his shoe into an opening that is closing in front of him.

"I want you to tell it to me again."

Night after night, for years, the two of them had sat, like yeshiva students, bent over the fragrant, leather-bound photo album, elegantly engraved with Latin letters. When he was a little boy, he'd sit on her lap, and when he grew up, he sat beside her encircled by her arm. Over and over again, in the same voice she used for other fairy tales—until they knew the sentences by heart and would say them in unison—she would tell him the story of his father and the story of his mother and the story of their meeting, their love, their happiness which grew greater every day until, when it was absolutely perfect, a child was born to them, the most beautiful child in the kibbutz and perhaps even in the entire area. He grew and became their pride and joy until his sixth birthday party, which was memorialized in the last picture of the three of them. It was taken in the children's house and showed him squashed between his father, standing on his right, and his mother, standing on his left. All three are looking happily into the camera to the great satisfaction of the photographer, who also managed to include the magnificent layer cake in the picture.

That's where the story ended. They never mentioned the tragedy: he didn't ask and she didn't reply. Devora sometimes thought he'd grown up right before her eyes—as in one of those time lapse shots on the nature channel of flowers blossoming— becoming a young man as they held the album, his shoulders broadening, his chin sharpening, his feet lengthening, his cheeks sprouting bristles, his eyes filling with shadows, all while he was still bent over the pictures, touching their edges gently, examining the details with eyes growing wiser, lingering silently, unmoving, on the picture of his sixth birthday party three days before his parents were killed, then closing the album between his hands, as if to signify that the story had ended.

She couldn't hide her surprise. "You want me to tell you your parents' story now?"

"If you don't mind. Picture by picture. The way you did then."

"That was so many years ago, Melech," she said, wondering what the connection was between his request and the menacing signals she'd been picking up from the minute he appeared.

"That's exactly why."

"Are you starting to forget them, is that it?" Clinging eagerly to this new explanation, she reached out to stroke his cheek, stubbly now where once had been the soft, velvety cheek of a child.

"No. I never forget them."

"So what's this request all about? Why now?" She dropped her hand.

"It's *because* I never forget them."

"What's wrong, Melech? You can tell me. I can see in your eyes that something's happened."

The murky glance turned toward her again, a gleam in it now, as if he enjoyed tormenting her, trying to evade her ability to read what was in his heart. To her surprise, she could see a spasm of pain pushed deep down inside him.

"It's all right, Melech, it's all right." She soothed him as she had so many times in the past, but this time she knew it was definitely not all right.

He shot a question at her. "And how's Aharon?"

Like someone being attacked from behind, she tensed, as suspicious as she always had been when asked how Aharon was, a reminder of the stabbing, seemingly innocent questions from the time her husband used to chase the women on the kibbutz and all the occasional female visitors, too. People would whisper and gossip behind her back, but to her face, they'd ask with pretended casualness, "And how is Aharon?" as if they didn't know that she was the last person who could answer that question. It seemed to her that, over the last few years, the snickering had stopped and the questions about Aharon's well-being had grown fewer, and she understood that it wasn't only in her bed that things had become boring. Nevertheless, when she heard the unexpected "And how is Aharon," the old scar throbbed.

But Melech, like his parents, was outside the circle of kibbutz gossipers, and he didn't seem to be inquiring about Aharon's love life. On the other hand, Melech never asked how her husband or her daughters were, as if he had drawn a line between her and her family, inviting her into his life and keeping them out. As soon as the week of mourning for his parents was over, Devora had taken him into her bedroom where her large closet stood. Each of her daughters had been allocated three shelves in that closet, and she showed him the three shelves she'd emptied for him. He went straight to his parents' house and brought back the picture of his sixth birthday party with the layer cake and put it on the middle shelf. But the peaceful atmosphere was spoiled that very day. In the afternoon, in Melech's presence, Yarden protested at the top of her lungs that Devora had claimed there was no room when she had asked for another shelf, and now three whole shelves had suddenly appeared out of nowhere. Furious about the offense to Melech, but before she could explain, Melech tore out of the house. Later, at her mother's command, Yarden apologized to Melech, spewing out the words as if they were curses. In a further attempt at reconciliation, they all sat in oppressive silence and even Aharon was careful about what he said. After that, Melech refused to come to their house, and most of his meetings with Devora took place in the clinic at the end of the workday.

"Why are you suddenly asking about Aharon?"

"Because he's your husband."

"He's fine."

"And the album's at your place?"

"I have no idea where the album is."

"I thought it was in your bedroom, on that shelf."

"Only the birthday picture was there, and later on, I put it back in the album."

"So it's in your house. If no one took it."

"Why should anyone take it?"

"How do I know? Maybe someone felt like having an album."

"So?"

"So he went into your room and took it."

"What's wrong with you, no one would throw away someone else's pictures so they could have an album."

"Probably not pictures of Aharon. But they'd throw out pictures of my parents readily enough."

She thought she was getting closer to the mystery of the thing she'd sensed inside him: he'd never spoken so bitterly about people's attitude toward his parents. What does he know about it?

Who told him? What brought him here today, unannounced and uninvited? What is it that she read in his eyes: Rage? Affront? The desire for revenge?

"Don't you trust me anymore, Melech?"

"You're the only person left in the world who I can trust."

"So why aren't you being open with me?"

"I will be, after we look at the album."

"Swear?"

"On my parents' grave." His chuckle sounded like a strangled sob.

Fourteen years after his parents' death, neglect had overtaken the cultivated flowerbeds, and an uncared-for bit of sand had replaced the garden of marvelous, flowering bushes in front of their house. Neighbors had filled the empty porch with pieces of broken furniture, rusty bicycles, and old baby carriages.

Melech, his expression unreadable, looked at the junk blocking the door.

"I'll make sure all of this is gone tomorrow," Devora said quickly. "I'll send one of the maintenance crew to come and throw it all away. I'll ask him to paint the walls, too."

"It doesn't matter." Melech pushed his way through to the locked door and put the key in the keyhole. The door opened onto a room as gloomy as a forbidding cave and it smelled of mildew and things long untouched. The first few years after their death, no one but Devora and Melech had dared go into the place. Several years later, the house had been offered to young men after their military service and they had refused, preferring a small shack or a storeroom. And later on, Devora prevented its being given to anyone by claiming that Melech was approaching draft age and he had the right to his parents' house.

Devora put the bowl of plums on the table and was again seized by a vague feeling, a strange and oppressive uneasiness, as if the ghosts of the dead couple had taken over the place. They found the dust-covered album easily at the bottom of the closet, on a shoebox.

"Maybe we should take the album and go somewhere else, Melech?"

"Where?"

"My place, or the clinic."

"I'd rather stay here."

Devora picked up the familiar album, took a tissue out of her pocket and gently wiped off the layer of dust, feeling time retreating, returning Melech the child to her. She touched his hand with the old naturalness, sat down, and pulled him close. On her lap she placed the album of black cardboard pages separated by silky, transparent papers that turned slowly, leafed through it, found the picture she'd always begun the story with, summoned up the voice she'd used then, and said, "This is David, Melech's father—"

"Not like that, Devora," he interrupted brusquely.

"Then how?"

"You know how. With 'Once upon a time,' and all that, like you did then."

"What's gotten into you, Melech, I can't . . . "

"I'm asking you."

"It won't work . . . " She protested against the trap he had set for her, that she had been led into from the minute he appeared at the clinic.

"Why not?"

"You know why not. Because it's strange, as if this were a play or something . . . "

"But that's how you always started: 'Once upon a time'."

"That was appropriate when you were six. Now, I don't know . . . it's a little contrived . . . "

"Not to me. I want to try to feel like six again."

She looked at him, deliberating.

"Please, Devora."

"Okay . . . " She cleared her throat and tried to give her voice the same intonation it had had the hundreds of times when she'd told the boy on her lap his parents' story as if it were another fairy tale: "Once upon a time there was a man, and his name was David, Melech's father—"

"That's it," he said softly, encouragingly, and the fingers of the boy that lay hidden within the fingers of the second lieutenant clasped her arm.

"This is Melech's father on one of his first days here, on our kibbutz . . . " As she grew accustomed to time moving backward and
turning Melech into a child in her lap, she was transported into the
old story. "It's lucky someone took his picture and we have such a
lovely souvenir of him. Here he is standing tall and proud with a
pail in one hand and a pitchfork in the other. He has very beautiful eyes, just like Melech's, and you can see how light they are even
when he's standing in the shade. He's happy because he found
work doing something he loves—"

She stopped, hesitated, wondered if time hadn't made a mock-
ery of the next line, which she remembered quite well.

He was waiting breathlessly, and when she hesitated, he quickly
helped her out, imitating in a whisper the intonation of her voice,
"So what's the moral of the story?"

"So what's the moral of the story?" she repeated with a smile, as
if all that delay had not come from hesitation, but from a conscious
decision to test his memory, and now she was waiting, as she had
then, for the expected response, which always had a declamatory
ring to it, and when he didn't reply, as sometimes happened, she
herself did: "That in order to be happy you have to find work
doing something you really, really love."

"Look at this idiot—a complete idiot." Haimke pushed the photograph into Devora's hand and collapsed onto the chair. "I ran to
the office especially to get the camera, and Michael sent in the film
to be developed right away, so we'd have something for posterity:
the face of an idiot, the blue eyes of an idiot, the posture of an
idiot, even the pail of an idiot. A perfect idiot. Sticking out his
chest as if he's about to get a medal. That's what he looks like.
Tonight he'll tell us about himself. I invited him to the clubhouse.
Come one, come all, and you won't believe what an idiot a person
can sound like."

That evening, along with a handful of members who had been
tempted into coming by the promise of some good entertainment, Devora heard David tell the story of his dismal life, heard
him get tangled up in it, lose the thread and try desperately to

find it, stammer an inarticulate description of how he was born in a DP camp in Europe after the war, how he came to Israel with his parents and they opened a small grocery store in Bnei Brak, how he found it difficult to understand his teachers and in the end, dropped out of school and spent most of his days in his parents' grocery store, how his mother died and he and his father kept the store running together, how terrible his life was in the city and how he begged his father to look for a store out in the country, but his father refused, how his father had died a year ago, how he tried to manage the store himself but had problems with customers who bought on credit and then disappeared, with strangers who suddenly turned up, claiming that his father had borrowed money from them, with suppliers who sent him phony bills, and the bank, which pretended to help him but made things worse with its high interest, and then he was forced to close the grocery and sell it to pay off his debts, and how a soft-hearted neighbor, may God bless him—David kissed the tips of his fingers and threw a kiss to his good neighbor—a teacher, told him about the kibbutzim that were looking for hard workers like him, and even took the trouble to get the information and arrange a meeting for him with the kibbutz representative and even escorted him to his office door. There, David told the man about himself and his love for the countryside, but the man showed no enthusiasm or interest until David mentioned the apartment his parents had left him and promised to turn it over to the kibbutz.

David fell silent, bent as if bowing, and took a noisy sip from the glass of water in front of him.

Everyone, embarrassed by his child-like frankness, stared at him.

"And you've been single the whole time?"

"The who-o-le time." David stretched out the word to emphasize the eternity of it and shrugged, as if apologizing.

"Why? Didn't any girls come into the store?" Aharon dared to ask.

"Sure they did. They came in and bought stuff and went out."

"But with you religious people, matchmaking is a mitzvah.

Nobody tried to arrange a match for you?" Mathilda joined in, as
if she were angry at those who hadn't come to his aid.

"They tried, but none of the girls wanted me," David said simply, spreading his arms to the side as if proving that he had nothing to hide.

Mathilda wouldn't let it go, and continued sweetly, "But you're
such a good catch, why—"

"I'm not such a good catch. People are always cheating me."

"Why do you say you're not a good catch? You could easily have
finished university, found a rich girl—"

"Enough—" Devora stood up and placed herself between David
and the others, a symbolic gesture of the task she'd be performing
over the years to come. "That's enough. Let's take a break, David.
Come with me, we'll make ourselves some tea. And there's cake."

"Once upon a time there was a happy man who tended cows in a
kibbutz in Israel and his name was David. You can see from his
smile how happy he was from the very beginning. He came here
by accident, completely by accident. In fact, he was actually on
his way to another kibbutz, but the bus stopped at our stop,
which just happens to be right opposite the cowshed. And when
he saw the cowshed, he decided he wanted to stay here, in our
kibbutz. He wouldn't take no for an answer. Melech's father was
very stubborn. He held a kind of sit-in at the cowshed, and that's
what finally convinced everyone on the kibbutz, because they
realized how much he wanted to stay. It wasn't easy to arrange,
because the people in the kibbutz he was supposed to go to
fought for him and refused to give him up, but there was no cowshed there. And Menachem, who was the kibbutz secretary then,
promised him work in the cowshed and traveled all the way to
the city especially to arrange for him to stay with us, and David
never forgot what Menachem did for him, and every time he saw
him, even years later, he still thanked him for traveling all the
way to the city especially for him. That's how he came here and
that's how he stayed here in our kibbutz. And what's the moral
of the story?" Devora broke off the sentence and immediately

completed it herself—"That's right: if you want something and really really fight for it, you'll get it in the end. Because where there's a will, there's a way."

Through the bus window and the door of the cowshed, David saw, as if it were a dream come true, a row of cows' heads, and it took his breath away. With uncharacteristic decisiveness, he got up and pulled his suitcase excitedly off the rack above the seats. The driver, who saw his passenger's head lower and disappear into the back stairwell, jumped out of his seat, got off the bus, and grabbed hold of the excited passenger to stop him and to explain slowly, the way you explain to a child, that all kibbutzim look alike, but that wasn't the kibbutz whose name he'd shown him written on a slip of paper when he'd gotten on the bus at the central bus station in Tel Aviv. But David, deviating from his usual obedience, refused to hear the rest of what the driver had to say. With a few firm shakes of his head and in a brave voice, he said that this was the place where he wanted to stay, and to prove his resolve, he began walking purposefully toward the cowshed, although he was shod in his best shoes.

At the door to the cowshed, his suitcase on the ground at his right and in his left hand, the sweat-soaked bus ticket he'd clutched so tightly all the way from Tel Aviv, ready for the moment the ticket inspector would board the bus, David shouted a passionate "Shalom" and almost fainted from the impact of the delightful smell and the velvety eyes of the cows. He had no doubt, this was where he belonged, not in the dark, stifling air of the grocery store among the shelves overflowing with matchboxes and shoelaces and mayonnaise jars and chocolate bars and cigarette packs and candy bags.

How long he stood there, stunned with joy, he had no idea. At five in the afternoon—Yehuda, who tended to the cows, later recounted—a peculiar looking man stood in the middle of his cowshed dressed in city clothes, a shabby suitcase at his feet and tears in his eyes. When Yehuda asked him what he was looking for, the man said that he'd stopped looking; he'd already found it. This was where he wanted to work. Right here in this cow-shed. And when he was told that, at the moment, they didn't need anyone else to work with the cows, he burst into tears, unintentionally knocked the suitcase onto its side on the muddy, dung-covered floor, stepped into the water ditch with his city shoes, threw his arms around the neck of the cow Attalia, and said that he was ready to give the kibbutz the apartment his parents had left him, and anyway, there was no way they'd get him out of there alive. Yehuda looked helplessly at him for a minute, then went to get Menachem, the kibbutz secretary. He did not forget to mention the matter of the apartment, and they both came running back to the man who was still clinging to Attalia's neck, and coaxed him into letting go of the cow and telling them how he'd gotten there and what apartment he was talking about.

"Once upon a time there was a very kindhearted man and his name was David. He left the city and came to live on the kibbutz. Here he is a few months after he arrived. He'd already gotten used to the people here and everyone liked him very, very much. He grew huge dahlias in many beautiful colors, the kind of dahlias no other gardener could grow, and he would give them to anyone who wanted them. He didn't know how to say no. He really loved people to ask him for the flowers, and there were some people who didn't even bother to ask, they just came and picked his flowers because they knew he wouldn't be angry. You can see him sitting on the ground, surrounded by his dahlias, and you can see the joyful smile on his face. Look, Melech, at his feet. What do you see? Yes. He's pulled his big toe over onto the little one."

The taunting began immediately, and from almost the first moment, was completely unembarrassed and guilt-free. At first, they made an effort to find a polite way to cover it up. Months later, they no longer bothered to disguise it, and the children who bullied David weren't scolded, a sign that it was permitted and done good-naturedly. But on that first day, a few minutes after the three of them went into the office and David, still in tears, gave a muddled account of how he'd seen the cows' heads, how he'd been overcome with the tremendous need to reach out and touch them, how he'd grabbed his suitcase and rushed off the bus even though the driver told him it wasn't his stop, and how, when he went into the cowshed, he almost fainted at the sight of a cow and her calf standing there so peacefully, as if all was well with the world, and how the calf pressed up against its mother—

At that point in the flow of the story, which lurched along with the seesawing of his choked voice, Menachem lost his patience and asked a direct question about the apartment he'd mentioned earlier. Right then, Yehuda saw Aharon pass the shed on his bicycle. He went to the window, whistled sharply, and gestured with a quick wave of his arm and a wink of his eye for Aharon to come over. And Aharon, recognizing the cheerful urgency of the signals, dropped his bike, hurried to the window and stuck his head between the bushes, and as he stood there listening, a happy smile spread across his face.

"But we're not religious here, you'd better get that straight—" Menachem said threateningly, waving a finger in the air and looking sideways at Aharon, who was nodding outside.

"Me too, I'm not religious either," David said, alarmed.

"But you said the apartment's in Bnei Brak."

"On the border," David moaned, "the border of Bnei Brak, a building next to a building in Ramat Gan."

"On the border," Menachem raised his voice, "on the border is something else. Isn't it dangerous to live on the border?" The edge of a smile began to creep across his face, and he didn't try to suppress it.

"The border of Bnei Brak, that's not dangerous, a building next to a building in Ramat Gan."

"I see," Menachem turned his head, "so the matter is closed. Now let's hear what you're willing to do here."

"Anything, anything," David said, spreading his arms to the side, "whatever I have to."

"Will you dance?" Menachem asked carefully, testing limits, and caught the surprise in Yehuda's eyes.

"I'll dance too, if I have to," David kept his arms outspread.

"You have to, of course you do," Menachem said quickly.

"So if I have to—I have to," David reconciled himself to his fate.

"And where will you do it?" Menachem groped, not sure he and his interlocutor were headed in the same direction at the same pace.

"Wherever you say," David extended his wandering hands.

"What, in the cowshed?"

"In the cowshed, wherever you say." David yielded again, as if he understood that a new place has new customs, and he had to adjust himself to them.

"I didn't mean the cowshed"—Menachem caught Aharon's glittering smile—"I meant in our dancing class, but if you want the cowshed, then okay, maybe you can dance with the cows."

David didn't respond, as if he were considering the idea.

"So the matter's closed. What else do you know how to do?" Menachem asked.

David gave him a puzzled look, as if he were still immersed in thoughts about the earlier matter, or had just realized that they were ridiculing him, or was trying to decipher the question.

"So what else do you know how to do?" Menachem repeated.

David hesitated. "You mean like tricks?"

Menachem remained unflustered, didn't blink an eye. "Exactly, you hit the nail right on the head. We like tricks here. What tricks do you know how to do?"

David suddenly smiled a big, mysterious smile that exposed his gums, and his pale blue eyes crinkled and were swallowed up by the lids. He raised his right foot to his left knee, took off the shoe that was filthy with cow dung and hay stalks, pulled off his sock, presented his clear, virginal foot, took hold of his big toe with two fingers and pulled it, as flexible as rubber, over the others until the pad of his big toe touched the nail of the smallest toe. Then he lifted his head, as overjoyed as a child, and waited for the applause.

That evening, in the dining hall, from two tables away, Devora looked at David, who was totally engrossed in spreading cheese on his slice of bread. Her husband, Aharon, sitting beside her, was telling the people around the table about the two acres of newly sown hay, in addition to the hundred acres already planted, and about the stevedores' strike at the Haifa port that had caused them to stop harvesting for three days. When at that moment, his glance happened to fall on David, he burst out laughing and described the conversation he'd heard and the phenomenal big toe he'd seen as he stood at the window. David, as if he'd heard the words, raised his head and fixed his round eyes on Aharon. Aharon hesitated for a moment, lifted his hand to him, regained his calm, and said, "You're invited to the clubhouse tonight."

"Tonight?" Even from several tables away, you could see how upset he was.

"Yes. I told everyone about you and they'd be very happy to meet you."

"But I can't tonight." David squirmed with the refusal.

"Why not?"

"Because I have to fix up my room. And I start working tomorrow."

"So we'll wait a few days."

"That's wonderful," David said, gratefully.

Two weeks later, David's medical file came in the mail, completely empty, indicating that he hadn't been to a doctor in almost thirty years. Devora asked him to come to the clinic, and he arrived freshly showered, his wet hair plastered to his head and his eyes shining. As soon as he sat down, he said, "A new calf was born today."

"Congratulations."

"Thank you," he exulted.

She felt the urge to reach out and touch him, to calm his excitement, to prepare him for the insults he would have to endure in this place, insults that the blind joy he was feeling now temporarily shielded him from.

"I'm glad you came to the kibbutz, David."

"I'm glad too. Very, very, very glad."

"Did I already tell you that I'm in charge of—"

"I don't remember," he admitted readily.

"I'm in charge of the kibbutz clinic. I asked you to come because your medical file arrived and I wanted us to get to know each other."

"I have no medical file. I don't go to doctors."

"Why not?"

"Because they killed my sister when she was a baby."

"And you never went to a doctor?"

"No. I'm afraid of doctors."

Devora looked into his colorless eyes, and she felt anger rise in her at the injustice, at nature, which had washed its hands of him and had left even his eyes defenseless. She put her hand on his arm and heard herself say, "Listen, David. I know quite a few things about you already, and I want to tell you a little about myself. My name is Devora. I'm not a doctor. I'm a nurse. I want you to know that you can always come to me, anytime. Not only about your health."

He looked at her with searching, suspicious eyes that gave away the fact that he wasn't so oblivious to what was happening around him, that he was used to being treated unkindly, which perhaps explained why he found it difficult to recognize good intentions. He asked cautiously, "So about what?"

"Whatever you want, David. I'm always here."

Not out of malice, but out of a lack of a generosity, after first teasing David, the people on the kibbutz began abusing him, and it didn't happen quickly, but in an imperceptible, ongoing deterioration that blurred the horror of it. And because David was amiable and seemed not to always understand the affronts, the kibbutz members could tell themselves that they teased him out of their affection for him. At first, they merely added salt to his coffee and sugar to his salad. Later, they involved him in escapades that provided them with hours of laughter: how he slept on the rickety roof of the cowshed from midnight till dawn, his socks full of ice, to protect his cows from thieves; how they stood him in front of a pan of Atida's dung to look for a precious stone she'd swallowed; how they starved him for a whole day so he could do his part to help cut expenses. He was an eager participant in their schemes, keeping awake with the help of the ice he'd poured into his socks, bringing the lumps of dung close to his eyes, enduring hunger without complaint for the sake of the kibbutz budget.

Devora, observing the revelry surrounding the new member, tried to stop it, and argued with them fiercely. They laughed and denied that they were abusing him, trying to mollify her with the assurance that it was just good-natured fun. And when that didn't satisfy her, they swore up and down that they'd stop. But they never seriously considered giving up the toy that had fallen into their hands. Two months after he arrived, apparently tired of the way people provoked him even during meals, David took his plate and moved to an isolated table far from the serving cart and he sat there, quiet and pensive, eating and looking out at the silent landscape of tree trunks and empty children's swings. Devora watched him from where she was sitting, saw the way people walked passed him and made comments, the way David stayed bent over his plate and didn't respond.

"What's wrong with David?" she asked Yehuda, who was in charge of the cowshed.

"Nothing," he replied.

"He looks a little depressed."

"If I was without a woman for twenty years, I'd be depressed, too."

"And he's working as usual?"

"Works and kisses the cows."

"What do you mean, kisses the cows?" She tensed.

"Exactly what I said. French kisses. If I didn't have a woman for twenty years, I'd kiss the cows, too."

At suppertime the next day, she carried her plate to the isolated table.

"Can I sit with you, David?"

He didn't reply, only pointed to the chair opposite him, and she took this as an invitation.

"Can I tell you something, as the clinic nurse?"

"What?"

"You look very sad to me. I have the feeling that something's wrong."

"What?"

"I don't know, but if you tell me, maybe I can help."

"You can't, because he threw them out already."

"Threw what out?"

"The pictures."

"What pictures?"

"Of my family."

"From where?"

"From the apartment."

"What apartment?"

"The apartment in Bnei Brak. He bought it and threw everything out. What they sold, they sold, and what they didn't sell—he threw out."

The stuffed peppers flipped in her stomach and a sourness rose up in her throat. The apartment in Bnei Brak had been sold and the money had been swallowed up into the kibbutz budget, as the last kibbutz bulletin had explicitly stated.

"They didn't take you to the apartment so you could get what you wanted?"

"No. They said it was a shame to waste a day's work."

"You could've taken a Saturday."

"They said they needed me to help with the peanuts and then with the roof of the feed containers."

"And they threw out everything that was in the apartment?"

"Not them—" he came to the defense of the kibbutz members, and his colorless eyes opened wide. "Him. The one they sold the apartment to. He threw everything into the city dump."

Devora watched Aharon all evening, wondering how the young man who'd written her poetry had disappeared and in his place had appeared this coarse stranger who ate the sandwiches she made.

"Is David working in the cowshed, or is he doing all the jobs everyone tries to get out of?" she asked at the end of the evening.

"Who tries to get out of what?"

"Out of the peanuts, for example. Out of the feed containers, for example."

"About the peanuts, they needed people to plow and fertilize two hundred acres. And there's a leak in the feed containers because the metal at the top is rusty, so they recruited people to put up an asbestos roof."

"And why is it that he's always being recruited for everything?"

"He's not the only one."

She tried to calm down. "Okay, let's say that's true . . . You were involved in selling David's apartment, weren't you?"

"What do you mean, 'involved'? What does 'involved' mean?"

"You know what 'involved' means."

"I went to the notary public with David to have the irrevocable power-of-attorney notarized."

"And while you were at it, you couldn't take him to the apartment to get the things he needs?"

"What does he need? He has everything here."

"Are there pictures of his parents here?"

"Is that what this is all about? I thought I killed someone."

"You know, some things aren't funny. Okay, so you stole the apartment from him. Yakov and Bella inherited apartments and no one touches them. Okay, so you didn't wait a few months to see if he would fit in here, and if you broke him in the end, at least he would've had someplace to go back to. His parents were Holocaust survivors, did you know that? All they had was seven pictures from before the war. You couldn't give up a day's work so he could go there and get the pictures of his family?"

"He himself showed me a picture."

"He has one picture, of himself as a child. The new tenant threw everything out. He doesn't have a single picture of his parents left."

"That tenant is really not a mensch. And about David, I can tell you that there's some really good news, but it's still a secret. Can you keep a secret?"

"Don't get me involved in your secrets," she snapped.

"Still, to prove how much I trust you, I'll tell you: Michael found him a wife."

*

"Once upon a time there was man called David who married
Rachel and they loved each other very much and they were very
happy together, like in a fairy tale. This is Melech's mother, she's
in the tire storeroom, so the picture looks a little dark. She lived
with her parents in Haifa then, and Michael met her in the garage
when he went there to buy parts for the kibbutz trucks. Melech's
father saw the picture, and he didn't really like her because in that
picture, you couldn't see how nice she was. But Michael invited
her here and she came one Friday, and the women dressed her up
and did her hair—here, in the picture they took as a memento,
you can see how pretty her hairdo is. And she met David in the
clubhouse, and the minute he saw her, like in a fairy tale, he
changed his mind and in the end, they fell in love. And after he
went to see her in Haifa a few times, they decided to get married,
and the kibbutz made them a beautiful wedding and they
brought her whole family here from Haifa on a bus. Her grandmother and grandfather came, and her aunts and uncles and
cousins, and all the sweet little children. And after the wedding,
she came to live with him on the kibbutz. She was employed in
the sewing shop, and on the holidays, she'd bake in the kitchen
and everyone was so happy, because her cakes were the most deli-
cious, and she watched over David, she even watched over the
flowers he grew and didn't let people come and pick them whenever they wanted, the way they did before. Here, in this picture
they're standing next to the flowers and holding hands. They'd
hold hands everywhere, even in the dining room. They'd eat with
one hand and with the other, they held hands. They were very,
very happy together. So what is the moral of the story? That if you
don't like someone when you first meet them, you should give it
another chance, and not say 'no' right away."

Michael shoved the picture between David's eyes and the trembling udders of Pnina the cow.

"What do you say?"

David drew back. "What's that?"

"Not 'what's that.' *Who's* that. That's your bride."

David blinked and grimaced. "Who says?"

"The kibbutz," Michael asserted. "You're marrying her next Wednesday."

"I can't!" David burst out in a sob.

"Why not?" Michael sounded disappointed, as if he'd been denied the opportunity to do a good deed.

"Because she's black as a Negro," David said despairingly, afraid that his fate had been sealed. "I can't marry a black woman."

"Why, David, why not?"

"Maybe she's not Jewish."

"What happened, did you suddenly turn religious on us? You said you lived on the border, not really in Bnei Brak."

"Even if I did, so what?"

"And if I prove to you that she's Jewish?"

"Then I still can't."

"Why can't you?"

"I don't know why. I just can't."

"Explain to me why."

"I don't know how to explain."

"Try."

"No one in my family married a black woman."

"So what? That's not a good reason. Give me a better reason."

"I don't have one."

"And besides, she's not black. She's dark because she was born in Iran. Do you know that after the wedding, you get a three-day honeymoon? And besides, if you don't take her, someone else will come along and snatch her up."

"So let him."

"With the honeymoon and everything."

"It's okay. I don't want her."

"But she wants you." Michael held out both hands, palms up, in a gesture of "Don't even try to top this."

"She doesn't even know me."

"Not yet. But I told her about you and she said she wants you."

"She wants me?" David stole a glance at the picture.

"Yes."

David was silent for a moment, letting the information seep in. A woman, even if she looked too dark for his taste in the picture, had said explicitly, in actual words, that she wanted him.

"Did you tell her that I don't have the apartment in Bnei Brak anymore?" David's forehead wrinkled with his fear.

"She didn't ask about an apartment."

David thought for a moment, stroked the skin of the silent cow, drew strength from her, stuck out his chin, and said in a brave voice, "I still don't want her."

"That's your right. It's a free country."

"Exactly," David said, proud of himself for his new firmness, and his courage grew. "And I don't want her."

"So tell her yourself. She's coming on Friday."

Rachel arrived at the kibbutz on Friday afternoon. She sat swaying in the front seat between Michael's shoulder and the truck driver's, keeping her knees together and her head facing forward to make sure the truck didn't suddenly turn its nose into a side road, as the garage owner had cautioned her. When they arrived, she looked around inquisitively and immediately asked to see the room she'd be spending the night in, and if she didn't like it, she waved her finger in warning and demanded that they take her back to Haifa right then and there. Michael took her to the room of a member who'd gone to visit his children at his ex-wife's house in another kibbutz. He waited at the door and watched her step purposefully into the room, take a look at the bed, examine the mattress with twenty outspread fingers, open the closet, thrust her head inside and sniff, rummage around and find clean bedclothes, go to the bathroom, open the door, check to see if the floor and the soap holder were clean, open the plastic shower curtain, come back in and close the door, put her bag on the bed, and say in the tone of a customer pretending indifference so the salesman will lower the price, "So far, so good."

"Good. The women have invited you to have your hair done now," he said.

The business of the hairdo kept the kibbutz buzzing for quite a few days, and they even wrote about it in the kibbutz bulletin, publishing pictures of the work in progress along with the article. Three women did the job, struggling to choke silent laughter, running one after the other to the bathroom to release their stifled screeches of laughter, covering them with the noise of the water flushing in the toilet. Rachel watched them suspiciously, but every time she raised a doubt, they assured her that that's how it was done in the kibbutz, and each woman in turn recounted how the old-timers had gotten her ready for the first meeting. First, they loosened her tangled, coarse hair, tried unsuccessfully to comb it, pulled it to the right and pulled it to the left, and then, when they despaired of giving it a shape, they made a thick band of hair, lifted it over her temples, arranged it high on her scalp, pulled it over her nape and straightened the wavy surface.

"Like a runway," Shosh spluttered, and ran off to the bathroom.

"A bird's nest," Hemda said and stuck her fist into the middle of it.

And then they made her up. Rachel was ordered to close her eyes, and Yael took advantage of the moment to get the small egg the children had taken out of the pigeon's nest in the window box and place it carefully in the indentation at the top of the hill of hair. Rachel, whose suspicions had faded, enjoyed the pampering hands, abandoned herself to them with closed eyes, and didn't see Shosh appear suddenly and pull out the egg, which had already settled down into the bed of hair. Finally, on command, Rachel opened her eyes. The women held up a mirror before her and turned it slowly so she could see herself from every angle, and exclaimed their admiration. Rachel saw the beautiful lips they had drawn and the line of her throat that had been exposed, and as she moved her head from left to right, she said to the women standing over her, waiting for her response, "So far, so good."

Yael, in whose house the preparations were made, took Rachel under her wing, and in the evening, when the kibbutz members had gathered in the clubhouse and the young men had come especially to tell them that David was already there, she escorted Rachel there. She led her like a bridesmaid past the curious members, who were suppressing smiles at the sight of the hairdo, and, with a nod of her head, indicated the ornate chair under the lamplight where David was sitting. Rachel examined him from a distance, her expression giving away nothing. That evening, David was led to the chair next to hers and pushed into it. One of the members stood beside him and held his shoulder in a pseudo-friendly gesture to keep him a prisoner in the chair. David sat there for several minutes, frozen with fear, and then summoned up the courage to say something to Rachel, his eyes downcast. He got up the minute the members left and escaped to a corner of the room, from where he stole glances at her all evening, afraid of her yet attracted. He saw Zevik bend down and talk to her, was tormented by the sight and terrified that she might prefer Zevik, who would promise her to leave his wife and marry her. And so, tossed between the contradictory new feelings churning within him, David became captivated. At the end of the evening, his eyes were riveted on her despite his shyness, and he knew that he'd fallen in love with her, and when Michael came over to him at the end of the evening and whispered, "She said she's interested," he said with a sigh of joy, "Me, too."

The wedding ceremony was modest as far as food was concerned, and noisy as far as people were concerned. The bride's large family, who had despaired of finding her a husband and were unwilling to reveal her age until they had to present her papers at the Rabbinate, arrived in a bus that was parked for hours across from the cowshed, arousing the curiosity of the cows. The female guests wore gold-embroidered, velvet dresses and the male guests, clean-shaven, were clad in fancy suits. An endless number of children ran around screaming and chasing each other on the grass and among the tables and chairs, overturning the Styrofoam cups and banging into people's feet; the adults couldn't control them even when the bride and groom were being led to the chuppah. When the groom shattered the glass with his foot, the guests burst into cheering and crying, and trilled loudly between hands beating against their mouths as the kibbutz members looked at them and sniggered.

The bride and groom spent their three-day honeymoon in their room. They sealed their shutters and closed their door, but apparently weren't able to tell each other many of their stories, and probably didn't make love, because kibbutz members kept entering unannounced and without knocking. On the second day of their honeymoon, after hearing that the members had coordinated their visits to continue until midnight so the young couple wouldn't have a minute alone, Devora went to see them, bearing a tray of food, a key, and a "Do Not Disturb" sign, and instructed them to lock the door and not to open it for visitors. David, exhausted from the previous day, so happy she'd come that he almost cried, said to Rachel, "This is Devora the nurse. She's my best friend on the kibbutz." And Rachel fingered the key and said, "So from now on, she's mine, too."

In a short time, Rachel began managing the sewing shop efficiently and strictly, and turned out to be a suspicious, bad-tempered woman who showed generosity only to David. It didn't take long before she stood as a buffer between the abusive kibbutz members and her husband, fighting his fights energetically and fearlessly. Sometimes, she went out to look for people in their houses and shouted at them in front of their children. But most often she'd ambush most of them in the dining room and admonish them in a loud, childish voice, despite David's attempts to silence her. A note she wrote in large letters and hung on the bulletin board forbade the members to pick flowers from their garden, and when she discovered that the flowers were still being picked, she scrunched down behind the low wall of the porch to lie in wait for the thieves, and when she heard the sound of a stem being pulled up, she leaped out onto the person doing it, who turned out to be Shosh, and beat her severely. Half an hour later, she attacked Zetooni with a broomstick, injuring him, and he rushed to the clinic stunned, his back bleeding. One by one, she drove the kibbutz members away from her house, allowing only a few to pick dahlias or to enjoy her marvelous cakes, their sweet aroma floating like a cloud over great distances.

From the day Rachel came into David's life, the members were forced to relinquish the fun of overtly abusing him and went back to covert methods. Devora, from where she stood, could see how relieved he was: someone was protecting him again, standing between him and the world, as his parents had done when he was a child.

Some six months after the wedding night, Rachel appeared at the clinic, her hand on her stomach, and declared she was pregnant. Devora, a while before that, had taken it upon herself to consult with a specialist about the chances that the couple could have a child of normal intelligence, and he'd convinced her to plead with them not to foster dreams of parenthood. Now she looked in confusion at Rachel's radiant face and wondered if she had been right not to find the courage to talk to them about it. But when the test results came back, it became clear to Devora—to the puzzlement of Rachel, who thought she was pregnant because she'd gained weight—that Rachel knew less about pregnancy than her eight-year-old daughter did. In an oblique description, using words she'd chosen years before for her daughters—the specialist's words constantly in her mind, although she never found the right moment to speak them—Devora explained to Rachel how the sperm and the egg try to meet in order to create a baby, and added that cats and even the cows in David's cowshed become pregnant the same way. Rachel, disappointed by the test results and determined to remedy the situation, expressed an interest in knowing more than what Devora was describing so circuitously and asked questions that made Devora wonder what they did in their bed at night. And after more answers, still evasive, had been given, Rachel asked very directly to learn exactly how to make a baby as if she were asking for a cake recipe.

The next day, Devora let Rachel into the clinic, locked the door, and showed her an illustrated book she'd found in the library of one of the children's houses that explained the reproductive process, stage by stage, through drawings and simple descriptions.

Rachel looked at the drawings, eyes wide in astonishment, and asked to borrow the book for a few days to show to David.

"Don't tell anyone about the book," Devora said, as she sealed it in a brown paper envelope. "And tell David not to tell anyone in the cowshed about it either, so they won't laugh."

Apparently the book, and perhaps also what David had learned in the cowshed, was effective, because three months later, tests showed that Rachel was pregnant. Devora locked the clinic immediately, hung a sign on the door that said, "Be right back. In an emergency, look for me at David and Rachel's house," and with a bursting heart, hurried to give them the news. And there, in their room, with the specialist's opinion still clear in her mind, as the couple was still hugging her and Rachel was wiping away David's tears, the connection began between Devora and the child who had signaled his existence on the papers she was holding in her hand.

In the months that followed, Devora occasionally went to their house with a book of photographs and explained in simple language the present stage of the pregnancy and the fetus's new developments, praying silently that the fetus was following her explanations and that every part of its body was conforming to the illustrations she was showing its parents. David and Rachel listened in wonder to her explanations, ran the tips of their fingers over the photos like children learning amazing things. Devora always left their room, brimming with warmth and concern and excitement, loaded down with a bouquet of dahlias and a cake that Aharon demolished in an hour.

Several days before the birth, Devora reminded them that it was time to look for a name for the baby, and David announced that they already had one: Melech. He'd been called to the kibbutz office, where Menachem informed him that, as kibbutz secretary, he was in charge of giving names to new babies and he'd chosen a name worthy of their baby—Melech (king). Devora, controlling her anger, asked in a restrained voice why they had agreed, and Rachel, her arms hugging her stomach, explained with great seriousness that Melech was a lucky name.

That evening, Devora burst into Menachem's house and spoke harshly to him in front of his wife and children: "The father wasn't enough for you, you have to do it to the baby, too?" Menachem's wife—who, according to the stories whispered among the members, was also Aharon's new lover—became pale and dumbstruck the moment she saw Devora at her door. Menachem knew immediately what the fuss was all about and said, "What's wrong with you, Devora'le. It's a good name. She herself said it was a lucky name."

"Why didn't you call your son Melech if it's such a good name?"

"Believe me, I'm really sorry I didn't think of it."

"Why don't you let him be born before you start abusing him too," she said, not backing down.

"I'm starting to abuse him? I don't mean to cause problems between you and your husband, but I have to tell you—as long as you're talking about it—that it was Aharon's idea."

"Then I want you to know that I'm going to raise a stink about this. It's a name that invites abuse," and burning with anger, she left the house and went back to Rachel and David's place, formulating tactful sentences in her mind. But Rachel insisted on the name. Her grandmother's name was Malka (queen), she said, rejecting Devora's good intentions, and she was a healer. The baby would be named after her saintly great-grandmother.

Ten minutes after he was born, Devora held Melech in her arms, running quick hands over his body under the tight swaddling, checking his features close up, almost bursting into tears of relief at the sight of the healthy, perfect baby whose facial expression was completely normal. The baby, seeming to know why she was on the verge of tears, opened his eyes and looked at her. She flinched at the expression in his clever eyes. And she worried about what Aharon and his pals would prepare for the *brith*, as if she could foresee the small crown that would be taken from a Purim costume and placed on the baby's head, the red velvet cushion he would lie on when Menachem said festively, "As befits a king."

Three years later, as if the future had been revealed to him, David brought Melech to Devora and made her swear to take care of the child for him. One evening, they both appeared at the clinic, holding hands. David sat Melech down and told him seriously, as if dictating a will, "You know that Devora is Mommy and Daddy's best friend on the kibbutz, and she'll be your best friend too, and I want her to hear, and you to remember, that if anything happens to me or to Mommy, she'll take care of you. Now you can ask." Devora considered apprehensively what David had promised in her name as Melech asked all the questions his father didn't know how to answer: why don't airplanes fall; why do birds have a beak and people don't; who made the night; why does the moon have a face; why do some flowers close up at night and others don't; what makes apples red; how do eyes see; why do cows give milk and dogs don't—

She was bothered that evening by the burden of a curious child and by a mysterious uneasiness caused by David's terrible prescience, which she didn't dare look into. But several months later, she found herself waiting for the boy in the clinic, standing at the door, reaching for him and gathering him to her breast in the same strong encircling motion that the monkey in the pet corner used to scoop up her baby as it leaped toward her from all over the cage. Or while sitting in her chair, she'd suddenly see the small hand, pressed against the window from outside, crawling up the glass like an insect with all its five antennae quivering. And they'd spend an hour together, far from the mouths gossiping about Aharon's indiscretions, mouths that would suddenly fall silent the minute she appeared, far from the little girls so attached to their father. He would describe all that had happened to him that morning and afternoon, and the questions he bombarded Devora with moved her and filled her heart with love. It was the brightest hour of her day.

Seven years after his parents died, when his class was assigned a family history project, Melech asked Devora to take him to Beersheba to see his father's cousin, a very old man whose address he'd found in a letter in a drawer in his parents' room. The old man, as if he'd forgotten that only two people were coming, had covered the table with fruit and candy in their honor. He welcomed them with childlike excitement, gave Melech a long hug,

marveling at how handsome he was. When he'd calmed down, he
took out an old album that contained some black-and-white pictures of gloomy-faced people wearing dark clothes and, pointing
to the photographed figures, told Melech about the hard-working,
God-fearing grandparents David had never told him about, and
about his father's aunts and uncles and their children and babies,
who, with the exception of one who survived and went to
Australia, were murdered by the Nazis, may their name be cursed.

"And they're all dead?" Melech's eyes roamed over the photographed people.

"E-ver-y sin-gle one," the old man said, as if, in his imagination, he were moving from image to image in a long row. "Except
for your grandfather and me and the one in Australia."

"Why didn't anyone save them?" Melech looked at the picture of
a girl with a boyish stance, wearing a middy blouse, her eyes smiling.

"Because there were a lot of other bad people, not only the
Nazis, may their name be cursed."

"And there weren't any good people?"

"There weren't enough good people." The old man reached out
and caressed Melech's head, saying in amazement, "So you're
David's boy—what a handsome boy David had."

They ate and drank and looked at pictures for hours, and the
old man spoke, while Melech and Devora wrote down what he
said, about how he was saved when the Nazis, may their name be
cursed, shot three-hundred and fifty people from his town,
including a few in the photographs, and piled their bodies in a
clearing in the woods, and when night fell, two figures rose from
the dead: he and a nine-year-old boy. They looked at each other as
if they'd seen a ghost and stayed together until the end of the war.
Then the old man began to cry when he spoke of his daughter,
who'd died of an illness before the Nazis, may their name be
cursed, loaded the women and children on trucks, and Melech
cried along with him, weeping even harder when the old man
asked about his father and mother. Then Devora stood up,
thanked him for the refreshments and the stories, and apologized,
saying that she didn't see well in the dark and the drive back was

very long. The old man was sorry the visit had been so short, insisted that they take the candy with them because no one would eat it anyway and it was a shame to throw it out, crushed Melech to his body and gave him a gift of two pictures that showed his grandparents clearly as a bad-tempered young couple. Melech pressed the picture to his chest and the old man again smothered him in his embrace, until Devora, gently at first, then forcefully, separated them.

"Did you see the way he hugged me?" Melech said excitedly as he sat next to her in the pickup truck, holding the two photographs in his hand and the bag of candy on his lap. Devora turned to look at him, imagining that someday he'd say that the biggest hug he ever got was from a man he didn't really know.

"Of course I did. And he gave you lots of material for your project. Did you notice that I wrote down all the names of the people and places when you stopped writing?"

"Yes. But did you see how hard he hugged me?"

"Of course. And I felt it too. It was hard to separate the two of you. I didn't know your father had such a large family. He never talked about them."

"But they died because of the Nazis, may their name be cursed. Now only you and he are my family."

She tried to think of someone else fast—one of the people on the kibbutz, a woman who looked after the children in the children's house, a teacher—to expand the list of people who loved him.

"And that one from Australia." Melech added the nameless man to the short list. "I even hurt from his hug." He rubbed the back of his neck.

And she said with a mixture of compassion and resentment, "That must be the way Holocaust survivors hug."

"Once upon a time, there was a lovely couple: David and Rachel. They had an adorable, handsome and smart little boy, and that's why they called him Melech. Everyone especially loved Melech, who was the youngest in his class because he skipped two grades, and when he grew up, he won many medals in sports and all the kibbutz members were proud of him, but when he was still small, the proudest ones were his mother Rachel and his father David, and another woman whose name was Devora, who fell in love with him as soon as she saw him, ten minutes after he was born—"

Melech jumped up, agitated, his face dark. He crossed the room in large steps, turned and walked quickly to the opposite wall, hurling himself at it as if he wanted to knock it down. Then he turned around, tense and menacing, and walked toward the kitchenette.

"Maybe now you'll tell me what's wrong, Melech. You promised," she shouted, frightened by his agitation.

He stopped suddenly, as if he'd just decided to abandon the detailed plan he'd devised earlier. "I'll tell you everything," he said quietly. Now she was terrified by the calm, measured voice so at odds with the madness in his eyes. "But before I do, I want you to know that no matter what, you are the person I care most about in the world, the *only* person I care about in the world. Your love for me from the day I was born—and even before I was born—until today is important to me, and I'm grateful for it. You've been the most stable thing in my life since I was six. Without you, I wouldn't have survived in this place."

"You're sick, aren't you, Melech?" She stood up. "What did they find?"

"I'm perfectly healthy, and I said that as an introduction, because I'm going to hurt you, Devora. Very much."

Her throat dried up all at once and she was suddenly frightened for the safety of her baby granddaughter.

"Why do you want to hurt me, Melech?"

"I don't want to. Really I don't. But I have to."

She sat down again, and as she pressed her legs together and felt the uncontrollable trembling in her thighs, it upset her to notice wrinkles in his forehead she hadn't seen before, wrinkles of maturity come too quickly, and she thought that none of the children in his class, two years older than he, had wrinkles like that.

"What level of retardation did my father have?"

She choked. "I don't think . . ."

"This conversation is going to be hard for both of us, Devora." For some reason, she interpreted the slowness of his speech as threatening. "So it's a good idea not to make it complicated."

There was a brief silence as she thought about what to say, preparing herself for what was to come, confused by the thought that the menace being suppressed by such strong powers of restraint was directed against her.

"Mild retardation."

"Did anyone check his intelligence level?"

"No. He wouldn't let anyone check him. It was mild retardation."

"And my mother, also mild retardation?"

"Your mother was diagnosed as having environmentally-related retardation."

"The kibbutz agreed to accept my father because he had an apartment, right?"

"He loved the cowshed, and he was an excellent worker."

"Yes, but he was accepted because of the apartment, right?"

"Yes."

"Until he got married he used to get the hardest shifts, right?"

"I don't know."

"And not a single day off for months, right?"

"I don't know."

"He was the kibbutz circus, right?"

"The word circus is—"

"Exactly right, isn't it?"

"Everyone liked him."

"They insulted him, took advantage of his retardation, stole flowers from him, abused him. Their wedding, my *brith*, it was all part of the kibbutz entertainment program."

"You can't know that."

"I know a lot more than you think."

"From where?"

"We'll save that for the end! So you could say that they were the kibbutz entertainment team?"

"Don't say it like that . . . "

"Aharon picked my name?"

"Yes."

"Is it funny to call the son of retards 'Melech'? Is that a kind of humor?"

"Your mother loved the name. Your grandmother was called Malka."

"Do you know many kids with the name Melech?"

"No."

"I'm grown up now, Devora, I can deal with the truth. The stories you told me about my parents all those years—in a singsong that people use to tell stories to a sad little boy or a retarded big boy—was that to protect Aharon?"

"No. That was to protect you. I thought there were things that should be kept from a child, that you have to create the picture of a world that is easy for him to live with."

"If you'd helped create a reality that was easy to live with, you wouldn't have had to make up stories."

"I couldn't create a reality like that."

"Why not?"

"Because they were stronger than I was. I'm much weaker than you think. I couldn't change things in my own life either, even though I wanted to. I could only protect you."

"But you didn't succeed."

"Until today, I thought I did."

"My parents were killed in an accident, right?"

"Yes."

"With the John Deere tractor, right?"

"No. The John Deere was dangerous. It wasn't used. I think it was the Oliver."

"That's what the police report said, but someone gave them the wrong details."

"Where did you get that from?"

"And they switched the tractors, too. They took away the John Deere and brought the Oliver."

"What are you talking about?"

"Aharon was there, did you know that?"

"Of course."

"It's hard for you to hear that he lied to the police, altered evidence."

"No one lied or altered, Melech. It was an accident, a terrible tragedy."

"Don't you care about why I said he lied to the police?"

"It's over, Melech. There's no point in digging it up again."

"No point because of Aharon?"

"No point because of you."

"But I want to tell you exactly what—"

She leaped up. "I don't even want to hear!"

He grabbed her shoulders with the two strong pincers of his hands and pressed slowly until he'd sat her back down.

"But I want you to hear. It's important to me."

"Why is it so important to you? It happened a long time ago and it can't be changed."

The eyes she'd seen ten minutes after he was born looked at her now, hard, cruel, scrutinizing, hellbent on finding out who she was covering for. That expression still in his eyes, he kneeled in front of her and took her hands in his, his voice out of kilter with his expression, and, paralyzed with fear, she listened to him, completely unable to recognize the eyes, as he said, "Because now it's my turn to tell you a story. Listen to what a nice story I'm going to tell you: Once upon a time there was a beautiful place, like in a fairytale, that was called a kibbutz. The people there were very hard-hearted and mean-spirited, and more than anything, they were very bored, and that's why they were always looking for entertainment. One day, a good, hard-working young man who was mildly retarded came to their kibbutz. He loved the cowshed and the cows, and he loved the people and their kibbutz, but that didn't make them really like him, because they had a great need for entertainment. Part of their entertainment was quite cruel, but he was lucky enough not to see it, because he was mildly retarded. And one day, they decided to double the fun and brought him a woman who would entertain them, too. Messengers were sent urgently throughout the kingdom, and one clever messenger found her in the spare parts storeroom of a garage. The people brought her to the kibbutz in all her glory, made her up to look like a circus clown, married her to the mildly retarded man, and everyone was very happy. A year and a half later, the couple had a boy. On the kibbutz, they thought that now their fun would be tripled because the circus had really expanded, and they also found a perfect name for the little clown: Melech." He said his name loudly, a proclamation, then lowered his voice suddenly like a skilled actor and whispered to her, "But alas, the boy didn't suffer from mild retardation or even environmentally-related retardation. He was a pretty smart kid, and that's why he was also very sad, because unlike his parents, he understood very well what he saw."

Devora was crying so much that her eyes were crisscrossed with red capillaries, but she thrust the tears back into her body and held them there by force, and Melech looked at her eyes and went on with his story in a quiet, rhythmic voice, astonishing her with statements she was hearing from him for the first time, accounts that mocked the stories she had told him with so much love when he was a child.

"One day, a new tractor arrived at the kibbutz: it's name was John Deere. How disappointed they all were when they discovered that the tractor was dangerous to drive and completely unsuitable for work because a defect in the engine made it suddenly lurch. One day, one of the kibbutz leaders, whose name was Aharon, had a naughty idea: they'd have a bit of fun by sitting the pair of circus clowns on the tractor. That Aharon took his two friends, Menachem and Zetooni, and the three of them went out to have a good time. That was the circus people's last and best performance. I have to say, to the credit of the merrymakers, that this was an absolutely normal bit of entertainment and their intentions were no worse than usual. The three friends never thought it would end in death."

"That's not true, Melech!"

"How do you know?"

"It just can't be."

"How do you know? You weren't there."

"Neither were you."

"Of course not. If I'd been there, I would've been murdered with them—"

"Don't say 'murdered', Melech!"

"Murdered, Devora. Someone who was there told me it was murder."

"Zetooni?"

"Exactly."

"Did he come looking for you?"

"No. We met by chance near my base, at the mailbox I sent the invitation to the ceremony from."

"And you believe him? He's a pathological liar. Everyone knows that. His medical file was full of psychiatric opinions that *I* read, not you. If his story was true, someone would've found out sooner or later. You know you can't keep secrets on a kibbutz."

"It was a secret that only three people knew. One went crazy and died less than a year later. The second decided to leave before he went crazy too, and eventually became very religious. He made himself keep the secret until he met me by chance and saw it as a sign from God to tell me the truth. And the third stayed on the kibbutz with his beloved wife and two lovely daughters as if nothing had happened."

She looked at him, dumbfounded, trying in vain to let the words pass through her without hurting her, suddenly understanding with profound clarity—a rare occurrence—the things that had simmered at the edge of her consciousness all those years, never flowing over the edge but never subsiding either, things that had happened between her and Aharon after David and Rachel had died, and that she had attributed to reasons she herself had contrived.

"I had no idea, Melech. I hope you believe—"

"I know that the murder—"

"Don't say that word, Melech, please."

"But that's the word, Devora: murder. It was murder. And you didn't know about it. But you knew all the rest and you kept it from me, covered it up with stories."

"To protect you, Melech."

"I'm sure."

The good intentions, she realized now, too late and with the well-known sadness of things understood too late, the good intentions can't always be explained at the moment of truth. How easy it is to turn things around from the safe distance of time, until even the well-intentioned person himself no longer remembers how pure his intentions really were. And sometimes, from the distance of time, new questions suddenly arise, like the one about why she invested so much of her heart in that child of the retarded couple from the time he was a baby until the time she joined the "Four Mothers" anti-war group out of fear that he would be sent to Lebanon. What consolation had she found in that, what deliverance from the unspoken anger she felt toward her husband and his lies, toward her daughters who had rebelled against her from the time they were children, toward the soul-crushing kibbutz. And only now, too late, did she realize how high a price she'd paid for the gamble she'd taken by investing her strength in this child.

"What are we going to do now, Melech?" She stared into the clear, clear blue eyes.

"What do you want us to do?"

"What can we do? What has been done can't . . . And so many years have passed . . . You know how much I loved your father . . . "

"I'm sorry, Devora. I think we have to—"

"What?"

"You know."

"What?" she shouted.

"Go to the police," he said quietly.

"Why, Melech? You said yourself they didn't have bad intentions."

"They had very bad intentions, but they didn't plan murder."

"So why go to the police?"

"For my parents, who were so mildly retarded and environmentally retarded that they thought they were members of the kibbutz, a couple like all the others, a couple with a child. They didn't know they lived here to be the kibbutz clowns. They didn't know they were taking risks that circus people take. They probably didn't even know they were actually murdered and didn't think their murderers should be punished. They wanted to live here in peace with the cows and the flowers and the plum cakes, and their little boy."

His expression unreadable, Melech bent down and closed the photo album carefully, put it into his bag like a businessman who'd just closed a deal, stood up, and turned to go.

"Melech, Melech, I'm so sorry. . . " Devora cried loudly, unable to stop herself, not daring to get up and press him to her, recognizing in him the determination to settle scores.

"Is this how you're leaving, without a goodbye, without—" The familiar taste of betrayal assailed her.

At the door, he turned to her. "But with the beginning of a new story for you: Once upon a time there was a child who found out that his parents had been murdered for the fun of it. Once upon a time there were a few bad people and a few indifferent people who tried to hide it from him. There was also one good woman, but that wasn't enough. Told right, it could be a story with an intriguing moral."

Hiroshima

THE FIRST THING Idit asked to see in Hiroshima—right after the hotel bellboy, an overgrown toy soldier in a uniform and gloves, marched in and placed her suitcases neatly next to each other in her room—was the fountain in front of the Atomic Bomb Museum.

And during the years to come, all nine of her years in Hiroshima, whenever she had an attack of loneliness, homesickness, or emotional turmoil, she'd slip out in the middle of a lecture or leave her office on some pretext and hurry to get to the giant fountain before the museum closed. There, she'd kneel in front of the pool, her head bowed over folded hands as if she were praying to the god of water. Then she'd look up at the canopy bubbling at the top of the tall column of water and let the streaming flow run over her arms— caressing in summer, icy lashes in winter, but always able to instantly calm her racing thoughts.

And so she'd gone there the last time too, right after Nancy's murder, arriving ten minutes before the museum doors were locked, stunned and frantic, her heart pounding like a hammer in her ears, and so frightened that her vision was dimmed. She had groped her way to the edge of the pool, collapsed onto her knees at her usual place, dipped her fingers in the water as if trying to wash away incriminating evidence. Amid the flashing dark crescents that precede a faint, she looked at her reflection quivering on the water and had seen in horror the water turn pale pink, dark pink, reddish, red, crimson, dark purple, almost black. From the sky, a voice as muffled as the echo of fading thunder had called to her, as if God himself were speaking to her from deep in the heavens: "Can I help you, Miss?" And she had pulled her hands out of the water and quickly spoke her wish out loud: "I want to go home. To Natan."

*　　　*　　　*

But still on that first day—before she checked out the wonders of the heated toilet seat, before she read the contract that had been sent to her from the architects' office, wrapped like an expensive gift, before she went down to the basement floor to take a look at the famous rock baths where men and women bathe naked separated by a perforated bamboo fence—she stopped for a moment near the door to look at the gorgeous fruit and flowering branch arrangement on a carved tray in the corner of the room, then hurried down to the reception desk in the lobby. The only clerk who spoke understandable English greeted her impassively, not a single feature of his face giving away his surprise that she wanted to go out only five minutes after he'd handed her the key to her room or that, of all the city's attractions, she asked for directions to the Atomic Bomb Museum. On the glittering counter, he spread out an advertising pamphlet for a company that organized tea ceremonies for tourists, which included a map of the city. Squares marked the location of the hotel and the Museum. He added perfect circles around the stations near both places, wrote down the price of a ticket for public transportation, and without being asked, added the price of a taxi ride, pointing out that they would take about the same time, and then he translated the yens into dollars.

Hours later, weak with hunger, still sitting at the edge of the pool and gazing up along the length of the column of water that touched the sky, she thought, for some reason, of her classmate Tsila's mother, who used to spend days and nights scrubbing walls and washing floors and polishing silver like a worker ant, and of

Natan, who'd said, "She's a Holocaust survivor. Cleaning is the obsession of Holocaust survivors."

As her hands became white and wrinkled in the water, Idit thought about her father and about Natan. She thought about how she'd sworn to her father on his deathbed that she'd go to his childhood home to see the town square where he'd been separated from his mother and his sisters and that she'd look for the Polish man who'd taken care of him all through the war. And about Natan, she remembered how, at the end of their junior year in high school, he had stood at the blackboard in front of his class-mates—who were all putting their heads on their desks, undone by the heat and the weightiness of the subject—and had enthu-siastically delivered the lecture he'd labored over for so many months: "The Jewish Holocaust vs. the Japanese Holocaust." He had told them about the Atomic Bomb Museum in Hiroshima and described in great detail "The Fountain of Prayer" that was built in memory of the victims of the bomb who screamed for water in their last moments. The fountain—Natan had said, ignoring his classmates' eyes closing in entreaty—is ten meters high, and at night, one hundred and fifty-three colored, underwa-ter lights illuminate it.

Now she thought: Natan, Natan. I'm in Hiroshima, who would've believed it. I never made it to my father's town, but I did make it to the museum in Hiroshima. The water of the fountain spouts about ten meters into the air, just like you said. I can't count the colored lights now. And actually, who cares whether there are a hundred fifty-three underwater lights. What does this place have to do with me anyway? What am I doing here without you? When I casually mentioned the idea of going to school in Hiroshima, I only wanted to test you. I never dreamed of coming here without you. How did you manage to turn things around so I couldn't change my mind? Why didn't you stop this needless trip for my sake? Why didn't you suggest coming along? Look, I found your fountain, but where are you?

Where are you?

For the first few days, she wandered the streets of Hiroshima

on foot, resenting the city, firing off suspicious looks at everything around her. But the resistance she'd brought from home
and her anger at Natan faded and, despite herself, she was
amazed at the beauty of the parks, at the sounds, the colors, the
remarkable Hiroshige prints from the mid-nineteenth century,
the flower arrangements in the shop windows, the weary sadness
in the eyes of the old Japanese that were so like the eyes of the
people from her father's town when they met at Holocaust
memorial day services. She wandered for many hours with no
plan and no map, carried along by the host of men and women
with waxy features and unreadable expressions, dressed in tailored suits, some of them with surgical masks on their faces.
Only the young girls were lively in their colorful clothing and
frills, twittering away at each other. Again and again, her glance
would rise to the tops of the buildings and linger on the upper
windows or on the flickering electronic billboards. Drawn along
by the sights, she went into an origami exhibition she happened
upon and into the bookstores, and she stopped to watch garden-
ers who were laboring over their trees the way artists do over
their sculptures, meticulously trimming the branches of the trees
that lined the avenue. She went into the huge arcades where men
and women played games like children, clapping their hands
when the metal beads fell into place, and she ran her enchanted
fingers over shiny silk embroideries—peacocks, ducks, water
lilies, and cherry flower buds. She ate roast chicken in one of the
snack bars run by work-weary, angry women, a counter and several stools in front of a small kitchen that opened onto the sidewalk. As she ate, she watched in amazement the careful steps of
the women passing by, their feet turned inward, the tips of their
big toes threatening to collide and cause them to stumble, and
she stared impolitely at short-limbed, scar-faced, blind people,
wondering if those were marks of the poison that had been
dropped onto the city. When she tired of the sights and the noise
of the crowds, she'd stop people on the street, open a map and
point to the hotel, and they would bow again and again, directing her wordlessly to the bus stop.

During the second week, bewildered by the disappearance of her resentment toward the city and filled to the bursting point with impressions—hieroglyphics of sights and unfamiliar sounds her senses had not deciphered—she began work at the American company her teacher in the Technion had recommended. She'd signed a contract to work full time, until the academic year began. Then she'd divide her time between the university and the office. Ensconced in the soothing, familiar American bubble, from her desk she could see the sign in English and Japanese, "Those who know do not speak; those who speak do not know." She slowly got used to the light from the high window, the noise of the barking language that she was already beginning to understand, and the sounds of music and the cries of peddlers that filtered in from outside. And she became so absorbed with and so proficient at her work that she was immediately rewarded with a move to a larger space.

As if she had smuggled in a part of him, Natan seemed to be with her the whole first year. In the office, at lectures, in the night school where she studied Japanese, in her wanderings through the city during her limited free time on the weekends, in her bed, and once in the middle of an exam, she'd find herself communicating through that stolen part of him: Natan, Natan, where are you now? Are you driving your car to your mother's house? Washing the dog? Standing on the salad line in Mensa? Shaving over the cracked sink? Reading my last letter? Planning to write to me? Burrowing through the Yad Vashem archives? Lying in bed on your sunken mattress? Lying in bed alone? Lying in bed not alone? Today I moved to a tiny apartment with a wooden floor that creaks horribly, but one word from you and I'll leave everything here and fly back home. Just like that, in the middle of moving, in the middle of everything.

When they were last together, they'd agreed to correspond, both afraid of betraying themselves in a phone conversation. The letters they'd exchanged the first year were groping, attempts to detect what went unwritten. She'd read his letters over and over until she knew them by heart. She wondered if his highly acute senses, which had been directed at her since they were children and easily discovered her secrets, had also reported to him on everything she hadn't written about: her loneliness among the Americans in her office and the people of the Japanese city; the survivors of the bomb she met in the museum who reminded her of her father and his friends; the sudden longing for forgotten things, including, for some reason, the citrus grove behind their elementary school; and especially about her longing for him—his smell; his mocking remarks; the ease she always felt in his presence, even though he knew all her secrets or perhaps because he did; and the odd way he held her pinkie, his four fingers wrapped around it and his thumb closed over them like a lock.

Sometimes, at night, memories of distant times besieged her: her mother, who was hard of hearing, receiving the news of her trip to Hiroshima, her hand squeezing a handkerchief that was as thin as a bandage, "That's in the United States, isn't it? No? In Japan? Since when is Arizona in Japan? Ah, not Arizona? Hiroshima? Of course I know. Who doesn't know? Hiroshima from the atomic bomb. You have to go all the way there to study? Isn't there anyplace closer? Are there even any Jews there?" And immediately after that, leaping years back, she had a totally out-of-context memory of the pretty, arrogant gym teacher who was mean to the eighth-grade girls, refusing to exempt them when they had their periods no matter how much they begged her, and who then suddenly appeared in the rows of parents at the ceremony marking the end of basic training, the mother of the ugliest girl on the base.

Then the amusing memories dwindled and the memories related to stories of her father's childhood increased. That surprised her because before she came to Hiroshima, she hadn't let them into her mind. Again and again, she recalled Tsila's mother, who used to serve them chocolate balls on pretty saucers and gather the crumbs from the starched tablecloth with hands dry from contact with so many detergents. When Idit saw her name on the obituary page, she couldn't remember that quiet woman's face or smile, only the circular movement of her hands as she wrung out the dripping cloth she used to wash the floors. And suddenly came the memory of her weeping father, his tears wetting the letter he held in his stiff fingers: thirty years after the war, he had located his Uncle Meir in Tashkent, and the whole family bent over the atlas as her father's finger moved eastward and further eastward, feeling its way across the Caspian Sea, Turkmenistan, Uzbekistan, almost to the border of Kasakhstan, and there was Tashkent, at the end of the world. For the time being, they airmailed each other pictures and her father scrutinized the ones he received, trying to match the bald man in the picture to the little boy in his memory, hoping they would see each other someday, maybe in the town of their childhood, not knowing that before then, they'd both die prematurely of an inherited genetic defect they shared.

It was only toward the end of her second year in Hiroshima, when she met Edward and was surprised at how easily he pushed Natan away, that she dared—like a person contemplating a danger that had already passed—to write explicitly to Natan: "I've thought about you quite a lot the whole last year and nine months," and he, picking up the farewell tone, sensed the change taking place in her and sent a letter consisting of four words: "Who's the lucky guy?" And she replied in a telegram: "Edward."

By then, the last memories of her childhood and youth had subsided, like water ebbing at low tide, lying inertly in the distance. She understood then, with a mixture of shock and guilt, that the threads connecting her to the country of her birth were thinner and frailer than she'd thought. Witness how quickly, like a cured patient happy to part with her respirator, she had been weaned from the need to scan the pages of the newspaper every morning looking for Israel in the headlines.

Natan, aware of all this without her telling him, did not give up easily. Knowing that she was slipping away from him, he tried to set a trap from a distance. He bombarded her with letters recounting military events—descriptions of Kiryat Shemona after Katusha rockets had landed on it, as well as names of the injured. Then, sporadically, amid the military news, he sent the kind of letters he hadn't written earlier, full of pleading and lewd fantasies, letters swearing to fix up the bedroom for her, to welcome her like an exiled queen returning to her subjects, to settle her in a room where Japanese wind chimes would hang by the door and where the air would be scented by vanilla incense. And there his hands would roam from her hair to her temples to her eyelids to her cheekbones to her nose to her mouth to the hollow in her neck. In her imagination, Idit could hear his voice uttering the written words, and it excited her for days. If he had sent that letter a few months earlier, before she had grown strong and before Edward had become an anchor in her life, she would have packed her things in five minutes. But her powers of resistance, she discovered, had increased, as if she'd succeeded in becoming immune to Natan. After months of her stubborn silence, he sent her a letter promising not to write to her anymore and signed it: "Sayonara, Diti. Pray for us in the nearest temple." But still, he couldn't control himself and on Yom Kippur eve, he sent her a postcard with a picture of a blooming squill on it and congratulated her on her twenty-sixth birthday, and a year later, on an ordinary day in November, he succeeded in amusing her by sending several Biblical verses he signed as if he'd written them himself, and he didn't ask a single thing about Edward.

She had met Edward in the office. She'd raised her head from her drawing board, saw his extended hand and stood up and bowed out of habit. She found herself looking into the trust-inspiring eyes of Gary Cooper. Edward smiled, amused by the woman with Caucasian features and Japanese gestures, and said, "I saw on CNN yesterday that Israel is making new gas masks," and she replied, "I must be the only Israeli in the world who tries not to watch the news." At the end of that workday, wearing their coats and about to leave, it was clear to both of them—as they learned later—that they'd be spending the next weekend together.

In the empty rooms with the tatami floors, watercolors, and rice-paper screens that bore absolutely no resemblance to her mother's house—which was packed with dark veneered furniture, oil paintings of inanimate landscapes, and collections of dolls in national costumes—she began a new life with Edward in Hiroshima. And it was easy to do so in the company of a man who had inspired trust from the first moment, with whom she found the comfortable formula of living in separate apartments for seven years, who was—from the stories of his childhood on the family estate in Tennessee to his sex organ—completely different from anyone she had known. And she was introduced to new things, as she had been with the books she'd read as a teenager: stories about his church; quotes from his uncle, the priest; his experiences at college in Boston; the songs of his childhood that she tried to find equivalents for in Hebrew. He also regaled her with stories about the deeds of the grandmother he admired. She had been a friend of William Faulkner's mother, whose family had exchanged slaves with hers during their shared history.

On her first visit to his home, Edward introduced her to Hidiao-San, an old Japanese homeless man who had built himself a cardboard room between a park fence and the path leading to Edward's house. It was roofed by six open umbrellas, advertising gifts from Sony. In front of the entrance, as round as the mouth of a cave, stood Hidiao-San's shoes like soldiers in a military formation. His underpants and socks were laid out flat to dry on the umbrellas. Edward introduced her to Hidiao-San as if he were a close friend, but the man, pretending to be deaf, did not respond. "He's always like that," Edward explained, unoffended. "He doesn't respond to people, but I bring him food almost every day." His loyalty to the strange Japanese man who, without a word of thanks, ate the food Edward bought, warmed her heart, suffusing their first meal with the feeling that they were a family. You'd like him, Natan, she said to herself, a Righteous of the Nations with Gary Cooper eyes, and you'd be interested in the Japanese man, almost certainly a survivor of the bomb.

In the sixth year of her stay in Hiroshima, she'd become part of the city. She'd placed the Buddhist altar and the shelf of Shinto gods she'd bought in an antique store in her bedroom. Most of the time, her legs moved automatically along the city sidewalks and subway passageways. The landscapes and faces of the people were already engraved on her retinas. The customs that had seemed so strange to her when she'd first arrived were now clear. And the course she'd been invited to teach at the university had made her famous: the first foreign woman to lecture on Feng-Shui. Her Japanese was fluent and all her conversations and even most of her thoughts were in English, and when she paused occasionally to look for a word, she'd find that she didn't have it in Hebrew either. She spoke Hebrew rarely, with her old friends, and every week with her brother, passing on to him the things she wanted to say to her deaf mother, hearing from him again and again in a reproachful voice that if she didn't come to visit as she'd promised, they'd come to her in Hiroshima.

With the years, her Hebrew was relegated to rare dreams, to phrases that would suddenly pop into her mind and that she'd say aloud to herself, unable to recall whether she'd ever spoken them before.

Sometimes she heard people speaking Hebrew: a gray-haired couple quarreling in a shop about what to buy for a child, apparently their granddaughter; two jewelry sellers at their stand in the street, conversing in Israeli slang about a man who had gotten very rich; an Israeli guide leading a small group through the Atomic Bomb Museum; a woman calling loudly from the far end of the vegetable section: "Mica! Come look at this—sixty dollars for a melon you can finish in two bites!" She'd stop then, moved, quelling her desire to help the couple choose a gift for their grand-daughter, to trail after the group in the museum.

And it wasn't only the language that was replaced by other languages, but her thinking changed too, and the movements her body had adopted automatically—the slight bow she'd make unthinkingly, the *arigato* that suddenly came out of her mouth while she was speaking to her brother, causing an outburst.

"What was that?" he demanded.

"I got confused. The Japanese word for 'thank you' slipped out."

"Slipped out? Words in Japanese slip out in the middle of a conversation in Hebrew?"

"What are you getting so hot and bothered about? I hear Japanese all day."

His agitation filled him with resolve and the courage to ask a question about a subject that was rarely raised. "What about the plans to come home?"

"What's wrong with you, I can't plan anything now. I told you that the office is in the middle of a big project and I committed myself to the university for two more years."

"You know what I want from you? A picture. I want you to send a picture so I can see whether your eyes are already slanted."

Her glance, as if by chance, fell on the nature photo on the calendar: a hill whose peak disappears into the fog, plants hanging doggedly onto the rocks of the slope, river water flowing gently like the gray hair of a once beautiful woman. She could see what the river did not yet know: a new crevice would open in an earthquake or from the rush of water during the rainy season and soon the water would diverge, like a playful child leaping aside; it would stream into the fresh channel, leaving the old one dry. She felt the urge to console the river: the past is not always worthy of our longing.

What it was that caused her, a year later, to feel an unending, abysmal emptiness, she did not know. Perhaps it was that week she gave her brother and his family her small apartment and went to live with Edward, for the first time waking up with him seven mornings straight, enveloped in warmth every morning. Perhaps it was her four-year-old niece who arrived in Hiroshima with her parents in the spring and made Idit tremble with the sweetness of her touch, with her screams of joy at the sight of the cherry trees in blossom, with the song she'd sing to herself, hopping from one foot to the other: "The almond tree is blooming, the golden sun is gleaming . . . " Perhaps it happened because of the preparations for the end of the school year, when she would part from her students, especially one young girl she'd grown fond of. And perhaps it was something else entirely: her body had ripened. In any case, that spring she began to desire a child. Even before, she would find herself at the shrines of the Mizuko, the water children, those Japanese babies who never got to live, whose mothers, filled with guilt and regret, paid for nurturing the regiments of faceless wooden children wearing bibs. Or her legs would stop on their own in front of shop windows displaying baby clothes or in the children's department of the enormous department stores, where she found herself rocking cradles covered with canopies printed with spotted mushrooms.

That year, her eighth in Hiroshima, her brother did what he'd been threatening to do for so long and came to visit her with his wife and his young daughter. The child latched onto Idit from the minute they met at the Hiroshima airport, when Idit handed her a little Hello Kitty doll that Japanese girls pinned on their clothes, on their schoolbags, in their hair, on their shoes. Her brother gave her a bear hug and a scrutinizing look, then asserted, "It's you and it isn't you."

And seven days later, when she came to drive them back to the airport, as if he'd been troubled the entire week about that "It's you and it isn't you," Idit found him looking through a picture album he'd taken down from one of her shelves.

"You toured Japan a lot," he said sadly, turning pages on which she saw herself several years younger, her hair still long, lying in the red barley fields of the island of Hokaido as if she were stretched out on a flaming blanket, and in another picture, Edward standing with legs spread wide against the background of Tsurugi-dake Mountain in the Japanese Alps, the equipment he'd borrowed for the picture from climbers he'd met on the way lying at his feet like an animal at the feet of the proud hunter who captured it. On the next page, they were embracing at the entrance to the Meiji Shrine under the huge wooden entrance gate in the gray rain, and in another photo, holding hands under a cluster of lights on the wall of the Imperial Palace in Tokyo.

"We did tour a lot, yes."

"In Israel, you didn't like to tour."

"When did I have time in Israel? I was in the army and right afterward, I started school."

"You just didn't like to tour." He was looking at a gorgeous photo of one of Okinawa Island's turquoise beaches showing her and Edward, in bathing suits, lying side by side on a blanket, like

Barbie and Ken. "Eilat has beaches that are just as beautiful and it has rare coral reefs, but you just didn't like to tour in Israel."

"What's going on, are you insulted on behalf of the Israeli landscape?"

"Yes, the truth is I am. I've been going around the city with you for a week and I see how impressed you are by every door, every statue of Buddha, who looks like a person with an IQ of thirty, and every shrine that is pure kindergarten kitsch. Your apartment is full of paintings by that Hiroshiga, and at home, you never had a good word to say even about the coral reefs in Eilat that National Geographic sends photographers to take pictures of."

"Actually, I really loved the road to Jerusalem."

"Here you love all the roads." He opened a page at random on which all the pictures were of the gigantic statue of Buddha in Kamakura, and in one of them, their heads not even reaching the edge of the base of the statue, two dwarves smiling into the camera: she and Edward.

"Here,"—he looked indifferently at the photo—"another one with the IQ of a baby."

Something in the way he made himself a spokesman for the landscape of her childhood touched her heart, and she sat down in front of him and reached for his hand, which was holding the album.

"So you don't love home anymore?" he asked.

"It happens sometimes that people wind up in far-away places, and for all kinds of reasons, they can't go back home right away, and after a while, they realize that they feel pretty good where they are. It isn't—"

"Do me a favor, Diti, don't give me any lectures. I'm talking about you."

"So am I. I wasn't lying when I promised you I'd finish my degree here and come home."

"How many years does a degree take? Three? Four?"

"Something like that."

"Eight years have passed and you're still here. Without family, without friends, in an apartment with a floor that squeals as if it's being slaughtered. What's so good about this place?"

"Maybe it's good enough and not bad enough."

"So that's it, not bad enough, and you stay here, making do with not bad enough, that's what you've chosen?" He tried to turn the vague things she was saying into clear statements.

"I haven't chosen and I haven't not chosen. I landed here by accident and somehow, I must feel at home."

"So what exactly is it that keeps you here?" he persisted.

"The beauty—"

"Beauty? Beauty is the most important thing in life? Germany's beautiful too—why not Germany?"

"The work is interesting." She sailed onward without responding about Germany.

"You're here because of work?"

"And because of Edward."

"Edward, Edward, I honestly don't understand this kind of life. You're in your apartment, he's in his apartment. Sure, there are no fights that way, but there's no life either."

"You sound like Mom, you really do."

"Because I'm worried about you. He looks okay, yet what do we know about him? He can tell you a million stories about himself, but how can you know if they're true? Maybe his uncle the priest is someone he made up? Maybe he's a Mormon who ran away from his five wives? Do we know anyone in Tennessee who can verify what he tells you? In Israel, you give me a name and in an hour, I fax you the story of his life. And besides, people should live with people of their own kind, who speak their native language, who think like them, who live in their homeland. This is not your home and there's no chance it ever will be. I don't believe you feel like you belong here. It's good for a visit, to get away from things for a while, but not for life. People need to feel they belong to the place they live in. Beauty or no beauty—you have to come home."

"My home now is here."

There was a decisiveness in her words that she too was hearing for the first time: words spoken in a more determined tone than the words of her thought.

"Do you know why I came, Diti?" he suddenly asked with great seriousness, slamming the album closed.

"To tour Japan."

"No. I've got more interesting and cheaper places on my list."

"To see how slanted my eyes are."

"I wanted Sheli to get to know her aunt," he said, not falling for the facetious bait. "We're a small family. Small families like ours should not spread out this way. My kids only have you and Mira's crazy brother and his even crazier wife, so I'm not going to give up on you, because my daughter only has one aunt. The twins remember you, but she has no memory at all. And every year I tell her, This year, Aunt Idit is coming—and Aunt Idit doesn't even bother to send her a present on her birthday."

"I'm sorry, really. . . "

"You promised to come visit every two years."

"I didn't know then how hard it would be for me."

"I promised to pay for the tickets."

"It's not the money. I'm not stable enough to deal with home."

"Home or Natan?"

She stared at her brother, surprised by his quick response, as if he'd been waiting the entire conversation for the opportunity to mention Natan's name.

"You know which Natan. The one you loved the road to Jerusalem because of."

"I know which Natan. The one you could never stand."

"I couldn't stand him from the first minute, that's true. And rightly so. He's bad. There's been something bad about him since he was a little kid, and it's grown worse with time. And he had a bad influence on you, since then too. Until he came on the scene, you had girlfriends, normal relationships. But from the age of eight, no boyfriends, no girlfriends—only Natan and Natan."

There was no point continuing the argument that had gone on for years at home.

"Why'd you mention him all of a sudden?"

"Because he got married."

As if she were participating in some martial art, her heart

received a quick, unexpected and fatal blow as if delivered by an iron fist, and a second later, but already too late, her hand rose to protect the place that literally hurt, as if it were bleeding, and for some reason, she recalled the carp that, every Friday, would convulse, its eyes almost bursting out of their sockets, under her mother's right hand, a little of it under her left hand, which held the knife with the thick wooden handle.

"Why are you telling me this now?" she whispered.

"I thought you knew, maybe he told you himself."

"Natan and I are not in touch," she said, succeeding, to her surprise, in stabilizing her voice. "Did he invite you to his wedding?"

"The world could stand on its head twice before he'd invite me—I found out by chance."

"How by chance?"

"Believe me, by chance. I didn't send detectives after him."

"Who did he marry?"

"Some veterinarian."

"Suits him. He read *Doctor Doolittle* a thousand times."

She managed to pretend that her heart had slowed down and put her hand back on the table as a declaration that nothing had happened that was worth getting upset about, but her imagination —like so many times in the past—was already feverishly drawing a picture of their house in one of the neighborhoods on the hill, far from the center of the city, an old house made of Jerusalem stone nestled among grapevines and ferns where they'd live in tranquility, he and Doctor Doolittle and their children, charming children of nature, surrounded by a multitude of animals.

"Is that why you came? To tell me that Natan got married?"

"I told you why I came: so Sheli could finally meet her aunt."

"So thanks for bringing her." She patted his hand. "I don't how you managed to have such sweet children."

"Maybe they take after you," he teased.

"They're nicer than I am. Maybe—"

"I shouldn't have told you about Natan, right?" She realized that she hadn't succeeded in hiding her shock from him.

She pretended nonetheless, reconciling herself to the fact that, for the time being, she wouldn't be able to uproot Natan from inside her. "He doesn't interest me anymore."

"I'm glad to hear it. Maybe I told you so you'd know you're free, if by some chance you were waiting for him. I never understood what exactly was going on between you."

"I'm free, don't worry. Free as a bird." The years she thought she'd pushed Natan away disappeared all at once, spreading clouds of dust, and as time moved backward, his young face appeared, smiling mischievously, as if he'd been waiting all those years with uncharacteristic patience under the growing piles of dust for the moment his face and the "I knew it" expression on it would be revealed to her. Months later, over her drawings at work, in front of her students at the university, in Edward's bed, like the pounding of drums in the background, the words struck at her: Natan's married, Natan's married, Natan's married.

A week after she'd met them at the airport, Idit drove her brother and his family back there. On the sidewalk in front of the departures hall, they hugged tightly and Sheli, surprising all three of them, threw her arms around Idit's thighs and burst into tears that attracted the attention of passersby. Idit, embarrassed by the intensity of the sadness their parting was causing her niece, bent down to her, and Sheli came close and buried her face in Idit's neck, stabbing her shoulder with all her Hello Kitty pins. And even after they separated, even after she disappeared with her parents behind the automatic doors of the glass divider, the child was still crying.

During that week, Idit became aware of how much she longed for a child, as if she were a young girl at puberty who'd suddenly discovered the nature of a secret yearning that had possessed her for some time. For a few days, she kept it to herself, fantasizing about Natan during the day, seeing him in her dreams at night, children always skipping around them, sometimes Natan himself as young as a child. When she'd wake up, she could easily figure out what the dream meant, recognizing the wish that Natan would be the father of her child. Sometimes, she'd grab the tail end of the dream, and sometimes she'd continue the story while she was awake, telling herself about how she'd leave Hiroshima for a while and go to him unannounced, find him in the stone house without his new wife, peer over the hedges and see him reading or hoeing, sneak over to the windows and find him sleeping in his bed—and she'd ask him for a child.

One day, breathless with the expectation of Natan's reply, she saw Edward leaning across his desk in the office, looking at her in concern, and he asked again if that sadness came from missing her brother, because ever since he'd left, she'd been looking troubled, and she replied, "I only miss my niece."

"Maybe he'll give her to you if you ask nicely." He was trying to amuse her and apparently failed because, suddenly, in the middle of the office, among the legless people passing by on the other side of the low divider, their torsos floating back and forth, she became very serious as she managed to grasp the futile wishes from within the vagueness of her wandering thoughts and understood that her brother would not give her his daughter and Natan would not give her a baby, and she said quietly, as if she'd memorized the words, "And what about you, what if I ask you nicely?"

"Then I'll answer nicely, 'no,'" he said very loudly, alarmed. He burst out laughing like someone who'd been slow to understand a joke, and two heads sailing past turned to look at him. Warning lights apparently flashed in his mind at the sight of the look she shot him and her lips clenching, so he said quickly, "Let's continue this conversation at home," stroked her cheek fleetingly, and left.

That evening, she asked, "Why did you laugh?"

"Because you took me by surprise. It was a Japanese laugh. I didn't think you were that type."

"What type?"

"Career and family, you know. I thought we'd both run pretty far away from that cliché."

"I don't know what you're running away from,"—she thought of the Mormon and his five wives—"but if I'm running away from something, it isn't from a cliché."

The heady smell of a blooming citrus grove assailed her without warning in the middle of Hiroshima, suppressing the affront.

In her mind she saw a multitude of trees, like a herd of green sheep dotted with orange, and recognized the grove behind the elementary school, cut down a few days before their graduation ceremony. Even many years later, in the spring, the ghostly smell of citrus tree blossoms lingered there.

"I'm sorry," Edward said as soon as her saw her expression growing distant. "You never mentioned children. I was surprised, that's all. I didn't mean to laugh."

Her nostrils sought the smell to capture its sweetness.

"But if that's what you really want,"—he put a warm hand on her cheek—"I don't object."

"I'm not sure anymore that I do." The citrus grove vanished.

In the days that followed, it was Edward, seemingly by chance, but with a persistence reminiscent of the beginning of their relationship, who would raise the matter of the pregnancy, and she wondered if all he wanted was to pacify her, or if perhaps her secret desire had kindled his secret desire. She responded unenthusiastically, mainly out of defensiveness, but she let him talk, at first hesitantly and then with ease. He listed his conditions, which shocked her at first, but which she later understood and accepted, until in the end, they clarified the smallest details of the clauses as if they were entering into a business transaction. And as befits people entering into a business transaction, they wrote a contract and signed it in the presence of a lawyer: their agreement to have a child together will not change the fact that they will continue to live in separate apartments; the child to be born, whether a boy or a girl, will be raised in the mother's home and the responsibility for raising the child will be hers; if the mother decides to leave Japan and return to Israel or to live somewhere else, the father will be permitted to visit his child whenever he wishes and to invite the child to whatever country he resides in, at least once a year; the father will support his child financially with a sum that does not exceed one quarter of his salary, until the child reaches the age of eighteen; the child will be exposed to both Jewish and Christian education, and when the child comes of age, the child will be free to choose his religion; the language to be spoken when all three are together is English, but the mother can speak Hebrew when she is alone with the child.

The agreement stood between them as a sign of a lack of faith, inhibiting passion, even freezing for a time the desire for a child. In her mind's eye, Idit saw herself sitting down in front of Natan and snatching away from him the book he was reading or crawling under his blanket and giggling into his ear, "You won't believe what I did: I signed a contract for a child."

One morning, she was standing at the bedroom window, looking at the cherry tree that grew just outside. It had been so late in blooming that she'd almost given up hope. But then the tree had suddenly erupted into a plethora of magnificent, fragrant purple blooms and she—like the parent of a child she'd thought was lagging behind until she discovered his genius—was filled with joy at the remarkable beauty of a tree made of purple butterflies. It crossed her mind that Natan had never seen cherry trees in bloom, and without understanding what caused her to put her hand on the phone at that moment, she said to Edward, "I'd like to start implementing our contract tonight, if you don't mind."

She didn't conceive that night, or many nights after it, and the two pregnancies that did take hold in her womb months later ended in early miscarriages. She'd had to stay in bed for several days each time to recover from the sense of defeat and to let her empty body gather strength—and all the while her thoughts wandered to the water children made of wood. From her window, occasionally, she thought she saw a slight haze, like an omen, as if the vestiges of the dust of August 1945 had still not gone, and a line about Jerusalem came into her mind from a song that in the past, used to move her to tears, "Mountain air as mellow as wine . . . "

"What are you thinking about?" Edward asked.

"Wine."

"Chicken in wine, that's actually what you're getting today."

During those days, Edward took care of her with great concern, heeding the instructions of his friend, the gynecologist from San Francisco. Once, after he had fluffed her pillow like a pampering, southern black nanny and put a tray of long, symmetrically arranged vegetables in front of her, she noticed the knot of the apron tied around his waist and burst out laughing. "Did you bring that apron from home?"

"No. I found it in a cabinet at your place, and I was surprised. It's probably your sister-in-law's," he said, going into the kitchen to squeeze fresh juice for her. As she looked at his back affectionately, a terrible idea began to gnaw at her, that those miscarriages were related to Natan, who was watching her attempts to become pregnant from afar and cursing the fruit of her womb, which wasn't his.

A month after the fourth miscarriage, which was the most painful of all and left her depressed, exhausted, and constantly picturing the blood-reddened sheet, Nancy and Kumo entered her life.

The beginning was ordinary enough, offering no sign of what was to come: a phone call from old acquaintances at the moment when they were discussing plans for a trip to Kyoto. When the phone rang, Edward picked up the receiver, listened, paled, and said nervously, "Did you really decide? . . . When . . . I'm very glad, really. Can I call you later, or tomorrow? I'm writing down the number. . . No, not you. I'll call, if that's okay. . . . Bye."

And later, while he was in the middle of reading the pamphlets he'd brought from the travel agency, but distracted, he told her about Nancy and Kumo for the first time. He was Japanese and she was American, old friends from his college days in Boston when Nancy and he were students and Kumo was their lecturer in Japanese art. The two fell in love and got married, and now they'd arrived in Hiroshima from New York.

"On a tour?" Idit asked.

"We didn't really talk."

"Why'd you hang up so quickly?"

"Because you and I are busy."

Occasionally, in the evening, Edward would remember something about Nancy and Kumo, as if a hidden spot in the depths of his brain had been stimulated and was beginning to transmit pictures to the surface.

Although she'd planned to stay with him that night because of warnings of an imminent earthquake, Idit left early, knowing that the minute she closed the door behind her, he'd rush to the phone. A message from Edward was already waiting for her on her answering machine: It's too bad she hadn't stayed. On the news, they said there was going to be an earthquake. Kumo and Nancy had invited them to dinner at Kumo's mother's house. Was Thursday convenient for her?

Over the next few days, it seemed to her that Nancy and Kumo were constantly in Edward's thoughts, but for some reason, he stopped himself from telling her. It wasn't until they were on their way to Kumo's mother's house that he told her about the enormous effort the ambitious young Japanese man had made to adopt America and the American mode of thought, even though he didn't admire the lifestyle. His marriage to Nancy, daughter of an eminent New England family, Edward said, as he was parking the car, was part of Kumo's desperate effort to become assimilated.

At the door to the house, Kumo and Nancy fell into Edward's arms with joyous shouts and vigorous pats on the back and shoulders, delighted to see him. Interspersed among the sounds of greeting were the words "Edward-San," "Kumo-San," "Nancy-San," like the continuation of an old joke. Standing a step behind them, the bouquet upright in her hands, Idit caught sight of a Japanese woman's face looking at her—obviously Kumo's mother, her eyes wide with fear and her brow furrowed with concern. When the joy of the meeting had abated, the woman whispered something to Kumo, and he bowed and whispered a brief reply through clenched lips, shaking his head irritably.

A strange silence fell, and Idit noticed the clouded faces of Kumo and his mother, which were turned to her and Edward, and the pleading in Nancy's face as she moved aside, studying the four of them standing opposite each other. Idit glanced quickly at the bouquet in her hands to make sure it didn't contain four flowers or nine, which are signs of bad luck, that it wasn't tied with black-and-white ribbons, which are used only for tying gifts for a funeral, and then raised her eyes again in a question.

"Is there a problem?" Edward asked Kumo in English.

Kumo and his mother whispered twice more to each other, and shot two quick glances at Idit.

"Can you tell me what the problem is?" Edward asked.

"There's no problem," Nancy said and made her way over to the guests, took the bouquet from Idit's hands, pulled out three pink orchids, counted the white ones quickly and handed the rest of the bouquet to Edward. Then she took Idit by the arm and pulled her into the inner room. It wasn't until she'd closed the door, tossed the orchids into the waste basket, changed her mind, took them out and put them on the table, that she extended her hand for a handshake and said, "I'm Nancy-San and you're Idit-San and we're going to be friends."

"Really?" Idit said in surprise.

"Yes. And we'll help each other not to get swallowed up into Japanese culture."

"I'm not sure that Japanese culture is interested in swallowing us up."

"That's another good reason to be friends." Nancy smiled with dancing eyes.

"What was that problem at the door?"

"The pink flowers—which it would be a shame to throw out, so you'll take them home tonight because I know how expensive they are—and your pink blouse. Pink clothes are not allowed in this house."

"Why not?"

"Because of Kumo's grandmother. You couldn't know that, of course. Even the people who know about Japanese craziness aren't ready for this. Can I lend you one of my blouses? I have a few brand new ones." Nancy was already standing in front of her closet, pushing the waves of fabric left and right, until she pulled out three hangers and lay blouses in shades of blue and green on the bed.

"Why isn't pink allowed?"

"Because on the day of the bomb in Hiroshima, Kumo's grand-mother saw pink animals, cows and horses, whose skins peeled off and they turned pink. I reacted just like you." Seeing that Idit was so shocked that she had to sit down on the bed, Nancy laughed.

"Kumo's grandmother is a survivor of the bomb—"

"And it seems that lots of survivors saw pink animals. Nothing pink is allowed in this house. I stopped using pink nail polish, and obviously, all my pink clothes have gone underground. Not even pink soap or a dish trimmed in pink is allowed here."

"And what happens if she's out in the street and accidentally sees —"

"She doesn't see any streets. She doesn't leave the house and doesn't look out the window. Can you imagine. She has a black-and-white TV in her room. She can't watch color TV."

"And what happens if, by mistake, she . . . "

"I'm curious about that, too."

Until Kumo's mother and grandmother joined them at the table, one from her room and the other from the kitchen, the young people spoke English. Nancy and Edward laughed loudly, Kumo choked back his laughter, and Idit waited tensely for the appearance of Kumo's grandmother. Edward told them about Hidieo-San, who'd upscaled his cardboard house and opened a window onto the park, and Nancy talked about her problems with an especially generous neighbor, who'd welcomed them with candy the day they arrived. Nancy had quickly reciprocated, in the accepted manner, with a more expensive gift: a small basket of fruit. The neighbor continued the game and bought them a glass vase decorated with jade. Nancy, whose American logic told her to put an end to the escalating contest, raised her hands in the gesture of a surrendering soldier and declared that she was the middle of a culture war.

"America will win," Kumo reassured her.

"Before or after we spend all our savings on gifts for the neighbor?" Nancy lowered her waving hands.

"After, of course," Kumo said.

"I just don't understand the Japanese mentality!" Nancy said and turned to Idit, "Edward said you're Israeli."

"Yes . . ."

"Do you understand the American mentality?"

"I think I understand Edward's mentality."

"But she didn't pick me because of my mentality." Edward shot Nancy a look and their eyes locked.

"Why *did* you pick him?" Nancy laughed, prying her glance from his.

"No!" Kumo shouted. "Please don't answer them. I've heard that Israelis have no inhibitions—"

"But why? I'm ready to hear it." Nancy banged her fist on the table.

"Tell them," Edward urged Idit, but his smile stopped her, was directed against her.

"Because of my eyes." Edward revealed what she hesitated to say "They reminded her of Gary Cooper's eyes."

"Really!" Nancy said with pleasure, and leaned across the table toward Edward to look into his eyes. "She's right! Gary Cooper eyes! How come I never noticed it before!"

"Because you were busy with other eyes," Edward said.

"Because they don't look anything like Gary Cooper eyes!" Kumo said.

The three of them burst out laughing in practiced unison and Kumo asked, "And what exactly does it mean to have Gary Cooper eyes?"

"It means you're someone who can be trusted," Edward said as if boasting.

"And as we know, that's really true!" Nancy cried, and the chorus of laughter rang out again, embarrassing Idit, though she didn't understand why.

At that moment, a very old woman appeared at the end of the hallway, and Kumo got up and went to her, extended his hand as if he were inviting her to dance, and led her to the table. The others fell silent, stood up immediately, and bowed. They did not sit down until the old lady, the skin of her face cracked like scorched earth, was seated in her place of honor furthest from the door and Kumo's mother came out of the kitchen, put a large bowl of rice on the long table, and signaled the beginning of the meal. There was a brief silence as the four young people groped their way into the renewed conversation in Japanese. Edward apologized immediately, saying that his Japanese was terrible because he didn't need it at work; Nancy announced that she understood it perfectly, but found it hard to speak; and Kumo was impressed by Idit's fluency.

Sullen and short, her black, beady eyes sunken in their bony sockets, the old lady sat in her chair, shooting suspicious looks at the strangers, lingering on Idit's ring inset with an Eilat stone. Her daughter helped her to hold her chopsticks and her teacup, to wipe her mouth, and mainly, to pour water from the large pitcher that stood in front of her. Every once in a while, she'd mutter to herself and stick out the tip of her tongue, a small snake poised to bite but then thinking better of it. Idit glanced at her from the corner of her eye, as if watching for any abrupt movement or sudden leap, recognizing in the old lady the agitation, the constant restlessness of her own father. Suddenly, the old lady pulled Kumo's arm, and he leaned toward her. She mumbled something in his ear, and he whispered something back to her that caused her to give a short cry. Kumo's mother watched them the whole time, her eyes tense, and the others looked at them in polite silence.

"What's going on?" Nancy asked in English.

"Japanese!" the old lady screeched at her, and Nancy recoiled.

"She wants to ask you something." Kumo turned to Edward and Idit, reluctance in his voice.

The old lady looked at Edward, her eyes narrowing as if they wanted to penetrate to what lay behind what she saw.

"Were you a soldier?" she finally asked.

"No."

The old lady turned her invasive glance on Idit: "Were you a soldier?"

If Edward hadn't known that she'd been in the navy, she would have lied. "Yes. In Israel, women serve in the army," she said, almost apologetically.

"Aah," the old lady said, the slits of her eyes narrowing even more, "that is very bad."

From that point on, the conversation stumbled along, occasionally interrupted by questions the old lady asked about the army, the number of airplanes in the Israeli Air Force, the age of the youngest pilot.

Earlier than planned, Idit and Edward got up to leave, discomfited by the strange atmosphere. The old lady's eyes followed them to the door, never leaving them for a moment, as if she were trying very hard to understand the words of the young people crowded at the door, who had gone back to speaking English as soon as the farewell bows were over, to understand what Nancy was whispering to Idit as she explained to her how to get under the window through which she'd throw the orchids and the pink blouse.

They were shaken when they left there, so they decided to go to Edward's apartment for a last drink, and in the end, Idit stayed the night, and they fell asleep after midnight. Edward was excited by memories of college in Boston that had been revived and were making him nostalgic, especially for the giant hamburgers they served in the restaurant there; Idit was seized by a new, vague emotion, a low flame fraught with danger that Kumo's grandmother had ignited in her.

"Do you know why I changed my blouse?"

"So Kumo would like you."

"I'm serious. I heard about a similar case in Israel. It's a post-traumatic response."

"So is mine."

"I'm talking about Kumo's grandmother."

"I'm talking about Kumo. As for his grandmother, I agree that 'post-traumatic' sounds more respectable than just crazy old lady.'"

"Nancy told me that it started with her ten years ago, after she saw a documentary about the day of the bomb. Kumo was in Boston then."

"Kumo told me that he talked to a specialist, and maybe she never actually saw any pink animals. She adopted someone else's memories."

"I also heard about a case like that in Israel."

"Lots of miracles happen in Israel because of the feeling of holiness there, but here—I don't think she was even in Hiroshima on the day of the bomb."

"She was. The skin on her back is completely ruined, full of scars. Nancy said that Kumo remembers that from when he was a child. The bomb caught her on her way to work, near the Asanosentai Park. The trees in the park were on fire and soldiers were carrying an enormous picture of the Emperor through the park to the port. She told Kumo how the people had stood still and bowed to the Emperor's picture and how the wounded soldiers stopped and saluted. He remembers her stories from his childhood. Later on, he learned about the event at school. The Emperor's picture that the soldiers carried through the blazing park and the burned people who stood there is a famous story in Japan."

"How do you know all that? Also from Israel?"

"No, from here. From the Atomic Bomb Museum."

The four of them no longer met in Kumo's mother's house, but they did see a lot of each other in the evenings and they avoided mention of the old lady. Sometimes, Idit felt like a stranger with the three of them, especially when they went on and on about their college experiences in the code words of a secret society. They usually didn't bother to explain anything to her, but occasionally, as if suddenly remembering her presence, Edward would try in vain to include her in the complicated stories of their past. The stories were based on memories that caused them to burst out laughing together when they heard an ordinary word, to suddenly become serious when they heard a different ordinary word, or to fool around together, like the gang of kids in *Hasamba,* the book she read as a child, who were always having adventures. Idit smiled to herself, and Edward, noticing her mocking look, made a remark that kept her from talking to him for a week afterward: "Is that smart Israeli girl mocking the stupid Americans again?"

Some two months after their first meeting, when Idit had grown tired of the repeated stories of a life she had no place in and was considering suggesting to Edward that he see the couple without her, Kumo found a job that required a great deal of traveling, which put a stop to their evening meetings in the middle of the week and made their Sunday meetings rare. Since Nancy happily accepted invitations without Kumo, and Kumo agreed with Edward that it would be best for his wife to spend her time in the city with friends and not alone, they found themselves going out as a threesome. But the meetings without Kumo aroused a vague restlessness, and a sharp tension developed between Nancy and Edward, as if unexplained caution were required. Later on, Edward avoided the meetings with excuses that were accepted with understanding. Nancy and Idit, with a pleasant sense of liberation, went out once to wander around the market, where Idit bought Sheli a turquoise kimono covered with embroidered water lilies, and once they strolled in the park and participated in a literary evening at the home of the American Consul where Nancy found a part-time, volunteer job as an English teacher in a school on the other side of the city, and later, as if it were a tradition it would be unpleasant to end, they continued to meet for lunch at a restaurant near Idit's office or went out shopping together.

Nancy blurted out the first remark as they stood in a store in front of a rack of women's pantsuits.

"These are men's suits," Nancy asserted, "Look, the buttons are on the right side."

"The buttons on women's pantsuits are on the right side too."

"Women's pantsuits button right over left. The buttons have to be on the left side."

"Not in Japan. Only the special clothes they use to bury the dead in button right over left."

"Crazy Japanese," Nancy said quietly, as if confirming it to herself.

And later she added small, venomous comments about the taboo on passing food from one set of chopsticks to another; about a waiter who, like an automatic machine, kept putting the ashtray back in the center of the table; about Kumo, who had forbidden her to clip her nails the night before because of the belief that people who clip their nails at night won't be with their parents when they die. Idit took all that in, as well as the muted gleam in Nancy's eyes, and told Edward that Nancy was losing the unbounded enthusiasm she'd had at their first meeting. When

Kumo's name came up in the women's conversation, a shadow passed quickly across Nancy's eyes, as if a painful spot had been touched by mistake. He was away a lot, Nancy mentioned, going out of her way to present this as an untroubling fact. The trips to Osaka involved being away for a night, and soon Tokyo would be added to his itinerary, which was more than twice the distance Osaka was. She was trying to keep busy outside the house when he was gone, to come home late so she could cut down on the hours spent with his mother and grandmother, but sometimes he was asked to travel at the last minute. No one was to blame, Nancy said quickly, dripping coffee on her skirt. She'd been warned that the Japanese work long days. She moistened the edge of tissue with water and wiped away the coffee. And very often, workers have to go out in the evenings with their colleagues after work, but she never imagined—rubbing hard at the recalcitrant stain that had penetrated the fibers of the light-colored cloth—she never imagined that this is what her life would be like in Japan. And besides—giving up, she tossed the tissue into the ashtray—it's just that she's starting to miss New York.

"How many years have you been here?" Nancy asked Idit at their next meeting.

"Eight and a half."

"What happened, did you kill someone at home?" Nancy's voice was a whisper, promising to keep a secret. "How can you live here for so long?"

"I like their aesthetic sense, their quiet, the space."

"They're not normal, haven't you noticed? They're not real people. They're robots who look like people, programmed like in science fiction. And do you know why they're quiet and give you space—so foreigners won't catch onto it."

And one meeting later, again with her voice lowered, "Have you noticed their smell?"

"No."

"Like the breath of old dogs."

"Kumo, too?" Idit smiled.

"Especially Kumo. He didn't have it in America."

"And you told him?" Still smiling.

"No. I reject him gently. Maybe he'll understand."

"Don't get your hopes up. He won't understand."

"You're right, they're completely oblivious."

Sometimes, Idit would ask about Kumo's grandmother and hear in Nancy's derisive tone, hidden at first and then overt, about how she drinks whole pitchers of water and then pees for hours; how she spends entire mornings polishing the frame of a picture of the Japanese Emperor, a smaller copy of the picture she'd seen on the day of the bomb; how Kumo's mother empties whole jars of oil on her scarred back, and the stuff smells like the disinfectants they use in America to clean public toilets. As she spoke, Nancy would imitate the Japanese women, sucking in her cheeks, pursing her lips into a tiny circle, raising her eyebrows until they drew up into her forehead, and she pushed her toes together, making her legs crooked, and both of them would burst out laughing.

"You're very interested in her," Nancy commented one day.

"I once had a friend who wrote a paper about the Japanese Holocaust versus the Jewish Holocaust in Europe. And I know a few Holocaust survivors."

"Are they all as crazy as she is?"

"No."

Nancy averted her face so that the people sitting at the next table wouldn't see, and she sucked in her cheeks, made her mouth a circle, drew up her eyebrows, and said in Japanese, "He was a soldier? She was a soldier? They were soldiers? Very bad," and hooted with laughter.

"My father was a Holocaust survivor, too," Idit said, trying to sound matter-of-fact in her confession.

"Ah—" Nancy broke off laughing. "I suppose it's not funny, but it's really very bad, isn't it?"

Idit couldn't remember when Kumo's grandmother ceased being an amusing subject, but in any case, it was weeks after Nancy had begun talking about Kumo with a resentment she couldn't hide: apparently they were pressuring him at work to travel frequently and were dissatisfied with what he'd accomplished. She'd never seen him so upset, and the old lady was now sleeping during the day and wandering around at night, making him even crazier.

"So maybe you should move to your own place?"

"That's just it—" Nancy began crying quietly, the tears transparent stalactites dripping from her nose, and Idit drew back at the unexpected response. "The thing is, he doesn't want to leave. Anyway, his salary isn't enough for us to move—"

And Nancy's ridiculous salary, just enough for pocket money, barely covered the cost of her makeup and clothes. But he'd already told her that he won't leave his mother and his grandmother because they need him. Only now does he realize how much he wronged them when he went to Boston. Really—Nancy took the tissue Idit pushed into her hand—she was sorry she's carrying on like this in the middle of lunch, but she can't hide the truth any longer: she's miserable in that awful house with three Japanese she doesn't understand at all. Kumo's changed a lot since they came back, especially when it comes to the way he feels about America. His great admiration for American culture has gradually turned into loathing, and he refuses to explain to her what happened. Probably, she came to his defense, he doesn't understand himself. He's forcing her to speak Japanese not only around his mother and grandmother, but also when they're alone in their room, and she has to fight with him to let her listen to English programs when he's away.

Nancy started sobbing loudly, ignoring all the people around her, smearing her makeup with the coffee house napkins. And holding a handful of them stained with her reddish makeup, she grabbed Idit's hand and swore to be her friend forever, and begged Idit not to end their weekly meetings, which were the only consolation she had in this damned city.

Over the next few weeks, Nancy would keep apologizing for that sudden outburst and try to tone down her descriptions of the slowly worsening situation at home: Kumo expected her to learn how to cook from his mother and share the housework with her. His mother had begun treating her like a messenger girl, preparing a daily list of chores for her. Nancy took advantage of their moments of affection to beg Kumo to look for their own apartment, but the last time, he told her roughly not to dare raise that subject again. She asked if she could at least furnish their room in her taste so she'd feel at home in it, and he replied that in Japan, people know how to appreciate modest furnishings, not like in America, where they buy and throw out everything like madmen, a place without tradition and without respect for anything but money. His hatred of America had become such an obsession that even his English was deteriorating.

Idit could see less and less of the radiant young girl Nancy had been when she'd offered Idit her blouse on the evening they first met. Their meetings became more and more dreary and oppressive, and Nancy was so self-involved she almost never asked about Edward or Idit's attempts to get pregnant. But Idit, recalling Nancy's face, dirty with streaked makeup, and her declaration of eternal friendship, felt responsible for her and couldn't find the courage to cancel even one meeting.

By the end of that year, Nancy's eyes were already full of shadows. The old lady was losing her mind, she said in a crushed voice. In the middle of a meal, she'd taken the cucumbers out of her salad and put them on her face to demonstrate what the people injured by the bomb did to ease the pain of their burns. She didn't allow any food on the table that contained the innards of an animal because on that day she'd seen a dog licking the spilled intestines of a cow. Nancy had been sent to see to the heating because the old lady was forbidden to touch coal. When the old lady had run home on that day she'd seen a pile of coal, and only when she saw a lump that looked like a leg did she realize that she'd stepped on people who'd been burned to charcoal. Her descriptions of the horror were neverending. If she hadn't understood Japanese, Nancy would have been spared the stories, but the old lady made a deliberate effort to speak clearly. When they were eating and when Nancy was helping her in the kitchen, the old lady repeated over and over and over again the descriptions of what she'd seen right after the bomb was dropped: long rows of blind people, people with strips of skin hanging from their bodies, weeping school children walking around without arms or lying on the side of the road without legs, charcoaled people who looked like statues—those pictures haunted her in her nightmares. The old lady wouldn't leave Nancy alone, even when she escaped to her room. She'd stand at the door and continue with her descriptions of horror, and when Nancy locked the door, the old lady would stand behind it and bark out her stories through the keyhole.

"You absolutely have to leave that house," Idit said, horrified.

"That's no house," Nancy raged, "it's a madhouse."

She'd asked Kumo to go back to New York with her, and he categorically refused. She'd asked to separate from him and go back home without him, and he was furious. She'd told him she'd ask her stepbrother to send her a plane ticket and he said that if she dared set foot outside the house, she wouldn't make it to the airport alive. He had abandoned her to his mother's abuse and now his grandmother was also giving her chores to do. Two days earlier, she'd asked her to polish the frame of the Emperor's picture. The day before, she'd demanded that Nancy wash her back, tattooed with scars and rampant tumors. She'd complained to Kumo, but he rebuked her. The role of a daughter-in-law in Japan, he told her, is to be a *haniome*, to look after her *shutome*, her mother-in-law. And enough of her American nonsense. There, in Kumo's mother's house, they respect Japanese tradition.

Idit, in the middle of her ninth year in Hiroshima, felt that she had finally found her place there: a project she had labored over diligently for two years won a national award that came with a generous grant; her relationship with Edward had deepened to that of a couple, accustomed to ups-and-downs, whose love has stabilized; his dedication to having a child together touched her heart; the anticipation of the next pregnancy was accompanied by a sense of certainty that this time, her uterus would succeed in retaining the fetus; thoughts of Natan had long since stopped bothering her. If it hadn't been for the feeling of horror Nancy had injected into her life, she would have felt an enormous sense of repose. But Nancy, like a child destined for catastrophes, appropriated all the maternal feelings that had grown in Idit and were seeking an outlet. Their conversations seemed less and less like a dialogue between friends.

"Be strong," Idit would whisper to her when they parted.

"I'll be fine."

"And take care of yourself."

"Don't worry. I'm a big girl."

"And call if you have to. Anytime."

Their next meeting gave Idit a tremendous sense of relief. From a distance, as Nancy walked jauntily toward the café, her full skirt flapping against her legs, Idit could see Nancy's bright face and happy doe eyes. She and Kumo had made up once and for all, Nancy said, smiling with joy. Then she kissed Idit and sat down. She'd cried in his arms the entire night and told him about how miserable she was living with his mother and his grandmother. He'd wiped away her tears and swore he'd take care of her as he'd promised he would in America, and that he'd never again frighten or threaten her. He apologized and explained that the pressure at work had blinded him and obliterated his love for her, but he'd had a good talk with his boss, who'd promised him a raise. Two days earlier, on March 14th, "the white day," he'd brought her a huge box of white chocolates shaped like bears, her favorite animal, and entreated her to agree to stay in his mother's house for another few months, until they could afford to move to their own apartment. As compensation, he agreed to let her refurnish their bedroom the way she wanted to. And this—Nancy's eyes shone— this is where Idit came into the plan. A western architect familiar with Feng-Shui is the ideal decorator for a mixed couple. So— Nancy recrossed her legs and looked outside—she'd be able to stay in her pleasant room, which will not have a single millimeter of tatami screens, and she'd listen to the country music the old lady had forbidden her to play in the living room. And since she'd put the TV near the door and turn the volume all the way up, the old lady could scream her stories to high heaven for all she cared.

"I'm going to make myself a little America here, not like your place with the tatami and the Buddhist altar and the Shinto crap."

With the point of a pencil, which was moving between the American catalogue she was holding and her pursed lips (a repulsive habit from her elementary school days), Nancy chose a rug, two curtains, a wallpaper pattern, a double bed, a desk, and TV stand, all of which would arrive within two weeks, packed well in huge sheets of bubble plastic.

Two weeks later, Kumo's grandmother stood grumbling as the packages were brought in and piled in the living room, and it wasn't until the porter took a pad of pink pages out of his many-pocketed overalls that she ran off to her room to the sound of Nancy's laughter.

The decorating work was simple and quick. The bed was put in the standard place, the headboard facing north. The other furniture found its rightful place after being shifted back and forth all morning. Kumo's grandmother walked up and down the hallway the entire time, lingering at the door as if she were doing a slow dance until Nancy's nerves frayed and she slammed the door in the old lady's face. Two days later, after the wallpaper had been put up, the carpet had been spread, the curtains had been hung, and the furniture stood in its place, they leaned their backs against the closed door and looked with satisfaction at the bright room, and Nancy, like a child who had been given a much coveted gift, kissed Idit on the cheek and said, "It's perfect. I plan to be happy here."

Happy and serene in her American refuge, Nancy didn't sense the approaching danger. She'd occasionally worry Idit with stories of the abuse she was inflicting on Kumo's mother and grandmother. At one of their meetings, she told Idit, as if she were a child confessing a prank, that she played country music in her room and deliberately left the door open, and as soon as the old lady appeared at the door, she slammed it in her face.

"Aren't you going a little overboard, Nancy?"

"About what?"

"About not being careful. This could be dangerous. She's probably not very balanced."

"She's completely crazy!" Nancy cried happily. "And this is making her even crazier! Once, she stopped talking suddenly and

I opened the door and found her on her knees, crying, sitting in her own pee."

"She peed?" Idit said, alarmed.

"She pees all the time."

"From fear?"

"From the water. She's a water freak. She drinks for all the Japanese who didn't get water on the day of the bomb. And yesterday—" Nancy burst out laughing as she remembered—"yesterday I told her that my father was a pilot in the war."

"You never told me that."

"Because it's not true. He wasn't even drafted because one of his legs was paralyzed when he was a child."

"So why did you tell her that?"

"To give her food for her nightmares. She's sure he's the one who dropped the bomb."

"That's not smart, Nancy, it really isn't."

"I'm getting back at her. She's been abusing me for five months, and it's the punishment she deserves."

"It sounds dangerous to me. You should stop it."

Nancy's cries of joy, which sometimes seemed to be signs of inebriation, continued that whole morning, and Idit's apprehension intensified.

"If something happens—" she said to Nancy said when they parted.

"Like what?"

"I don't know. Or if you feel that something is about to happen—"

"I believe in fate. I believe that if something bad has to happen to you, you can't escape it even if you run away to the end of the world."

"But still, if something happens—"

"Like what?"

"Like if you suddenly have to leave there—just take a taxi and come to me. Take my key in case I'm not home," she said, taking the key from her bag and thrusting it into Nancy's hand. "Just leave everything and come. Don't even lose time packing. I have everything you need. Next week, we'll look for a reading lamp and two pictures—and the room will be perfect."

After she'd taken ten steps past the store window, Idit realized that the painting she'd seen displayed there was a reproduction of Joseph Stella's "Brooklyn Bridge." Edward, determined to get her to like American culture, had shown her a book on twentieth-century American art and had lingered excitedly on that painting, expanding his explanation of its cubist construction, the crystalline spaces, the long cables piercing the sky, the meaning of the red cone at the bottom of the canvas.

Idit stopped in the middle of the street, an island among the flow of people splitting into two streams gliding forward on either side of her. Then she turned around and made her way back to the store. And two hours later, she handed Nancy the print wrapped in colored paper decorated with large paper flowers. Nancy held it with both hands and went to the window, still talking about the toilet she'd seen, the latest thing for hypochondriacs, that takes the blood pressure of the person sitting on it. "Those crazy Japanese," she said and ripped open the paper wrapping, against all the rules, revealing the crystalline and cylindrical shapes. In the light of day, the colors of the print were fresher than they'd looked from the depths of the shop. The blue spots of river and sky sparkled; the cables of the bridge stretched in strong diagonals, reflecting the glitter; and the red spot at the bottom of the picture looked moist, alive, like a puddle that had not yet stabilized.

Idit raised her glance to see Nancy's reaction and saw wide-open eyes in a shocked face.

"Do you like it?" Idit asked, leaning toward Nancy like a mother to her distressed child. "It's beautiful, isn't it?" she added when Nancy did not respond.

"Who bought this, Diti?" Nancy dropped the picture.

"I did, of course. You don't think it's beautiful?"

"It's very beautiful, but mostly it's weird." Nancy looked back at the picture. "Whose idea was it?"

"Mine. Why weird?"

"Not Edward's?"

"No. Edward doesn't even know I bought it, but it does have something to do with him. He told me he had this painting at college in Boston. And today I saw it by chance in a store window and decided to buy it for you, a souvenir of Boston. Why is it weird?"

"Because this is the exact same picture Edward and I had in our bedroom."

"What bedroom?"

Nancy pried her eyes from the picture, as if an unexpected and more pressing event that required her attention had suddenly taken place.

"Right opposite the bed."

"What bedroom?"

"Edward's and mine."

"I don't understand what you're saying."

"So Edward really didn't tell you. He swore he wouldn't, but I didn't believe him."

Many small puzzles were suddenly solved, like tiny pieces of a mechanism falling into place: the way the three of them burst inexplicably into laughter; the occasional furtive glances they exchanged when certain subjects were raised; mysterious remarks Nancy would make that Idit attributed to American culture, which was foreign to her, especially the recurring comments about coincidences in peoples' lives.

"It was when we were in college."

"Before you met Kumo?"

"Yes. In our sophomore year we took a course in Japanese art together, and that's where I met Kumo. He was the teacher."

"And you and Edward were living together then?"

"Yes."

"In the same bedroom?"

"Yes. We were married."

"You and Edward?"

"Yes."

"I don't believe you, Nancy. I'm sorry—"

"You can be sorry all you want. I still remember who I was married to. I'm not that deranged."

"And I know Edward well enough to know that he would've told me."

"He didn't tell you because of Kumo. Kumo asked him to keep it a secret."

"Why?"

"I have no idea. It's one of those things that happens in the Japanese mind."

"Edward and I have been together for seven years, long before Kumo asked or didn't ask him, long before you got here. He never told me he'd been married."

"Not even about the first time?"

"What first time?"

"The first time he was married, in Tennessee, to Gloria."

Idit looked at her, utterly still.

"So it really doesn't have anything to do with Kumo," Nancy said as if she'd just been exonerated of false charges, "because I was his second wife."

His ever-serious Gary Cooper eyes, even more serious now, were riveted on her. At the edge of the desk that stood between them was a collage of photographs in a frame decorated with painted cherry buds. The photographs crowded together as if trying to belong: Edward the child in a Peter Pan shirt with his parents and his sister sitting on a park bench blinking in the sun; his grandmother in a big Scarlet O'Hara straw hat against the background of the glittering white house at the end of the oak-lined path on their Tennessee estate; his baby nephew, naked; Idit and Edward, last summer, high in the air in the car of a Ferris wheel, their arms around each other. She was sitting across from him in his office, her face tense, the mosaic of photos to her left, her eyes focused straight ahead on Edward.

"Tell me it's not true. I also think she's starting to lose it."

Edward opened his mouth like a thirsty fish, changed his mind and smiled an artificial smile that exposed a great many teeth.

"Wait, wait a minute," he said, stalling for time, trying to organize his words, evading the eyes that were fastened on him.

"Is it true or not?" she demanded.

"This sounds like an interrogation by the Mossad. Am I being interrogated now?"

"So it *is* true," she said, stunned.

"Even with the Mossad, I have the right to remain silent and call for a lawyer, don't I?"

"Why didn't you tell me, Edward?"

"You didn't tell me you were with the Mossad either."

"Why did I have to hear it from Nancy?"

"Because Nancy's a blabbermouth."

"We've been together for so many years," she said in disappointment.

"Because it didn't mean anything to me."

"That's not true, it can't be true."

"The truth is that I wanted to make a good impression on you."

A feeling of affront, harsh and painful, rose in her about the way that he, like a grown up trying to fool a child, wasn't even trying to be clever about it.

"I wanted your child, that's how much I trusted you."

"And I agreed, that's how much *I* trusted *you*."

"I'm going." She stood up, suddenly exhausted, as if she'd suddenly come down with the flu, and he rose across from her.

"I'm going with you." He looked serious, and his eyes almost succeeded in leading her down the garden path once again. "I thought I wouldn't be able to explain, that's the truth, that I'd end up guiltier than I was. I wanted to tell you, but now... Let's go home, we'll talk quietly—"

The phone rang and, before picking up the receiver, he still managed to say, "Because it's still important to me to make a good impression on you."

Then he put the phone to his ear and his face darkened as he said incredulously, "What are you saying you did?... With your hands?... Maybe she's not dead, maybe she just passed out... Check her pulse... So what if she used to lock herself in the room with the TV... So what if she didn't listen to your grandmother? Wait, Kumo, listen to me. Wait, wait, let's not rush into any-

thing . . . You're sure . . . there's absolutely no chance . . . So wait.
First of all, calm your grandmother down. I hear her. . . . And don't
call anyone. . . . No. Not the police and not the hospital either.
You're married to an American woman and you're an American citizen. Don't move until I check out a few things at the embassy. . . . "

* * *

The ring of a telephone burst into a dream that was going round
and round in circles: she was at the edge of the pool at the Atomic
Bomb Museum, dipping her fingers into the water, blood streaming from her hands like ribbons in the flow, coloring the pool
gradually until the surface of the water blackened with old, bad
blood. "Can I help you, Miss?"—a distant voice against the background of the ringing phone, coming closer.

A man's voice broke through the drug-induced fog and the pro-
fuse, blinding light. "Are you all right now?"

"Hello, Natan," she whispered into the receiver, "I want to go
home."

"I know. When did it happen?"

"Yesterday morning. Did you dream it, too?"

"What do you mean, 'dream it'? I ran into your mother."

"I haven't spoken to my mother, I haven't spoken to anyone."
She woke up.

"So maybe I did dream it. What exactly happened to you?"

"I had a kind of breakdown."

"I told you that Hiroshima has a bad history."

"I remember what you said," she said, wanting to add, "I also
remember what you didn't say." Instead, what came out of her
mouth was, "And Jerusalem?"

"Jerusalem, too. But in Jerusalem someone's waiting for you."

She caught her breath. "But he's married."

"Temporarily. His wife is leaving on the weekend."

"Leaving temporarily?"

"Leaving permanently."

"Leaving alone?" She raised her head and straightened up
slightly.

"No. She's leaving with a lot of medical books."

She fell back onto the bed, glowing. So, with a lot of medical books and without a child. Children of nature were still possible, and meanwhile, from the weekend on, there'd be empty shelves and a yard full of grapevines and ferns.

"What about the bed?" she dared to say.

"The bed here is independent. It'll decide for itself who it wants to go with."

"Can you tell it something for me?"

"Absolutely. It's still in the making-up-its-mind stage."

"Tell it—" she looked at the landscape drawing of Hiroshima, then at the Buddhist altar of the spirits of the fathers and finally at the shelf of Shinto gods—"Tell it to wait for me. I'm on my way."

Tel Aviv

Y OU TURN AT THE PAVED SQUARE in front of the Cinemathèque, walk quickly toward Ibn Gvirol Street, cross against the light, almost collide with a girl wearing a hooded vest, apologize profusely without looking at her, and sweep forward, regaining your rapid stride, crossing the next two streets against the light, never slowing down for even a minute as you head toward city hall.

I rush along behind you, pushing my way past people, forced to cross two streets against the light, risking a ticket, stopping suddenly at the third traffic light to let the flow of traffic pass, getting worried as I see you pulling away, your trench coat flapping around your legs as if you were about to fly off. When the tail end of the last car passes me, I break away from the row of law-abiding citizens and race across the street, a woman running after a man to close the distance that has grown between us. You dash forward toward city hall, the corner of which is already visible in the distance. My eyes, unlike yours, are attracted by the shop windows, and when my gaze is drawn to a tailored green suit, I almost stumble.

As you get closer to the memorial where Itzhak Rabin was shot to death, you slow down like a horse being reined in. At the traffic light across from the site, I stand behind you, breathless, almost panting in your ear, almost touching your raincoat.

I've been your second shadow for almost two weeks now, walking behind you in the streets, following you into coffee houses, lying in wait in front of your house. You're easy to follow. You're either so focused on yourself, or so bored with what's outside you, or both, that you ignore the people around you as if they were transparent. If you were an animal—I'm amazed to find myself fearful for you—you would have been hunted down a long time ago. This morning, for example, at the Cinemathèque, I sat in the seat next to you for the entire lecture, the collar of the trench coat that lay on your lap rubbed against my thigh, my elbow touched yours on the armrest we shared, and I kept stealing glances at the notebook in which you wrote your comments, recognizing your handwriting with its well-shaped letters, the *l* pulled up to the line above it and the *p* dipping down to the line below it. You're blind to the people around you, to traffic lights, shops, street musicians. As soon as I realized that, I stopped trying to disguise myself by changing my clothes and my hairstyle. Now you are completely focused on Rabin's memorial stone. You take a notebook out of your bag and write in it. I move close enough to touch you. The scent that floated around you at the lecture, the scent of an elegant aftershave, is diluted in the open air. I read out of the corner of my eye: "Here in this place, the Prime Minister and Minister of Defense of the State of Israel was assassinated on November 4, 1995. His last will and testament—peace."

In another seventeen minutes, the tour you guide will begin, "Bauhaus in Tel Aviv: the International Style." The memorial site was set as the meeting place for the convenience of those who were paying for the entire series of tours in the city hall office. In another seventeen minutes, I will hear the voice that two weeks ago scorched my ear with a bolt of lightning from the telephone receiver in the bedroom when you tried to seduce Roni, who whispered his response to your murmuring voice from the phone in the dining room; in another seventeen minutes, I will stand in front of you in my yellow coat with the light-reflecting cuffs and collar, the one I've been wearing these last few days, the one that lay on my lap today in the Cinemathèque, and you will not recognize me.

Only buildings exist in your world. Buildings and young men.
Now you're standing and examining a piece of white wall like an
archaeologist standing in front of the discovery of his life. What do
you see there?

In the few minutes left before the tour begins, you walk past the
five large, framed photographs of the graffiti written by stunned
and stricken people after Rabin's assassination. You stop occasionally to get a sharper look at the details, press your forehead against
the glass. I'm impressed by your ability to project remoteness, by
your unintentional condescension. Since that phone call I accidentally heard—which paralyzed me for almost an hour and made me
search through Roni's belongings for the first time in my life until
I found the piece of paper hidden in the inner pocket of his work
portfolio—I've been following you through the streets of the city,
trying to see you through Roni's eyes, to smell you through Roni's
nostrils, to solve the riddle of the words you whispered over the
phone into the ear of my man and yours, Roni.

(Our first-grade, end-of-year photograph is proof of what does
not exist in our memories: the fact that we were in the same class.
Roni is standing stooped over in the middle row, on the far right,
his posture an indication of boredom or dejection. I'm sitting
stooped over, legs crossed, in the middle of the first row, my posture an indication of boredom or dejection. A symbolic omen,
deterministic proof of the future, and a clear sign that we came
from neglectful homes, we are the only ones wearing long-sleeved
shirts, as if we did not know, as all the other pupils in our class and
their parents knew, that summer had arrived. Years later, we wondered why we didn't remember each other from the first grade.
Maybe we had already recognized the alarming signs in each other.)

You're punctual. At the appointed time, you go to the meeting
place, and in a quick, measured voice, which has the gift of defin-
ing distance, introduce yourself to the people in the group that
gathers from all sides of the square and is immediately joined by
six people who get off a minibus, loaded with bags, cameras ready
for action hanging around their necks, and another four, two soldiers from the munitions corps among them, who file out of the

doors of city hall. I stand at the rear of the group, facing you, and hear your familiar, precise voice, a voice that is a stickler for details, matter-of-factness tinged with affectation, the voice I overheard trying to seduce Roni.

(Roni has been in my life since the second grade. On the third day of school, he was stung by bees as he walked past the blocks of hives that dotted the path lined with tall cacti near the ruins of the destroyed Arab village, and was rushed to the hospital where, our teacher told us, the doctors fought to keep him alive, and we all looked at her, thrilled by the heroism of the doctor-fighters. Later, Roni stayed home in bed for three weeks. Pairs of kids from the class were sent to visit him and bring him the homework assignments. I was last on the list. Since I was left without a partner, I went alone. I found his sister sitting in the kitchen playing with a cat crouching on the table. Without saying a word, she kicked her leg in the air in the direction of Roni's room. He was lying in bed, pale, his monster face looking up at the ceiling. I stood in the doorway, fascinated by that misshapen face. As if indulging some kind of evil whim, the swelling had gone from some parts of his body and had stayed in others, leaving one huge cheek under a closed eye and the other cheek flat under an eye that was open like the eye of a circus clown; his right hand looked normal and the left was swollen like a boxer's glove.

"It's nothing serious," he said and moved his clown eye toward me.

"I can see."

"And it isn't catching." The eye closed, as if it were winking.

"I don't care if I catch it," I said, looking at the first boy I'd ever met who looked more dejected than me.)

Curtly, as if warning us not to expect you to be a patient guide, you introduce the subject of the tour: houses in the International Style known as "the Bauhaus style," built in Tel Aviv at the end of the 1920s and 1930s. From the depths of your voice I hear your words coming through the phone like a relentless incantation: "Let's get it out in the open, Roni. What happened happened, and it can't and shouldn't be ignored. It's special for me, too, and it's going to affect both our lives. But we have to face the truth, we

can't run away from it. Like that man in the legend who ran from
death only to find death waiting for him at the place he had run
to." I know those lines of yours by heart. I spent a whole night
memorizing them like a diligent student, as I listened to Roni's
quiet breathing, wondering if they appeared in his dream, wondering how he could keep the secret of your fatal lines from me.

You turn your arm to the southwest and your superior voice says,
"We'll go from here to Chen Boulevard, circle the Mann Auditorium
and the Habima Theater, and continue along Rothschild Boulevard,
where we'll stop at some interesting buildings."

I know one of those interesting buildings on Rothschild
Boulevard, the building you live in, whose address I found written
in your handwriting with the tall *l* and the long *p*. I stood in front
of it for two evenings in the freezing cold, wrapped in a camel-skin
coat to keep myself covered and hidden, pretending for the few
people who hurried by on their way to a warm place that I was tin-
kering with the motorcycle parked opposite your balcony. Faint,
yellowish light, indulgent, like the glow that spills from a night
light, illuminated your room. I saw you walk past the door of glass
squares that leads onto the balcony, a book in your hand, wearing
a T-shirt, which says something about the quality of the heating in
your apartment. Then you appeared in the kitchen window, also lit
with a softer light than the fluorescent lights of the kitchen in the
apartment above you. Then the light went on in a side room,
apparently your bedroom. You came to the window with the telephone pressed to your ear, and lowered the venetian blinds by
shifting the angle of the string that holds them up. Were you talking to Roni? Were you explaining to him the nature of the thing
that couldn't and shouldn't be ignored? Were you telling him a
new tale about the need to recognize an exceptional fact of life that
shouldn't be ignored, a fact of life that excluded me?

I wake up from my thoughts as you are explaining Bauhaus,
which is not a style but an institution that existed for only fourteen
years and was studied by only seven hundred students. It generated
the International Style and such marvelous things as an aluminum
desk lamp with an adjustable shade, a folding table conceived by

Gustav Hassenflug, a ball lamp hanging from chains designed by Marianna Brandt, and Marcel Breuer's folding armchair. Demonstrating how knowledgeable you are also about the feelings of the dead, you say, Walter Gropius, the school director, would turn over in his grave if he knew about the misconception, because he once stated explicitly that it was not the aim of Bauhaus to advocate any particular style. And he was not the one responsible for choosing the name "the International Style"; that was the director of the Museum of Modern Art in New York, where the exhibit was held. That style, a new architectural language with high aesthetic standards, left its mark on the city of Tel Aviv.

You wave your hand in a military "follow me" gesture, look at the soldiers whose language you're using, turn your back to the people in the group, and walk away, leaving them slightly confused. Then you're already crossing the stone square toward Chen Boulevard, passing the Yigal Tumarkin sculpture stuck in the paving stones like a giant warhead fallen from the sky. The people hurry after you without looking at each other, like a contentious family in a funeral procession. You stop at the traffic light, not bothering to check whether your group is with you. Here, like someone determined to set an example for others, you stand still at the red light, then cross at the green like a law-abiding citizen.

I'm careful to stay two steps behind you, like a prison guard in charge of an unpredictable prisoner, and images race through my mind: you and Roni are in them together. In your designer apartment, let's say next to the lamp (Marianna Brandt?) or the armchair (Marcel Breuer?), or in front of the picture, on each of which you could give an hour-long lecture. Roni is panting with excitement. You hand him a wine goblet (a Bauhaus design?), which also has a history worth telling. Roni doesn't know how to say no, and he sips some wine and almost faints. You sit him down on the couch and sit down next to him. Is this when you move your head to his neck and inhale his young smell, the smell of rain and harvested hay, slide your hands under his clothes to his lithe body? Pull down the zipper of his pants, bear down on his loins? Do you do all that in your bedroom, where you stand

and admire the nightstands, the headboard, the statue you bought at an auction or in some antique market? Do you waylay him in the bathroom in front of the huge crystal mirror that reflects the image of your beautiful heads, the guilty expressions on your faces?

("I brought you the homework," I said.

"Too bad," he replied, ignoring my scrutinizing gaze.

"Do you want me to tell the teacher I couldn't come?"

He looked at me in surprise. Maybe it was then that he really saw me for the first time in his life. Maybe the naturalness with which I offered to deceive the teacher was what made him straighten up in his bed, making the swollen cheek stand out more and turn red, as if it were about to burst open.

"My sister'll tell on us."

"I can say I got mixed up and brought you yesterday's homework," I said, exchanging one lie for another without blinking an eye.

His face lit up, but then the light was immediately extinguished."

"She hasn't caught me so far."

He gave up on the idea. "I always get caught. Even my father says it doesn't pay to lie."

"So I won't." I thought, "So I won't, you coward."

"You can sit down," he said.

I sat down. From that angle, half his forehead looked huge too, and had a fiery red color.

"Why is your cheek so swollen?" I recognized the sing-song voice I used when I played the part of Little Red Riding Hood in the kindergarten end-of-year play.

"I was stung by bees."

"I was stung by bees once, too. I didn't swell up like you."

"I'm allergic."

"So why do you go near hives?"

"I was going to the Arab village, not to the hives."

"The one that was destroyed?"

"Yes. Its ruins talk."

"Don't be silly."

"An Arab once told me that, and I wanted to hear it."

"So, did you hear anything?"

"Yes."

"What?"

"Whispering."

"What did it say?"

"I didn't get to hear because the bees attacked me."

I looked at him with pity. "My aunt says you have to put a tomato on the sting and it goes away."

"That won't help. My father says I should live in the city. There are no bees in the city."

"Everyone in the city is a corrupt bastard," I said, quoting my aunt.

"No they aren't. My grandmother lives in the city. She's a Holocaust survivor."

My aunt's voice came from my mouth again. "Life in the city is dog eat dog."

"And here?"

"It's less here."

"No, it isn't."

"Yes, it is. My aunt says that in the city, people have their nose up each other's ass," I said, revealing once and for all the identity of the most important figure in my life.

"It's worse here."

Our first argument, as far as I can remember, was about the city. And immediately after it came the conversation about our fathers.

"When does your father tell you all the things he tells you?" I asked him.

"When I see him."

"Our teacher said he got religious and left the house and disappeared."

"Who did she say that to?"

"To the class."

"When?"

"When she told us why we have to bring you the homework."

"Why do you have to?"

"Because your mother works late. He doesn't support you, so she has to do it."

Roni suddenly wilted, but of course the swelling in his cheek didn't go down. The largeness of his face only intensified his sadness over the insult to him and his parents, who had been exposed in class in his absence.

"My father left the house, too," I said, trying to console him.

"He got religious, too?"

"No. The opposite. He found a new woman. That's why we moved here, to be close to my aunt. Rachel, who works in the village office, is my mother's sister. We moved here a little more than a year ago."

"Is that why you lie so much?"

"I lie because I'm going to be an actress. Meanwhile, I lie only when I have to."

"And you lie a lot?"

"As much as I have to."

"Like every day?"

I looked at him with pity, like a veteran survivor looking at a rookie who doesn't have a chance. "Are you kidding?" I said. "At least once a day to everyone I talk to."

"Are you lying to me, too?"

"Sure."

"About what, for example."

"About my father leaving the house, for example."

"He didn't?"

"We left. He stayed with his whore."

"What, a real whore?"

"My aunt says she is.")

In the middle of the boulevard, exactly in the center of the two rows of ficus trees that rise as high as the fourth floor, you stop, turn, and find yourself looking right at me. You signal to the others to gather around you, prompt the soldiers to move closer to you, look reprovingly at one of the gang of camera wielders who lit himself a cigarette while he was walking.

"Notice the columns." You point at the buildings on both sides of the boulevard. "The columns enable the sea breeze to flow freely under the house. Look at how beautiful it is," you say with pleasure, then suddenly become quiet, your eyes wandering, roaming among the columns of the house across the street, caught in a private memory. You are suddenly exposed to me, and I look at you with the discomfort of a voyeur, like someone who is walking innocently down the street and sees a couple making love near a window whose curtains they have forgotten to close. Your eyes wander among the columns of the building, ivy wound densely around one of them up to the ceiling, as if trying to choke it, and you are carried far away from the group you are supposed to be guiding, far from the two soldiers standing on either side of you like guards who have fallen asleep on duty.

Your dissociation embarrasses the others; it makes me curious. According to the itemized telephone bill I secretly sent for, you haven't known each other for more than four months. It doesn't seem likely that that memory is related to Roni. But still: Is this where what happened between you happened?

You wake up in seconds, take in the staring people around you and snap out of your reverie. "It's beautiful," you sum up in a matter-of-fact voice, as if you hadn't disappeared on us earlier, and your eyes fix on a scrawny pomegranate tree. "Look at how the street continues on into the garden under the columns, into the back garden, creating a single visual space. And look at what people planted in their yards then: pomegranate trees."

(Roni and I picked the pomegranates from the trees that grew along the hewn stone fence of the cemetery on the eastern side of the village. Then we sat down on his grandfather's grave, tore the thick crimson peels with our fingers, and chewed the juicy seeds. The liquid ran down our chins, dripped onto our bare knees, and sprayed onto our shirts and the headstone, leaving stains that would last forever.

"You can start wishing," I told Roni.

I got the idea of going to his grandfather's grave on Yom Kippur from a story in which the hero goes to his mother's grave on Yom Kippur and makes three wishes, which are granted imme-

diately. Since no one from my family was buried there, I coaxed
Roni into it.

"But why on Yom Kippur?" he asked, frightened.

"Because on Yom Kippur, the heavens open and He'll help you
get whatever you wish for."

"That's not true."

"Everybody goes to the cemetery on Yom Kippur. Everyone
knows that."

"Everybody goes to synagogue on Yom Kippur, not to any
cemetery."

"What synagogue? My aunt watches videos." Then I said, "You
can start wishing now."

"Let it rain a lot this winter," Roni said after some thought.

"What do we care about rain. It would be a pity to bother your
grandfather for no good reason. Wish for something for yourself."

"Like what?"

"Like your allergies should go away."

Roni repeated like an echo, "Let all my allergies go away."

"You still have two more wishes," I said, faithful to the plot of
the story.

Roni sank into thought and finally said, defeated, "I don't
know. You make a wish."

"I want you never to have any friends but me." I spit out the
wish that had been ready and waiting on my tongue for three
months.)

On the way from Dizengoff Street to Rothschild Boulevard, you
again forget that we exist and put one foot onto the crosswalk,
even though the light is red. You seem to remember us at the last
minute, pretend you're just stretching, return your unruly foot to
the sidewalk, and take advantage of the delay to turn to us.

"By any chance"—you hesitate for a second and then give in
once and for all to the desire the memory of the pomegranate tree
aroused in you—"by any chance, does anyone have a fruit-flavored
candy?"

(Thigh to thigh, we sat among the pomegranate peels on the
carved letters of the gravestone. I could feel Roni's body trem-

bling; I knew he regretted his promise to come to the cemetery on
Yom Kippur.

"Don't tell me you're scared."

"I'm not," he lied.

"He loved you, right?"

"Sure. And I loved him."

"You don't have to be afraid of someone you love."

"Of course not," he said unenthusiastically.

"But the people you don't love, you can curse. And the best
place to do it is in the cemetery."

"I don't think that's a good idea."

"Sure it is. The sky is open now."

I started cursing my father and his whore in a stream of curses
that flowed easily from me, quoting from conversations my mother
and my aunt had had not knowing that I was listening to them from
my hiding place in the yard under the open kitchen window, near
the cylinders of gas that looked like mezuzahs. When I'd exhausted
my repertoire, I stopped and said, "Now you curse your father."

"I can't."

"What happened, all of a sudden you fell in love with him?" I
shook him by the shoulder, trying to shake the craziness out of him.

"No. but I can't curse him."

"Okay, so let all the curses for my father be for your father too."

"Okay." He surrendered.)

I wake up in the middle of your lecture about the buildings'
windows. The large European windows, made to let in the sparse
sunlight, shrank in Tel Aviv to horizontal strips to cut down on
the abundant light. You point to the building—those strips of
windows are a trademark of the International Style and show
LeCorbusier's positive influence. Sometimes, they turn into the
long narrow openings of a balcony that shields the room from the
strong rays of the sun.

Bending your hand slightly toward your face, you surrepti-
tiously glance at your watch from the corner of your eye, pretending to be checking your shirt cuff, and say quickly, "The use of
glass was limited in Israel because of the light."

Are you distracted because of Roni? I'm supposed to be at a job interview now. Are you impatient because you arranged to see each other? His sister left a message on the answering machine saying that she and her twins would be coming to Tel Aviv today. Did he want to introduce his family to you? Will that be the next stage in your confrontation with the truth?

(My aunt fussed with my clothes before I left with Roni to visit my father, as if all our futures depended on how well-ironed they were. Her muttered complaints and uneasy sighs about his invitation were interspersed with curses, the most frequent one being, "He should only drop dead."

"Are you worried he'll kidnap me?"

"Just let him try it," she uttered. "If he has any ideas of saying that your mother doesn't take good care of you, then let him look at you and drop dead. That's all I want—that he should drop dead—" She tried in vain to hold back the rest of the sentence and it came out as a muttered hiss, so I wouldn't hear it: "—him and that whore of his."

"Roni will be with me. He won't get any ideas."

If it hadn't been for Roni, I wouldn't have said yes to my father's invitation to visit him. With a passion that was rare for him, Roni convinced me that it was important to stay in touch with family and that I shouldn't give in to what my aunt wanted. For four years—like a juggler holding a deck of cards spread in his hands, Roni held up my father's letters, which I'd kept in a drawer, some still sealed in their envelopes—for four years, he'd begged me to visit him and I never even bothered to answer. If a father invites his daughter—Roni collected the letters into a bundle again—she has to go, because he's her family. A father is more family than an aunt.

"His whore is there," I reminded him.

"Her name's Aviva." He showed me the name written in a letter he was holding. "And I don't think she's really a whore. Your aunt made that up."

At the Haifa central bus station, my aunt put me and Roni on the bus to Herzliya and waited, poker-faced, until the bus pulled away from the platform, and an hour later, across the street from the Herzliya central bus station, my father was waiting for us in his car. I recognized the car right away, but the man who got out of the driver's seat and waved at, the man I hadn't seen for five years, was shorter and fatter than the father I remembered, a complete stranger.

"There he is," I said to Roni, and I was neither happy nor upset to see him.

We stood on the curb and looked right and left twenty times before running across the street, holding hands, dodging cars. My father met us on the opposite sidewalk, alarmed and agitated. He held his hands out toward me and said, "Why didn't you wait for me? That's no way to cross the street!"

I stood trapped in his embrace for a minute. "This is my best friend, Roni."

Roni extended his hand and my father shook it, looking at me. "You've changed so much," he said.

"You, too." I slipped quickly into the back seat and made room for Roni.

"Won't you sit next to me?" my father suggested.

"I don't feel like it," I said, sprawling in my seat next to Roni, and we both sat behind my father like tourists in a taxi. During most of the ride, I ducked down so his searching eyes couldn't see me in the mirror, and rediscovered the streets of my distant childhood, a city childhood, and they filled me with a vague sense of unease. For a minute, I was sorry I let Roni talk me into coming. The obligation to remain indifferent to my father, wordlessly imposed on me by my mother and aunt, burdened me; the feeling I had that he was a stranger oppressed me; the way he tried to catch my glance angered me. The closer we got to the house that had been my house until I was six, the more apprehensive I felt about seeing my old room again, about seeing that stranger, my stepmother, who at that very moment might be baking me a poisoned cake, spreading it with colored candy sprinkles as bait. Roni, easily figuring out what was going on inside me, hugged me, and my father looked at us in the mirror.

Wearing a brown dress, the woman my aunt called a whore,

older and less pretty than I imagined from my mother's conversations with my aunt, opened the door and welcomed us happily.
From where I was standing on the threshold, I could see the living
room which, except for the long table that was covered with a
tablecloth I didn't recognize, seemed to have remained untouched
since my mother and I left. At the sight of the house, suppressed
memories stirred in me like quick slaps on the face: the armchair
I found my mother sitting in, crying; the bedroom door I saw my
father shove my mother out of; the new sofabed in my room where
my mother and I sat when she told me in a despondent voice disguised as a voice craving adventure that we were moving to my
aunt's village; the window I found her leaning out of as if she were
going to commit suicide, but it turned out that she was only trying to push a disease-carrying pigeon's nest off the sill.

Roni took my hand and pulled me inside, and we followed
the woman as if she were an usher in a movie house. She sat us
down at the table, which was set with napkins and saucers like
in the illustration of the mad hatter's tea party in *Alice in
Wonderland*. My father, sitting in the armchair in which my
mother had cried so bitterly, unaware that I was watching her,
looked at me with longing, asked question after question, as if
trying to catch up on five years in an instant, explaining again
and again what he had already written in the few letters I'd read
out of all the letters he'd sent—why he didn't come to visit me
in the village—and he told me again and again how happy he
was that I had decided to come, just as he had dreamed all those
years that I would when I got older and was no longer influenced—he found this indirect way of taking a potshot at my
mother and my aunt—and maybe I'd even miss him a
little . . . then, all choked up, he grew silent.

He grew silent, looking at me with the sad eyes of a puppy
who'd been kicked outside, and I hurried to point out that it was
Roni who'd convinced me to come as he'd dreamed I would all
those years. My father smiled at him as if he'd just discovered his
presence, and thanked him profusely, putting his hands together as
if in prayer.

My father's words neither moved me nor interested me, and I even forgot Roni. My eyes, avoiding the armchair, the bedroom door, and the window across from me, were drawn to Aviva, who was partaking of the refreshments she had served, and I immediately absolved her of trying to poison me. I directed the answers to my father's questions to her. Every time she offered me a plate of cookies or candied fruit, she smiled, hinting that she'd made them especially for me, and I took a cookie or a candy. She passed the plate to Roni, but he responded with a polite refusal that became an adamant refusal, and I didn't try to persuade him to take something. When my stomach started to hurt from eating so much and Aviva offered to make tea, I volunteered to go to the kitchen with her, evading Roni's reproving looks.

The kitchen, unlike the living room, was different from the one I remembered. The cabinets were new, the refrigerator had been moved to the opposite corner, and cheerful curtains printed with ears of corn hung on the window. I stopped on the threshold and looked at the two hooks over the doorframe, where, from pictures I'd seen, I knew my childhood swing had once hung. Aviva took my hand and pulled me gently inside, rolled the sleeves of my sweater up to my elbows, and asked me to fill the tea pot with four teaspoons of tea leaves from the painted metal box, which also looked like it had come right out of the illustration of the mad hatter's tea party.

While I was busy with the tea leaves, I glanced at Aviva, who, with a light step, moved easily between the refrigerator and the kettle, humming a tune that I didn't know. I said to myself that my father had probably decided to try a woman who was the total opposite of my mother. She asked me about the village, the school, my homework, and I answered her willingly.

When we went back into the living room carrying the tray together, she bending down a little to adjust her height to mine, our heads touching, I immediately noticed Roni's tortured expression. Even before we put the tray on the table, he got up and said, "We have to get back."

My father tried to calm him down, repeated the time he and my aunt had decided he would put us on the bus to Haifa, but

Roni, with a vehemence so unlike him, insisted that he and she had agreed on a different time, and claimed she would worry if we didn't reach Haifa within an hour.

I parted quickly from Aviva with a fierce hug, and Roni ripped me out of her arms into the hallway.

"You behaved very badly," I rebuked him when we were sitting in the bus and my father stood on the sidewalk, his arms waving and his eyes showing that he was embarrassed by the whole visit and the hasty departure.

"You're the one who behaved badly."

"It's not polite not to taste even a single thing that someone makes. And it's not nice to run away from them like that before tea."

"It's not fair to bad-mouth your mother."

"I didn't bad-mouth anyone."

"You told her your mother doesn't help you with your home-work because she doesn't know anything."

"She really doesn't," I said, realizing he had heard the conversation in the kitchen.

"You betrayed your mother."

"What are you talking about."

"Just like your father did."

"I didn't betray anyone."

"You should be faithful to your mother."

"If you hadn't made me, I wouldn't even have gone to visit him."

"You had to visit him because family is the most important thing."

"So why didn't you let her serve the tea?"

"Because your family is your father and your mother. She's not family.")

Two steps in front of me, you walk as if fighting the wind. The flaps of your raincoat get tangled around your legs. I picture a game of snipers, like a computer game, getting you in my sights, spraying your back with bullets, making you disappear from my life with the same suddenness you appeared in it. Because of you, Roni is unfaithful to me, did you know that? You succeeded in seducing him with your telephonic brainwashing and your tales.

Do you even know I exist? About Roni's baby, who is taking your whole tour with me, you can't know. Because of you, Roni was unfaithful to his baby, too.

Beside a gray building, rising up in all its ugliness on the beautiful boulevard, you stop.

"Don't tell me that's Bauhaus, too?" the elderly lady of the group says, panting.

You give the facade of the building a thoughtful, caressing look, window by window, and say slowly, "No. This is a city building built in the sixties. You can see how ugly it is." Your day-dreaming eyes linger on details, your mouth says one thing, your eyes another. "But sometimes even ugly buildings make one nostalgic," you say, as if reconciling the contradiction for me. "I once gave painting lessons here to pay for my studies at the Technion. It has nothing to do with our tour."

My breath catches in my throat.

"Seven years ago?" I ask, almost shouting.

Your eyes pass unsuspectingly over my face. "Yes, approximately," you say, and I stumble against the low stone wall and almost collapse beside it.

(We spent the vacation between our last matriculation exam and Roni's induction into the army separately: he in Tel Aviv, working in the mornings at a job his grandmother, whom he was living with, found for him, and the afternoons at a painting and sculpting class near her house. I was in London, at a boarding school where they taught English, including a drama class, a gift from Aviva and my father for my approaching army induction.

When I came back, Roni was waiting for me at the airport, standing one step away from my mother and my aunt. Something about the way he was standing was strange, new. His embrace was different too, cautious, and so was the way he rubbed his hands together when we were sitting in the car.

"What?" he asked in response to my gaze.

"Nothing serious."

"You're lying."

"Because I don't exactly know. Maybe you've gotten a little citified." I laughed, pushing his shoulder with my hand in that old gesture. "Kind of Tel Avivian."

Later, Roni went into the army and was swallowed up in army camps that were off limits to civilians. The few times we met, always in the presence of others, I saw the approaching breakdown in his look, in the nervous jiggling familiar to me from childhood. When I was home on my first leave from basic training, my aunt said she'd heard in the village grocery that Roni had had a nervous breakdown and left the army. Hurt that people in the grocery knew something about Roni's life before I did, that he didn't come to share with me what was happening to him, I went to his house. His mother told me, almost apologetically, that he was at his grandmother's in Tel Aviv.)

Was it you and the painting class that I saw in the way Roni stood, in the way he sat, in his embrace at the end of that summer? Was it then that you two discovered the truth that you could not run away from? And if so, why was your address in his portfolio? Did you move? Why did the phone calls to you begin only four months ago? Did you renew your relationship only recently and is that when what happened, happened? Were you secretly in touch during the years after the painting class, the years when he disappeared from my life?

I move away from the stone wall and trail behind you at the edge of the group. Was it to you he went after his early discharge from the army? Was it you who began filling the place that had become vacant when he got rid of me? Did he tell you about the letters I sent to his grandmother's house, and that he never answered even one of them? Did he spread them out for you like a deck of cards? Did he tell you he was punishing me for not having answered my father's letters so many years ago?

(Six years later, like in a scene from a melodrama, the luxuriant vista of mountains sunk in fog in the background—so appropriate to such a scene—and my heart pounding loudly inside me, I saw Roni in the Haifa University parking lot, his back to me, taking books out of a motorcycle box. My feet didn't move, as if they had suddenly put down roots in the ground. He must have felt my eyes boring into his back, because he turned toward me, and the books, in a fitting continuation of the scene, dropped from his hands into the open box. He took a step toward me, and I uprooted my feet and met him halfway, where we held out our arms to each other, and the familiar flow of heat blended with something unknown, exciting.

"Since when do you have a motorcycle?" My habit of worrying about him was instantly triggered.

"Since two years ago."

"It's dangerous."

"It's a little dangerous, but very convenient."

Our searching eyes never stopped moving.

"You've gotten so tall," I said.

"You've gotten so pretty," he said.

I quickly diverted the conversation, hoping the blood surging inside me hadn't reddened my cheeks with a blush. "What are you studying?"

"History and art. And you?"

"Literature and theater."

We both burst out laughing.

"What's funny?" he asked.

It isn't funny at all, actually, I wanted to say, it is annoying. I remember that you owe me answers to a lot of letters. But there was something about the touch of our hands that was reminiscent of something good, forgotten, yet it filled me with longing, imbued me with strength.

"Funny and sad. Because you were once my Siamese twin."

A tall, dark guy with a mustache so thin it looked like it was painted on, was coming toward the motorcycle. He saw us and stopped, his eyes flashing.

"Let me introduce you, Salah," Roni called to him, dropping my hand quickly. The guy seemed to sense my agitation, the obvious excitement Roni and I were feeling. He hesitated for a moment, suspicious, and walked slowly toward us, his head tilted, threatening, as if for an attack.

"Meet my Siamese twin," Roni said, and I heard the embarrassment clearly.

All through the next class, I was unable to control the tumult raging inside me. I kept remembering how they walked away, tense and silent, as if searching for a hidden corner where they could start a boxing match. Surprised by my confusion and the feeling of my heart rising in my body, puzzled by the blushing, afraid of what might happen to Roni in the boxing match that awaited him, tossed between fragmented memories and fragmented thoughts, I tried to bypass the unavoidable fact that had struck me at the end of the class like an axe: that Arab guy and Roni were a couple. Did his homosexuality explain the gentleness, the naiveté, and the submissiveness that had been part of Roni ever since he was a child? Had everyone sensed it, while I, his Siamese twin, privy to his childhood secrets, had needed so many years and an accidental encounter with his lover to understand? Was it true, as he once explained to me in a museum, that only from a distance can we see all the details of a painting correctly, and I had not been standing the proper distance from Roni?

Toward the end of class—as if I were an old woman looking back, puzzling out her life—memories floated up from some forgotten corner of my mind that explained the nature of my relationship with Roni: from the second grade, we were drawn to each other by the power of a vacuum seeking to be filled, I brash and unpredictable, he naive and cautious. In the world without boundaries I grew up in, he marked my boundaries; in the suffocating world he grew up in, I was his escape hatch to forbidden things.

I didn't stay for my next class. I took a taxi back to my rented apartment, dragged my bag up the stairs, out of breath and shivering as if I'd gotten very sick, and curled up under the covers without undressing. For the next few days, I didn't have the strength to leave my apartment or change my clothes. Suppressed memories rose, etched clearly, proving again and again how much love Roni was able to stir in me, confirming the fact that I'd never find anyone I could devote myself to so easily, that he'd left a frightening emptiness when he moved to Tel Aviv and did not answer my letters, that I was in deep mourning and I hadn't dared to acknowledge it. I stayed in my apartment for three days, lying in the dark, not knowing whether it was day or night. I also missed one of my exams.

Roni must have looked for me so persistently during those days that the faculty office took pity on him and called me to say I had a message from someone who wouldn't stop pestering them, begging them to give him my phone number. But students' phone numbers were not given out without their permission. And by the way, all the bulletin boards on campus were full of his messages for me.

Roni came to my room a week after that accidental meeting in the university parking lot. I waited for him, slouching in my chair, hoping to hide my convulsive breathing and clenched stomach. I left the door unlocked and the newspaper strewn over the desk to mislead him, to make him think I hadn't spent the morning cleaning the rooms and the bathroom and putting my nicest linens on the bed. We met with a hug that had something of the flavor of our old hugs and something else that was new. And in the end, we found ourselves sitting on either side of the tiny table, holding our cups of tea in that familiar way, exploring the changes we found in each other.

"You're pale," he said.

"I haven't felt well for a couple of days."

"Really?"

"Yes."

"Do you have a boyfriend?"

"Nothing serious."

"Did you have anything serious?"

"There were all kinds."

"Serious ones?"

"For maybe an hour or two."

"Not longer?"

"Maybe a year or two."

"Do you still lie?"

"When I have to."

"Do you have to a lot?"

"Less than I used to."

We smiled. Every word collapsed under memories. From the corner of my eye, I saw his hand move, and I pulled mine away.

"They told me you were looking for me like a madman. So what's up?" The directness was one of the things that hadn't changed, I saw him notice that.

"Nothing's up. I came to visit, to see how you are . . ."

"I'm okay now. But you aren't."

"What makes you think that?"

"Come on, say it already."

"Say what?"

"That you're gay. That that guy is your lover and he's insanely jealous."

A loose leg of the chair made it sway for a minute until I straightened it with my foot.

"How did you know?"

"I know you from the inside of your bones. I gave you my father's curses. Who would know if not me? Do you love him?"

"I don't use that word with him."

"Would you give him your father's curses?"

"No."

"I knew you wouldn't."

"What else do you know?"

"Whatever I have to."

"Do you know this?" He reached out and slowly began unbuttoning my blouse.)

"Look at the roof." You raise your chin and the people, like a flock of storks, stretch their necks in the same direction. "Look at how beautiful that pergola with the latticework concrete roof is. That is one of the characteristic elements of the International Style.

Something excites you, and I wonder if the others sense it. Did you take Roni up to one of the roofs with the beautiful, latticework concrete pergolas, and is that where what happened, happened?

I look at you as you listen politely to the questions asked by one of the women with a camera, the one you owe because she gave you a red, fruit-flavored candy. I can't hear her question, but your answer rings out: "You're right. I love this city very very much."

(And later I would ask Roni, but mostly wonder to myself: Why did we make love then, on the same evening he told me about his

complicated relationship with that Arab guy? From the age of fourteen, the age when I began fooling around with boys in secluded
places, why did Roni and I begin keeping our distance, and although
we still saw each other every day, why had each of us marked off an
area for ourselves that was off-limits, careful not to touch, as if close-
ness between us was incest? After all, we were together hundreds of
times, sometimes for whole nights. Why was it that in that rented,
ground floor apartment in Hadar Hacarmel, where we could be seen
by passersby through the window that didn't close properly, that I let
him undress me completely? I began undressing him too, taking off
his shirt and pants. And the minute before I pulled down his shorts,
I looked at the swelling under them. "Is that still from your allergy
to bees?" I asked, and we both roared with laughter on the mattress
under the window. Everything that came afterward was simple and
inevitable, a wonderful last-minute remedy, at the end of which you
breathed into my ear, "Let's get married."

Intoxicated by my victory over Salah and his like, flooded with
new, unexpected happiness, filled with a sense of perfect whole-
ness, diving into the smell I could never get enough of, the smell
of home, wrapped in arms surprisingly large, as safe in them as a
little girl in her father's arms, I said, "Let's.")

"This is where our tour comes to an end and we have to go our
separate ways," you say, as if fate has commanded you to leave us.
The frozen, arrogant man we met at Rabin's memorial has been
transformed right before our eyes.

"It is important to remember that Tel Aviv is the only city in
the world that has such a large concentration of buildings in the
International Style," you remember to add, like a devoted parent
sending his children out into the world fortified by a piece of valu-
able information.

I am fascinated by you now. I have never seen a man so in love
with a city, with buildings. I am enthralled by the way you let
your love affect you, as I follow the last, emotional glance you give
the row of windows dirty with the soot and dust of Tel Aviv.

Does the degree of someone's love for a city say anything about
his ability to love people? The woman with the candy holds the

box out to you like a witch tempting Snow White with a poisoned apple, and with a smile, you thank her and decline. Your
childlike smile is warm and captivating, and I find myself suddenly proud of you: this is the man who is in love with the man
that I too am in love with; here is the man that the man I am in
love with is in love with. A convoluted tie binds us, but you have
no idea who I am, the woman with the clipped hair, in a raincoat
with light-reflecting strips, who is swallowed up in the group of
people standing near the house with the row of windows in the
stairwell whose beauty so impresses you. I loved Roni a long time
before you did. Sometimes, we wake up holding hands. And you?
Do you sometimes sleep together? Talk about your love? Make
each other promises? Do you watch him sleep, as I do? Kiss his
sweat as I do? You are my unwanted partner, I remind myself, the
one I fooled myself into thinking I had vanquished. I force my
affection for you to evaporate, wanting to be infused only with
resentment toward you, toward Roni, toward Tel Aviv. I touch
the bottom of my stomach as if trying to stop the evil infusion
there, and watch you part from the soldiers with a handshake.
What do the three of us do now? What do we do with this baby
that Roni does not know exists?

*   *   *

"Did you cross the streets like a good girl today? Only at the green
light?" There is nothing in Roni's voice to provoke me, but my
nerves are frayed, and I'm looking for a fight.

"Why do you ask? Did you pay my fine?" I recognize latent
volatility in my voice, calling for a battle, and I wonder if Roni
recognizes it too.

"Seventy shekels."

"So, you're angry?" I offer an opening for an attack.

"Why should I be angry? It wasn't your fault. You grew up
without traffic lights." His voice is pure, simple, and I feel like
a boxer punching air. The anger that accumulated in me dissi-
pates all at once, and I'm left with the sense of defeat I've been
feeling these last two weeks. Reeling from the day's upheavals, I

go and stand behind him and, unable to restrain myself for more than an instant, I hug him from behind, bury my face in his hair, close my eyes and inhale deeply, the way we used to once, in fields of wildflowers. His neck is redolent of childhood, and I wonder if, by the time I'm old, I'll be used to the way his sweet seriousness and his country innocence, undiminished by the city, make me tingle.

"What am I going to do with you, Roni, you're so sweet," I say, wondering if he hears the despair in my voice.

He turns to face me and I see the sadness crouching deep in the bottom of his eyes. He gets up and we embrace, face to face.

"You don't have to do anything, just love me madly."

"And you?"

"Me? I've loved you since the second grade."

I take his face in my hands. "You'll never leave me, will you, Roni?"

"Don't be silly." He covers my hands with his, pressing them to his cheeks and making his lips protrude.

"Because I am the person who knows you best in the world, and that's something you can't ignore." It's hard for me to hear the pleading in my voice, but only Roni is there, and Roni will forget whatever needs forgetting for my sake.

"I know."

"So you won't leave?"

"Of course not."

"For sure?"

"What a question. Why are you even asking?"

"I've been having thoughts like that lately."

"Why?"

"You know, Roni. You don't talk to me because you're embarrassed, but you know, we have to get it out in the open."

"So tell me—" I hear the beginning of concern in his voice.

"Guess where I was today." I pull my hands out from under his.

"At a job interview."

"No. In the end, I didn't go. Guess where I went."

"I have no idea." He seems to pale.

"I went to look at buildings." My eyes fix on his like two snipers aiming at their targets.

"Since when are you interested in buildings?" Averting his eyes, gets up and moves away to the opposite wall.

"Since exactly two weeks ago. I joined a tour today."

"On the street?"

"Yes."

"What street?"

"Rothschild Boulevard." I quote from the brochure, "Bauhaus in Tel Aviv: the International Style."

"A tour with a guide?" He sits down and I can feel the pain climbing from his knees to his throat.

"All the tours have guides." I sit down across from him.

"And the guide —" he asks, without a question mark. His eyes cloud over, the way eyes do the moment before you faint.

"An astronaut, crazy about Bauhaus."

"And how... how was it, how was he?" His wide pupils disappear and reappear as he blinks. His hands are still, like in the game of statues we play. Where in the world will I ever find someone I can see through the way I can see through Roni?

Scenes of our childhood pass before my eyes. Against the background of winter's muddy fields, summer's dust curtains, the whispering ruins of the Arab village, our secret place buried under wild yam bushes behind the village meeting house, the huge expanses of corn, like the American plains, the valley of sunflowers, the hill of purple anemones, Roni and I, seven and nine and sixteen years old, walk side by side, sometimes hand in hand, and talk, and talk.

I look at him as if I were looking in a mirror. His facial expressions are more familiar to me than my own. His eyes freeze and his pupils are so enlarged, it worries me. And I can read his loneliness in his eyes amidst the new confusion I cannot share, because of all the people in the world, I am the one he is doomed to hide it from.

"I must say," I see his eyes pursuing my lips as if his life depended on what comes out of my mouth, "that he's charming, absolutely charming." I'm confirming it for him. We are trapped in each other's eyes. We've known these eyes for too long not to understand. And we recognize the pain of sudden maturity, his maturity, which is bound to my maturity.

"And I fell in love." I shake his shoulder in that old gesture and deliberately linger for a moment, smiling as always in the face of his extreme seriousness, digging at him playfully. "I fell in love with the city once and for all. You were so smart in the second grade. You knew that the city was the right place, and we didn't even know about all that Bauhaus then."

The muscles of his eyelids relax, as if a great danger has passed. He knows that I know. And I know that he knows I know. So many abstract conversations we've had in the past suddenly became realized in Tel Aviv. Like a prophet, I see the future spread out clearly before me: men will come and go, appear and disappear, be discovered and forgotten—and I will remain. They are guests and I am family.

"And what does that mean, what does that mean..." he wheezes, almost completely out of breath.

Something urgent, compelling, passes through me when I hear his wheeze of anxiety. It is the knowledge that now, the way in which the guests and the family live out their lives will be settled.

"What does that mean?" he whispers, utterly pale, that circus clown's eye rapidly swallowed up and reappearing under his eyelid. And for a moment, we return to being the boy and girl we once were, two little country children walking hand in hand from the village paths to the streets of Tel Aviv.

"It means that's the way it'll be in this city. That's the truth and you can't run away from it." I quickly update the picture of the past, incorporating the picture of the future into it. I go to where he is sitting and pull him close until his head rests on my belly.

Munich

THE FINGERS OF THE MUSLIM girl's right hand move across the cash register keys as if she were playing the piano. The lines of her eyelashes part as she looks up, creating a dark border around her elongated amber eyes, and suddenly an expression I've never used comes into my mind: "almond eyes." ("I'm turning into a poet in Germany," I think, wryly.) The almost unblinking almond eyes look puzzled. Maybe she's trying to decipher the foreign sound of my German again, maybe she recognizes my Israeli accent, maybe she's surprised at the strange choices I've made from the menu tacked on the gleaming board, and maybe the owner has told her to look directly into customers' eyes as a matter of politeness. Whatever the reason, with her left hand, she tugs at the ends of the white headscarf to tighten it and says in perfect, accent-free German, "Shish kebab salad and a beer—fourteen marks please."

Our fingertips touch when she hands me my one mark change ("You've just gotten an electric shock," I caution myself), and I wonder whether her religion allows her to touch the fingers of strange men. Maybe she hasn't even felt anything and is totally innocent, completely absorbed in giving change, and maybe this is the only form her rebellion can take, a furtive mutiny against the tight scarf that chokes her throat and covers her shiny hair. Whatever the reason, she says now, as if seeing me for the first time, although I've been eating here almost every day for the past five weeks, "Please go over to the counter on the right." Maybe she always says that because the customers' faces remain anonymous to her, a row of heads like objects on a conveyor belt, gliding past her above the cash register on their way to the counter on her left that gives off a spicy blend of cooking smells, and maybe she says it each time at the instruction of the owner, who believes that this is the way to respect the privacy of the customers, most of whom are on their way to or from the nearby train station, some of them gray-haired men with young girls who are not their daughters on their arm.

I sit down at my regular table, squeezed in at the far end of the restaurant near the kitchen, my back to the wall ("Like the hero of a western." I chuckle to myself). The sound of voices speaking Arabic comes from the kitchen, reminding me of the voices in the Middle-Eastern restaurant in Jaffa that I like so much, and with them comes a familiar smell, the smell of home. I'm looking out at the square, which is still filled with those long-legged German woman who are always so radiant, no matter how late it is. Like an army of women on their way to conquer the men of the city, they're wearing skirts and dresses with high slits that flap open with every gust of wind to expose, as if accidentally, the supple young thighs hidden under clothes that look so easy to remove: the pull of a lace, the twist of a button, and they'd drop to reveal the goddesslike body under them. Above the heads of those heavenly creatures rises the hotel I'm staying in, owned by a former Israeli. Through the open window of my room, I can see the shirt I hung up to air, and I suddenly notice that from a distance, it's khaki ("Doing reserve duty in Munich . . ." The thought amuses me), and I can make out the remains of the swastika drawn on the hotel door by an unknown hand every few nights, then scrubbed off quickly and violently by the chambermaids in the morning.

I glance occasionally at my plate, look up at the TV suspended between two flower pots overflowing with plastic ferns, scribble a few random ideas on the piece of paper that's always lying on the table in front of me, look over at the photos of Jerusalem among the pictures hanging on the walls—the Temple Mount, the Dome of the Rock, the Via Dolorosa. I gaze out at the women walking through the square as if they were part of a permanent stage set, but the corner of my eye is always on the Muslim girl standing with her back to the world, sheathed in her clothes and her head-scarf like a corpse in its shroud, enigmatic, unreachable, the antithesis of the brazen, alluring women crossing the square.

Looking out of my hotel window on my first day in Munich, I saw the restaurant sign, Orient House, about a hundred paces from the hotel entrance, and the next day, I sent an item to the paper in Tel Aviv on "The Munich Orient House," with pictures attached, and ended it with these words: "Here is the situation in a nutshell: In a cheap Middle-Eastern restaurant called Orient House, whose employees speak Arabic, located in the heart of Munich across from a hotel owned by a former Israeli, where the remains of the latest swastika are clearly visible on the door, sits an Israeli jour-nalist who is here to cover the trial of a Nazi officer and sees on TV a German volunteer in a Jerusalem hospital which is treating Jews injured in a suicide bombing carried out by a Muslim. How easy it is to get caught up in historical symbolism here."

Those few sentences put down on paper created one kind of chaos in my thoughts and another in my emotions. Almost every sight I see connects to the past, the present, and the future in the most amazing, frightening, and thought-provoking contexts. And in the middle of all this, I quickly established a comfortable routine for myself: from my very first day here, I've been loyal to the restaurant. Almost every night between eight and nine—after my daily visit to the courthouse, where I'm covering the trial of an old Nazi officer; after hours of poring over old newspapers and journals in the university library; after I've sent my story off to the paper in Tel Aviv; after my daily phone call home—I go to the restaurant, order this or that combination of dishes from the large selection: a sandwich and a rice dish, couscous and kebabs. My choices don't amuse the Muslim girl. Very serious, moving like a mechanical doll, her beautiful fingers dancing over the cash reg-ister keys, she informs me of the price of my meal in perfect German, hands me my change, and directs me to the counter on

the right. I remain standing there for a second, keeping my hand
in the air until it stops tingling from the touch of her fingertips
or her nails on my palm.

I've been in Munich for five weeks now, forcing myself to shut
out the beauty of the city, walking along the magnificent boule-
vards under treetops spread like canopies over astonishingly
straight rows of pastel-colored flowers, trying to contain my
excitement, reminding myself that I'm here on a mission and not
to have a good time. Every morning at ten I enter the courthouse
on Nymphenburgestrasse, sit down in the last row near the window ("So that if the Gestapo bursts in, I can make an easy escape,"
I say to myself) directly behind the defendant, Ernst Weindorf,
and watch as he confers with his lawyers, a man and a woman sitting on either side of him like bodyguards, elegant in their suits
and blond hair. Even from the back of the courtroom, you can easily see that he has Parkinson's disease, and as I stare at that old,
wobbling head and the wrinkled back of his neck, I imagine it
sixty years younger, sturdy and solid, the skin tight and supple,
the neck of the man who terrorized my father for the twenty
months he was interned in Stutthoff—Stutthoff, the terrifying
name that haunted my childhood.

The edges of his robe flapping, the German judge bursts into
the courtroom as if he were an actor in a television courtroom
series. I rise and stand at attention out of respect for the German
judge, for the justice that will be done here on behalf of my father.
As soon as the proceedings begin, I start translating and writing
rapidly in Hebrew, sometimes catching stares directed at my hand
racing from right to left across the page. I jot down single German
words, mainly legal terms unfamiliar to me, in transliterated
Hebrew. Back at the hotel, I'll look them up in the dictionary or
ask the helpful reception clerk. Then I'll punch holes in the pages
and add them to the swelling file, devote an hour to writing a story
about that day's session or some other subject that caught my
interest and send it to the paper in Tel Aviv. For the first few days,
I made do with dry, factual reports on the trial under the title
"Germany vs. Ernst Weindorf."

"The defendant's name."

"Ernst Weindorf."

"Year of birth."

"Nineteen seventeen."

"Were you a member of the Nazi party?"

"Yes."

"Did you serve in the army of the Third Reich?"

"Yes."

"What was your rank?"

"Obersturmbahnfuehrer."

"When did you arrive at Stutthoff?"

"In September nineteen forty-three."

Slowly, almost imperceptibly, as the German voices echo in the courtroom, as Ernest Weindorf dredges up details from the dim pictures in his memory, which is as shaky as his muscles, I find myself carried back to the gates of Stutthof, nineteen hundred forty-three. My father is twenty-nine. He has seen his parents, his twelve-year-old sister, and his beloved uncle shot dead right before his eyes by a German soldier who was either in a frenzy of murderous rage or simply bored. He learns that his maternal grandmother, his paternal grandfather, his pregnant sister-in-law, two aunts, and three young nephews have been shot and tossed into a pit they had been forced to dig themselves. His wife is ill when they are separated, their two-year-old daughter in her arms. A few days earlier, a Polish acquaintance agrees to find a hiding place for the wife and child at his sister's house in the country. Maybe the Pole managed to rescue them before they were loaded onto the trucks. Meanwhile, his own fate has brought him to Stutthoff, where Ernst Weinhoff and his whip await him.

When the proceedings end and court adjourns for the day, I remain frozen in my seat, my head buzzing with orders screamed out in barking German, my clenched muscles preventing me from moving, my eyes fixed on the old man ravaged by Parkinson's being supported on either side as he leaves the courtroom. I need a few minutes of total silence to return gradually to myself, as if I were regaining consciousness, sitting in the empty courtroom,

Munich, August two thousand and one. I cover the distance to the
Ludwigstrasse University library in twenty minutes of brisk walking, stretching my muscles, shaking off the oppressive atmosphere
of the courtroom with each step, preparing myself to read reports
on Nazi soldiers who had been tried over the last few years,
research for a series of articles I'm planning. Meanwhile, as I walk,
I debate what to write about today: sights of Munich; the art
museum; a literary evening with a Holocaust survivor; an argument with a neo-Nazi; a conversation with Leah Roche, who orig-
inated the plan to establish a Holocaust memorial; a gay couple
getting married in a church.

In the evening, fifteen minutes before Israeli television's news
roundup, I call home, hear from Galia that she misses me, that she
made this fantastic moussaka from a recipe the two fat ladies gave
on channel 8, she'll freeze it for me, the heat is awful, people are
dropping from exhaustion, fainting in the streets, an old man collapsed in front of the grocery at lunchtime and she took him to the
emergency room, the pipes in the bathroom off our bedroom drip
all night like Chinese torture and it's ruining her sleep, Yael
spends all day jabbering with her friends—they'd only just
stopped mourning the end of a soap opera and were already hooked
on a new one, getting together at one of their houses every day at
six to watch the episode, then arguing loudly about who's a bad
guy and who's a good guy and who's faking and who's cheating on
whom and who got pregnant by whom—it makes your hair stand
on end to see what preoccupies fourteen-year-old girls these days,
but it's better to have them at home than wandering around malls
where crazy suicide bombers blow themselves up. They were at our
place yesterday and all their screaming gave her a headache. The
Braun blender broke, could I go into a store and buy a new one?
Yuval decided after all to take one of those survival classes to get
into shape for basic training, today they rappelled down a seven-
story building and he's ecstatic about it. Some Arab managed to
drive to army headquarters in Tel Aviv so he could kill some soldiers, got out of his car in the middle of the intersection and
started firing an M-16 in every direction, it's a miracle no one got

hurt. A policeman and a soldier chased after him and killed him. And what about me? How was that Nazi today? Is that all I have to say about Munich, that the rows of flowers are so straight? How's the weather? Have I eaten yet? Did I buy Yael that poster she asked for? Do I miss them?

Of course, I can't tell her the truth: as always when I travel, I don't miss her or the children; all I do is worry about them and ask them to keep away from crowded places. The minute I fasten my seat belt in the plane, it's as if, through an ultra-modern remote control, I weaken the intensity of my connection to them and redeploy my energy like a military man preparing for what lies ahead. And Germany, more than any other place in the world, transports me to a new wavelength of reality where I have no commitments to others. Here, the only thing I'm committed to is my survival.

I dream about women most nights, but never about Galia. The women in my dreams are blond Germans, perfect duplicates of the long-legged women in the square. There is no romance in my dreams, no caressing, no longing, no foreplay, and no wasted time. The women are always in bed, ready, lying on their backs or crouching on all fours, naked or wearing lingerie as filmy as a spider's web, and I come to them and penetrate them and fuck them, in total control because I'm utterly focused on satisfying my lust, fucking them hard. The feeling's not entirely new to me, only the aggressive way I pound them, in and out, is new—savage and tremendous, and very often from behind or in one of the Kama Sutra positions Galia refuses to try. And as I fuck them, I'm aware that this is not an act of love, but an act of revenge. I enter them violently, empty out the whirlpool of emotions churning inside me, emotions that range from pure rage to adoration, and they scream those words familiar to me from German porn movies. In the morning, I imagine there are stains on my underwear or on the sheet, and I'm mortified at what the chambermaids will think, as if I were a teenager again and embarrassed because of my mother. Once, I recognized Ernst Weindorf's female lawyer under me and I woke up horrified. And the Muslim girl appeared in my dreams a few times, slipping into my room sheathed in her long clothes and her white headscarf, peeking at me from the side like a curious child, not the least bit repelled, and I tried to show off my skills, known to quite a few women, to justify the reputation I hoped I'd acquired among my colleagues, offering in evidence the moans of pleasure of the women under me or in front of me, and as I pounded them, I wondered if the girl had hair that fell to her waist and how her skin would taste ("Milk and honey," I promise myself in the dream).

Within a week, my life in Munich had fallen into a routine, taking place in four separate bubbles I enter and slip out of easily: Galia and the children are in one bubble that comes to life for the five minutes I spend surfing the Internet news from Israel after I've sent my story to the paper, and mainly fifteen minutes before the evening news on Israeli TV. Another part of my life takes place in the courtroom, where I'm hurled into a different time and a different place, lingering there long after the sessions end. In a separate compartment are my dreams about women, which are becoming wilder and wilder. The women I fuck are beginning to look alike, a uniform receptacle for my lust, which doesn't always subside when the dreams are over, and for the rest of the day, especially when my eyes are caressing the women passing through the square, I find myself toying with the lovely idea of turning one of the dreams into reality and inviting a woman up to my room, maybe even paying her, possibly with the help of the genial clerk, the way it's done in many hotels in Israel. And in a separate compartment is the restaurant, the anchor of my late evening hours, with the pleasant routine of my regular table; the dishes on the menu, all of which I've tried and enjoyed; the guttural, Arabic-speaking voices that are like background music for my evenings. At that hour, I'm relaxed after my phone call home and manage to ignore the familiar sights on TV of buildings being demolished and soldiers and scruffy children dashing along dirt roads or through narrow alleyways. In the heart of this kingdom stands the Muslim girl, whose hazel eyes wander from the cash register to the customers' faces or flick rapidly over the restaurant, but never turn to the world outside, the girl whose lips part only to say the price of the meal and never stretch in a smile. When our glances meet by chance, I wonder how she would react if I told her that she sometimes shows up in my erotic dreams, how she would react if I asked her to take off her headscarf and show me whether her hair actually does reach her waist.

About a month after the trial started, after everyone had gotten up to leave at the end of a session, I stayed in my seat as usual. A hand landed on my shoulder and someone asked me in English, "Are you all right?"

I leaped to my feet.

"I'm sorry, I didn't mean to startle you." A red-haired, bearded man held out his hand. "I'm Solomon Miller, correspondent for the New York *Times*. I gather you're from Israel," he said, looking at my papers, which were covered with Hebrew writing.

I shook his hand warily.

"It looked to me like you weren't feeling well."

"No, thank you. I'm fine."

"Sure?"

"Absolutely."

"So how about we go and sit in the cafeteria for a while?"

"Why?"

"Because I assume you're an Israeli newspaperman or researcher. I thought it might be interesting to share impressions."

Solomon Miller turned out to be a friendly, talkative guy. Toward the end of our conversation, he mentioned casually that he was Jewish. He was interested in my father's story, asked how I was reporting the trial, wanted to know what interested the Israeli public, what kind of responses I was getting, and said he was ready to give me the names of two female witnesses for the prosecution, one from Brooklyn and the other from Hamburg, and to set up a meeting for me with neo-Nazis, since I would most likely be reporting on the memorial rally they planned to hold on the seventeenth of the month. He himself had become friends with a twelve-year-old, the youngest in the neo-Nazi group, whose Jewish mother had abandoned him when he was a baby. The con-

versation flowed. Our journalist's instincts told us that there was
no danger in sharing information and being open with one
another. We parted with pats on the back and the promise to have
a meal together from time to time. I almost invited him to eat
with me at the Orient House, but something held me back, pre-
serving the boundaries of my privacy.

One night, I dreamed I was making love to the Muslim girl.
Never, neither in my life nor in my dreams had the act ever been
so tender, as if we were doing it for the first time and the last.
We're standing facing each other. I'm naked and she's completely
dressed. I reach out to her and our fingertips meet, as they do when
she gives me my change, sending currents through my already
taut, expectant body. First, I remove the white headscarf, exposing
the shining hair under it, a black waterfall that cascades to her
hips, covering her back and her breasts, giving off the faint but
rich fragrance of jasmine. We undress her together, I with single-
minded expertise, she shyly but passionately, pulling off the
sweater with its complicated fastenings from under that heavy
mass of hair, then the blouse with all its buttons, the long skirt
tied around her waist with an elastic belt, the cotton slip, the
brassiere made of some shiny fabric, the matching panties. Her
skin, hidden from sun in winter and summer, is snow-white and
silky, and she abandons herself to my touch instantly, sliding her
knee over my loins, pulling me to the bed. My chest crushes her
breasts and their pale pink nipples; hands roam over bodies as if
they were partners in some secret dance. The almond eyes close
under my tongue and the tight lips part, then her entire body
opens to me, and it's steeped in honey, and I plunge, plunge into
her depths, into the depths of the dream, the enormous sweetness,
enveloped by virginal flesh, abandoning myself to the gentle
movements that go on for half the night until I come and I'm
drained; I separate from her sadly, awaken in the morning lying in
semen stains.

In the restaurant the next day, I studied her over my plate as if
seeking traces of the night before, seeing her mask-like face
between flashes of scenes from my dream, searching her eyes,

remembering how they closed, looking at the headscarf that smothered her hair so cruelly, remembering the hair spread luxuriantly over the large pillow, gazing at her pianist's fingers, the fingers that cupped my balls. She shot me a quick glance of discomfort over the cash register and I turned to look at the square, where I saw a new row of pansies in astonishing shades of purple that must have been planted that day, straight as a row of soldiers standing at attention.

After today's court session, I have dinner with Solomon Miller. He asks about the terrible suicide bombing of a Jerusalem café, tells me that when he was a teenager, he'd spent a summer studying Hebrew in Jerusalem and still craves the hummus he used to eat in a little restaurant near the Mahaneh Yehuda market. Almost at the end of our conversation, he remarks casually, in response to something I've said, that he hopes it won't come as a surprise to me if he tells me that the entire trial is one big show.

"What do you mean, a show?"

"A show. Like in the theater. People saying their lines, knowing exactly how it'll end."

"How?"

"A private room in the Bernau jail. It's already been settled."

"By whom?"

"The prosecution and the defense."

I suddenly understand why I'd been feeling so uneasy at the trial, understand why there have been days I preferred not to report on it. I remember suppressing questions I had about proceedings, telling myself that I don't know enough about German legal procedures to develop suspicions.

"So why are they holding this trial?" I ask him anyway.

"To show that justice is being done. The Germans never wanted this trial, but they had no choice."

"What do you mean, they had no choice?"

"Well, they didn't actually catch him, and they definitely never looked for him. He just showed up one day at the German Embassy in Argentina and turned himself in. They ignored him for a while—they had no interest in him or this trial—but he

went to the media in Argentina and the Germans were forced to
bring him here and hold the trial."

"Why did he do it?"

"Because it was his only chance to get decent medical treatment. No hospital in Argentina could give him the treatment he'd
get here. His money was gone and this trial was a way of making
sure he's taken care of for as long as he lives. What do you think
they'll do with an eighty-four-year-old man who has Parkinson's?
Put him in solitary confinement? They'll give him a nice room,
three meals a day, and free medical treatment. Haven't you noticed
that the prosecutor isn't exactly exerting himself?"

"No."

He enjoys my naiveté. "That's because you're too involved on
account of your father's story. Sometimes that helps and sometimes
it gets in the way."

The journalist in me is suddenly aroused, alarmed: "And you've
written that this is a charade? Has it been published?"

"Are you crazy? Would I get the paper involved in a libel suit?
But I try to drop very subtle hints. So they won't think they're
dealing with idiots."

As soon as I recover from the insult to me and to my father, the
professional in me takes over, angry and slightly shamefaced, but
mainly worried. What had seemed to be an interesting subject
might turn into a scandal if I couldn't find a clever way of extri-
cating myself. Because I was the one who pressured the editor into
sending me here for two months. He tried to talk me out of it,
promised me I could be in touch with the correspondents in
Munich, but I insisted. In the end, he played his trump card and
said he suspected that I was looking for a quiet place to write the
novel I'd told him about years ago. I denied it and mustered all my
blackmailing skills, reminded him of how I'd refused a rival newspaper's tempting offer, how I'd endangered my life for the paper by
going into a house where an escaped convict serving a life sentence
was holding two girls hostage. I pointed out that this would probably be the last trial of a Nazi to be held in Germany, and no Israeli
newspaper could afford not to have on-the-spot coverage. I also

volunteered to cover another trial being held in Germany: the neo-Nazis' request to hold a memorial service for Rudolph Hess. And finally, without consulting Galia, I suggested that he take one of the two months off my vacation time. Now I was thinking about what a fool I'd made of myself professionally, how day after day for more than a month, I'd been sitting in the courtroom, idiot that I am, religiously writing down every word of a rigged trial. Solomon Miller was right: my eagerness to be there, for my father's sake, had dulled my common sense.

I toss and turn in bed that whole night trying to come up with a way to insert comments into my stories over the next three days that will make it seem as if I'd suspected these latest developments from the very beginning—which was why I'd insisted on coming—and now my suspicions are being confirmed. A journalist from Israel can permit himself to write what the New York *Times* correspondent can't. My editor won't buy this new story of mine, but no matter how pissed off he is at me, he can't expose the fiasco because he's had a part in it. It occurs to me that if I can get the scoop on some newsworthy event that happens here, in Munich, it would somehow make up for this ludicrous trip. As the hours pass, I become more and more angry and frustrated about Ernst Weindorf because the trap he'd laid for Germany has snared me as well, and exasperated by my impotence, I decide that if the whole business is really a show, I'll refuse to be the audience for it. My editor will definitely not insist that I stay, and the next time I talk to Galia, I'll tell her that the Germans have decided to drag out the trial endlessly and since I won't be able to stay for the verdict anyway, I've decided to come home earlier. She'll be glad. The night before she told me that not only is there a problem with the drainpipe, but also the lights in the front yard aren't working and sometimes the street is dark, too. and she worries when Yael comes home late, and that survival class is starting to get on her nerves. One of Yuval's friends was hurt and, if I came home, I could find out what's going on there, maybe even write an exposé on the whole business because she now thinks it's totally irresponsible, but Yuval is hooked and there's no way he'll give it up.

Carefully and cleverly, I begin working on my scheme to plant the new information about the trial. It will take some ingenuity if I don't want my fellow reporters to think I'm a complete idiot. After midnight, before I forget them, I get up and go to the desk to write down a few ideas that have come to me. When I raise my head from the writing and look out at the dark square, I see—as if God has decided to be generous with me in Munich—a motorcycle with two silhouetted riders race out of the main street and stop in front of my restaurant. The silhouette behind the driver gets off the motorcycle, and when it moves into the light of the restaurant's neon sign, I see that it's a man with a red backpack. He spray-paints the words ARABER RAUS in large letters on the window to the right of the entrance, then flings the backpack at the window to the left of the entrance. At the sound of shattering glass, a split second before the alarm sounds, he runs to his waiting pal and turns back into a silhouette on the motorcycle as it speeds away.

Before writing a single line in my mind, I call the paper in Tel Aviv. During the few seconds wait for the phone to be answered, the headline comes to me: "Kristallnacht at the Orient House" ("Brilliant, just brilliant," I gloat.)

"Who's speaking?... Hello, Shlomit, who's the night editor? Put him on right now... Hello, Micha, listen, this is Arnon from Munich. Is the front page closed?... Then run it as a short item, you decide where, maybe on the front page... It happened here, in a restaurant across from my hotel, not even Reuters knows, and the others definitely won't have enough time to get it in. Listen, I don't have it down on paper, I'm writing it out loud: After midnight today, a man spray painted ARABER RAUS on one of the front windows of the Orient House restaurant, near the central train station in Munich, Germany, and smashed another window... Yes, that's the alarm you're hearing in the background... The act appears to be motivated by racism, since the restaurant is run by Arabs, apparently Muslims. Recently, there have been numerous incidents of neo-Nazi graffiti against foreign residents. Large numbers of neo-Nazis have been gathering in

Munich after the party petitioned the court for permission to hold
a rally in memory of the Nazi leader, Rudolph Hess, Hitler's
deputy. Located opposite the restaurant is a hotel owned by a former Israeli where many Israelis stay. The hotel desk clerk reports
that there have been telephone threats and graffiti—swastikas are
painted on the hotel entrance every few days. What do you think?
I think it's enough, too... What do you think of 'Kristallnacht at
the Orient House' for the headline?... Okay... You're welcome... Listen, about a month ago, I wrote a short piece on that
restaurant and sent pictures with it. You should look for them in
the archives. I don't think any other paper has pictures... I'll
probably be coming back before the end of the month. See you
then, Micha."

At the university library, in the morning, later than usual and
still agitated from the night before, I finish collecting material on
trials of Nazis held decades after the war ended. The names make
me shiver, as if my father's hand were resting on mine as I write
them down: Friedrich Engle, residing in Hamburg; Michael
Seifert, known as Misha, residing in Canada since 1951; Julius
Viel, aged 82, now residing in Canada; Heinrich Schubert, now
residing in Damstadt. I'm planning to devote a special chapter to
Erich Priebke, who was extradited from Argentina to Italy and
tried for the murder of 335 people, most of them Jews. On March
7, 1998, he was sentenced to life in prison and then released
immediately because of his failing health. My father's hand trem-
bles on my fingers when I write, "released immediately."

I can still feel vestiges of that tremor as I walk to the Metro station, hurrying to the hotel so I can call the paper and Galia, and
then go to my restaurant, whose windows were fixed that morning.
As I'm trying to decide whether to have kebab with potatoes or a
rice dish that evening, I pass a newspaper stand, and before I know
what my eyes are seeing, I stop short like a horse rearing up on its
hind legs. On the front page of a special edition is a large picture of
a girl who looks amazingly like the Muslim girl from the restaurant, photographed as if a camera had infiltrated my mind on the
night I dreamed we'd made love: lying against a light background,

her almond eyes are closed, her black hair spreads around her face, her dark lips part. Above her, a large headline, thickly underlined in a blood-red smear, screams, "They've Killed Again."

Without looking at him, I pour a handful of coins into the puzzled vendor's palm, and he puts a newspaper into the hand I hold out to him. With my arm still outstretched, I cross two streets blindly and go into the railroad station, where I collapse, weak-kneed, onto a seat. As if I were suddenly far-sighted, it takes me a long time to decipher the letters, and when my vision finally clears, my eyes race over the lines, skipping difficult words, rapidly absorbing the details: At noon today, opening time, a young man in a suit entered the Orient House restaurant—the restaurant whose windows were smashed by unknown vandals last night—took a bunch of neo-Nazi leaflets out of his bag and put them on the counter, pulled out a gun and started firing in all directions. Bullets hit Salima Mansour, who was standing at the cash register, and her cousin, Mohammed Abu-Snein, one of the four employees in the kitchen at the time, and smashed all the front windows, including the new one installed this morning. Then he started running toward a motorcycle waiting for him outside the restaurant, but one of the workers and a passerby gave chase, caught him, and held him until the police came. A doctor, who arrived at the scene, resuscitated Mohammed Abu-Snein, now hospitalized in serious condition, and pronounced Salima Mansour dead.

Slumped in my seat, limp as a rag doll, drained of feeling, I stare at the picture of the dead Salima Mansour, remembering her charming vitality. Then I turn to page seven, as directed by the caption under the picture. On page seven, under photographs of the smashed windows and Mohammed Abu-Snein being rushed to Groshadem Hospital, is a story about the family who owns the restaurant, who opened it eleven years earlier. The father, Salah Mansour, was born in Jerusalem in 1946. His mother's family was also from Jerusalem. In 1948, when war broke out immediately after Israel was declared a state, the family fled to Gaza, where they found refuge with relatives. Most of the family is still living in the Jebalya refugee camp in the Gaza Strip. After Israel occupied the

Strip in 1967, Salah worked for three years, and saved enough money to go to Germany to study. He trained to be a food technician and worked for ten years in a noodle factory in Hamburg. In 1972, he married the daughter of Turkish immigrants, and they had five children, three boys and two girls. In 1990, the family moved to Munich, and the father and his brother, who arrived from Jebalya, opened the restaurant. The murdered daughter, nineteen-year-old Salima, worked as a cashier in the restaurant.

Despite my shock at the murder of the Muslim girl who had unknowingly become part of my life, despite the pain of losing what had not yet come into being, I'm enormously relieved: my professional reputation has been saved. That restaurant had been in my sights from my very first day in Munich. I grope clumsily for my cell phone, call the paper, arrange with the editor to send him copy on the restaurant and the incident in the next two hours, remind him of the pictures I'd sent, tell him I'll be coming back as soon as possible.

At seven forty-five, I call home. Galia's voice is excited. She already knows I'm coming home sooner than planned, the paper called her. She tells me the situation there is just terrible—we're shooting missiles into Gaza; two Palestinian brothers, kindergarten age, and their young aunt were killed; shots were fired at a car on the road to Hebron; and a Jewish woman in her ninth month was killed in front of her two daughters. She doesn't know how all this killing of women and children is going to end, Yael and her friends went to a movie in the Dizengoff Center mall and for four hours, she hasn't been able to think about anything else, but you can't ground a girl forever—she'll tell me about Yuval when I get back, there's no news, good or bad; in the end she had to call a plumber... am I still enjoying the peace and quiet of the library? Did I buy a new Braun blender? No? What happened, did I forget? Well maybe I'll find one in the duty-free store. When exactly am I coming in? Should she meet me at the airport?

My suitcase is on the hotel steps and I'm waiting, along with two Australian tourists, for our ride to the airport. The spectacled receptionist informs us apologetically that the minibus driver just called to say he'll be twenty-minutes late because of unexpected traffic. I report this to the Australians and they respond by inflating their cheeks to show their dissatisfaction.

A thin drizzle begins to fall, spotting the sidewalks, causing umbrellas to open. From where I'm standing, I see my restaurant, which is just opening. Newspaper pages are pasted on one window, and on the other, two large, square death notices. One of the workers is using a box-cutter to scrape away the excess putty around the large glass of the new windows. Another one is taking down, one by one, the chairs overturned on the tables. I'm drawn to the place and ask the Australians to keep an eye on my bag, which I decorated with a huge, yellow Star of David for easy identification, and for the irony of it.

From close up, I see that one of the death notices is in Arabic and the other in German. The name Salima Mansour, which I can read in Arabic, looks as familiar to me as the name of a relative. The young Arab man stops his work when I stand facing him and puts his hands together to signal "Closed." I raise my fingers in a pleading gesture and as I start moving toward the door, he seems to recognize me. Polite and solemn, he walks to the door, the box-cutter in his hand.

"I wanted to say how horrified I was about what happened to your restaurant and to the girl—" I point to the cash register and then to the death notice as if marking the route of her short life, and my throat tightens ("You're mourning her," I suddenly realize in amazement).

"Thank you," he says. Not a single muscle in his face moves.

"I ate here every day for almost six weeks."

"We're not opening today."

"I know, I know." I won't let myself feel insulted by the thought that he suspects my condolences are only a bribe to get me into the restaurant before it actually opens. "I'm leaving Munich in a few minutes. I just wanted to say goodbye because . . . I feel as if I knew her a little . . ." The memory of that night is absolutely vivid, the smells, the touch, the milk-and-honey taste of her body. He looks at me intently, as if he too were seeing the images of that memory.

"Bye bye," he says without warmth.

"She worked here. I suppose you knew her well."

"She is . . . was my cousin."

"Your cousin . . . ," I quickly make the connection between him and the details I read in the paper: his father is her father's brother, the one who came here from Jebalya, and the story of his childhood and teenage years is the same as her father's: Jerusalem, relatives in Gaza, the refugee camp ("*Shalom haver*," I chuckle to myself).

"I'm Israeli," I say, as if surrendering to the enemy.

He gives me a burning look and I hope that from the unapologetic way I said "Israeli," he can tell that I've participated in dozens of demonstrations against the occupation, I've even helped organize some of them, and that I've spent two months in an army prison for refusing to do reserve duty in the territories. A question takes shape in my mind, directed wordlessly at him: Of all the places in the world, why Munich? Why haven't you learned from our history? This is a terrible place. Here, the victims of the past, the future, and the present spin in an insane merry-go-round of death.

"From my hotel room, I saw them break your window the night before last. I called my paper right away and told them about the neo-Nazi graffiti too. I'm a journalist."

A car horn beeps from the direction of the hotel and I see that the minibus has arrived. One of the Australians hefts my travel bag with one hand, as if showing off, and with the other, waves at me to come. The yellow Star of David glitters in the distance like a golden stain, trapping the sunlight like the piece of mirror we used to blind passersby with when we were children.

"My ride is here," I say without moving. "I'm very sorry about your cousin . . . she was very . . . very—"

"Have a good trip," he says, his eyes fixed on my bag.

The Australian, whose arm is tired, is now holding my bag over his head with two hands, trying to catch my attention. The yellow Star of David floats high in the air.

". . . Take care of yourselves here."

"I think you have to go, sir," he says, and it seems to me that his voice isn't as cold as it was. We've touched on certain subjects—they can't be ignored, they need clarification—but I'm being sent away politely and those subjects are apparently fated to remain in need of clarification.

"Bye bye, sir." I think I hear his sorrow at our parting in his voice: the spinning cars of an amusement park ride we're trapped in haven't come close enough to touch yet, and they go zooming past one another, racing to their final destination, to more and more dizzy spins.

"Shalom," I reply in Hebrew and wave my hand, then add in his language, "Salaam" and walk toward my bag that is waiting for me on the curb.

Salaam German women, gorgeous goddesses of lechery, salaam public library with all your peace and quiet, salaam white swastika soon to be scrubbed off the hotel door, salaam hospitable restaurant with all your new windows, salaam Gaza and Jerusalem among the artificial ferns, salaam ruler-straight rows of flowers, salaam August rains, salaam German courtroom, salaam Ernst Weindorff, salaam Parkinson's disease, salaam sweet Salima Mansour, salaam Munich.

Jerusalem

On THE WAY TO JERUSALEM, passing the Latrun junction, Idit's eye caught the handsome monastery on the left side of the hill standing high against the background of the darkening, late afternoon sky, and a cry of wonder escaped her lips. As if releasing a bird from its cage, she unclasped her safety belt, which had grooved a diagonal line across her chest, and unpinned the snail-shell barrette that held her hair. Realizing she had come home and could now liberate her body, imprisoned for nine years and waiting patiently for this lovemaking, Idit inhaled deeply and abandoned herself to the male voice coming from the tiny cell phone, filling the space of the rented Autobianchi.

In a low, seductive voice, stirring quiescent memories, the man described in great detail the triangular hollow made by her collar bone, neck, and the line of her shoulders, and she— so breathless that her ribs hurt and alive to the pleasant, silent heat rising in her loins and the quickening of her heartbeat—could almost feel his breath collecting at the place he was describing and his hot, exciting mouth wandering from her neck to her shoulder, descending to the depths of that triangle, stopping at the narrow, satin strap of her bra.

The pounding inside her was so loud that his voice could barely break through it. She thought she heard his whisper flow into her inner ear: "From here, I can start talking to your heart without you interfering."

Her heart, a fifth column inside her body, turned over, threatening once again to betray the excitement she'd been trying to conceal from the moment she had called him at the airport in Israel as she'd promised him from the airport in Hiroshima, and he told her about the room he'd fixed up for her, the Japanese chimes he'd hung on the door in her honor, and the vanilla incense he'd light soon. And then he began the slow description of what he'd been planning to do for years, his hands reaching for her head, enveloping her hair, caressing her forehead, feeling their way to her temples, passing over her eyelids, fluttering over her cheek bones, moving down the length of her nose, outlining the perfect heart shape of her upper lip, sliding down to her chin, and when the car passed Latrun, his mouth took over from his hands and began its journey from her nape to that triangle from which the beating of her heart rose to his ear, now pressed up against the artery in her neck.

"And what does my heart tell you?" She continued to disguise her excitement with teasing, giving him her body, keeping her self for herself.

*   *   *

Months had passed, from the day at the beginning of the month of Nissan, when they told Ada that this year the old women had hearkened to her entreaties and, despite the dangerous roads, would give her leave to ascend to the Temple with her husband's family. Months had passed since a fierce longing, flowing from new springs, had seeped into her body, an invisible burbling that thickened the blood and carried messages in an arcane language from the top of her head to the tips of her toes, that entered her eyes and stimulated them with forbidden sights, that drained into the underground water of dream visions, pooling, pooling in the night. At night, she sometimes stole away from the tent where the menstruating women slept and, never frightened for a moment, flew to the hilltop, wild dogs at her heels, to look at the bewitching hills of Jerusalem in the distance. In the moonlight, they appeared to be naked men and women, bodies bent over each other, and she looked at them with trembling soul and yearning flesh, filling up, filling up, gathering strength. Soon she would come to the gates of the city, soon she would make a sacrificial offering and beseech God to fill her womb with a child. The nights were free for the passion that suffused her body and her fantasies, not so the days. The days were always filled with movement. On the days they journeyed, she tended the small herd of six goats and two kids. When they encamped, she set out the implements for their meal: pots of oil and plates made of clay and brass, and separately, carefully, she removed the lamb's wool wrapping that protected the four precious glass cups. She had been purifying herself for forty days, avoiding the touch of people, distancing herself from her husband, Yehuda Ben-Shaul, son of her mother's brother, abiding in the tent of the menstruating women, sequestered, bleeding in the night.

An irate expression had been fixed on Ben-Shaul's face for days, and he watched her intently as they walked or when they stopped on the road to encamp. He polished amulets made from the canines of wild animals and the leg bones of goats, rubbing and rubbing and never taking his eyes from her. She would buy the lamb in Jerusalem, in the market near the Temple. She had been able to save the three-quarters of a shekel and two zer for each priest, as required, by forgoing perfume and saving a sixth of a dinar from her weekly allowance. Before she had set out, her mother had given her a tiny coral stalactite amulet. The coins and the amulet were hidden in the hem of her robe. She would occasionally run her fingers over them and find them bound tightly in their place. There, on the stone altar in the Temple, she would spread the parts of the lamb's body as her father had told her. Along with the lamb, she would offer up all the empty chambers of her body yearning to be filled. Their longing would intensify under her wide robes and shake the very core of her soul and of the hidden mysteries of her body until the final shudder that would drive her mad with excitement. Her flesh would convulse, and a tremendous roar rushing from within her, as if escaping from the throat of a madwoman, would soar over the hilltops, as the blood of the lamb flowed on the stone, streaming, streaming into a small channel, gathering into a red pool in the heart of the stone basin of the sacrificial altar.

*   *   *

"So what does my heart tell you when I don't interfere?"

"The usual: the truth that your tongue doesn't dare reveal to me," he said. She recalled their last meeting in the café in Herzliya, when she hadn't yet known it would be the last, simply another of many meetings halfway between Jerusalem, where he was studying history, and Haifa, where she was studying architecture. Her fingers were mechanically crumbling a coconut cookie and his were rubbing an unlit cigarette when she told him with the portentous feeling of someone announcing a duel, "I was offered a scholarship to do my master's in Hiroshima," thinking: now things will be resolved one way or another, and we'll put an end to years of delay, years of letting things drag along on their own.

"A city with a bad, interesting history, Hiroshima," he said, and she understood that things would not be resolved easily.

"In other words, a place for me."

Reading her thoughts as if she had spoken them, he knew very well that she was expecting him to come between her and Hiroshima, to tell her explicitly that their weekend meetings were too rare, that it was time to move in together, that they should finally surrender to what had existed between them from the time they were children. And he also read her secret expectation that he would be excited and suggest going with her to Hiroshima to complete his master's degree in history, to see with his own eyes the museum and the famous fountain he'd lectured their twelfth grade class about as part of his end-of-year project comparing the Jewish holocaust to the Japanese holocaust.

"You said that, not me."

"And Jerusalem doesn't have a bad history?"

"A very bad one." He shifted his gaze from the whitish coconut worms, remnants of the crumbled cookie, to the signs of astonishment and affront that filtered through the mask she had quickly composed on her face. With forced lightness, he added, "And it doesn't have any geishas either." When she didn't respond, he went on, in an apologetic tone, "Good luck, Diti," and he pushed his hand under hers, his five fingers grasping the entire length of her pinkie in that strange, familiar grip.

"Thank you very much," she said politely, pulling her pinkie from his fingers. She knew she couldn't hide from him the sense of defeat she felt, the questions she was afraid to put to him—Had he fallen in love with someone else? Had he been sleeping with her between the weekends they met?—the fact that she felt he was sending her off with a sense of relief, that he'd been struggling with how to break off their long, complicated relationship, and now the unexpected opportunity to send her all the way to Hiroshima had conveniently appeared.

"No place in the world suits you better than Hiroshima." He left his orphaned hand on the sticky cookie crumbs.

"You think so?" She could almost count the organs of her body collapsing inside her, one by one.

"For now," he said, as if he could foresee that nine years later would be the right time to speak differently, that, as she drove along the Jerusalem highway, his breathing over the phone would give her goose bumps and he'd be able to nibble her satin bra strap and push it aside along with the thin fabric of the bra cup, causing the breast inside it to quiver with excitement. Then, his chin playing with the strap, he'd ask, "What's this, you've gone back to wearing bras?"

"Sometimes." She found herself amazed once more at that mysterious ability of his, which, many years ago, used to frighten them both.

"We shall overcome." He exhaled his warm breath into her neck.

"Easily." She prolonged the word deliberately and held the steering wheel with both hands, trying to control her breathing, hoping her heart would not give away the flashes of desire his fingers on her nape were sending to the depths of her body, to between her thighs.

"Like always." He chuckled, as if he knew everything she was trying in vain to hide.

"Like with the dolls," she suddenly remembered with a shiver. The fire in her body retreated all at once at the memory of the first time she'd seen him. He had been eight years old then, standing at the window of his room, looking at her with piercing eyes as she stood in front of her new home next to the truck full of the contents of their house that the movers had begun to unload. He'd caught her glance and called to her, alarmed, instantly infecting her with his anxiety: "Hey you, they're going to break your collection." Her big brother had given him a dismissive look and said, "Just some stupid kid, ignore him." But a few hours later, when she'd finally found the carton that held her things, she saw that most of the porcelain dolls inside it were shattered.

"Long before the dolls," he said now.

"We didn't know each other before the dolls."

"Sure we did."

She couldn't guess what it was in his words that caused her to tremble in a different way now, not with the stirring of hidden expectations, but with a shudder of fear that struck an inner vein. This fear was heightened by past discomfort, by its connection to her anger at the boy who had once scrutinized her life with his sharp gaze and at the man who was now scrutinizing it as if she and her secrets were apparent to him despite the nine years during which they had neither seen nor spoken to each other.

"Where did we meet before the dolls?"

"We didn't meet," he said, "I looked at you from afar. It was impossible to get close to you then."

She laughed with relief. "Why?"

"Because you had a crazy, insanely jealous husband."

"But that probably didn't bother you." She was giggling, carried away into the game whose rules had not yet been set.

"In the end, no."

"Maybe I was Cleopatra." She felt a sudden nostalgia for one long-ago Purim when she had dressed up as Cleopatra. The snake sewn on the front of her dress had drooped because it was heavy and she'd had to hold it with her hand to hide the khaki cloth lining.

"You were never Cleopatra," he said with a seriousness that surprised her.

"I wasn't?"

"No."

"And what were you when I wasn't Cleopatra?" She didn't know whether she was amused or terrified.

"I was someone with a special sense of smell," he said without hesitation, instantly dispelling his seriousness.

Surprised, she laughed with relief and whispered seductively, "Let's see if it can stand up to the test. Can you identify my perfume?"

He laughed. "On principle, I always like it to be standing up. And you?"

A provocative reply began to form on the tip of her tongue, but at that moment, just as she was passing the entrance gate to an olive grove, two hundred meters from the start of the steep rise to Sha'ar Hagai, the oil indicator on the dashboard of the Autobianchi lit up.

*   *   *

In the meantime, they are on the lookout for soldiers of the Roman army who have laid siege to Jerusalem. They follow the signs left by the two brave young men who go before the small group as scouts, examining the road to see that it is safe, searching for evidence of the army and of predatory animals, locating the caves where it will be comfortable to stop and in which to take refuge for the night. The straight road that leads to Upper Beit Horon is already behind them, and they are filled with apprehension, for here begins the gorge that leads down the hill to Lower Beit Horon. Even children know that this narrow slope is the most dangerous part of their journey, so they maintain a careful silence.

Two black maidservants and five new Canaanite slaves purchased by her husband's father for one gold dinar each walk with them, bearing their loads like beasts of burden. On the road, they occasionally see hungry, wide-eyed savages who fall upon the food offered them, eyeing the women lustfully, speaking of the horrors of starvation in the besieged city, of the diseases, especially the plague that was causing many deaths, mainly among children and old people, and of the dead bodies removed to the gate and piled along the length of the wall.

One day, they met a handsome Roman soldier who, astonished by the group of people approaching the besieged city, told them the roads ahead were crowded with pilgrims, and that, for months, the soldiers of the Emperor Titus had been deployed around the entire city, along the Kidron from the south and the Ben-Hinum valley from the east and the north, and along the wall from the north and the west. The soldiers had felled

most of the trees, destroying the orchards near the city, and were cata-
pulting rocks and lit torches into the city, day and night. No one was
permitted to enter or leave the city. Why were they taking women and
children on this dangerous road? They told him about the dream the
head of their family had dreamed. In it, the gates of the Temple had
opened before him, and a voice had whispered to him, saying that by the
time they arrived, the city would be liberated and they would be among
the first to offer sacrifices.

The Roman's face shone, and he told them that the Jewish God had
also been revealed to him in a dream. Not long before, he had gone up to
the city of Gamla with the Roman army and a terrible epidemic had broken out among the soldiers. He had managed to reach the city with the
army—some of the soldiers were already displaying the first signs of the
disease that would end in blindness—and had captured Mount Tabor.
There, on that night, the Jewish God was revealed to him. A voice echoed
from the sky commanding him to leave the camp, guiding him along the
safe path on the steep slope far from the Roman encampment, and he followed the mysterious voice as a child follows its mother, knowing for the
first time in his life that he was doing the right thing. Now he wanted
to be a Jew. The Jewish God, he said, his eyes glittering feverishly, the
Jewish God is the true God, the holy God, the eternal God. Through the
words of the translator, she could clearly see the fearsome trembling that
gripped the man, the same trembling she had been seized with for months,
and she looked at him, at his blazing eyes, seeing herself in him as if he
were a mirror.

In the late afternoon, she was visited by her husband's sister who, in her
own home (the home of wealthy people whose floor is stone and whose windows are glass), was accustomed to having a maidservant see to her every
wish, while here she herself was the keeper of the candles and lamp oil. The
flock was grazing on the side of the hill, and Ada sat high above them,
facing Jerusalem, staring, as if enthralled by the shifting light of the sunset spreading over the hills. This was the time to bring back the flock.
Several days earlier, she had been so mesmerized by the sight of the hills
that she had brought the flock in minus one kid. Now, from afar, she saw
her sister-in-law approaching, a bundle in her hands. As little girls, they
used to play together in their grandfather's courtyard, running about

between the legs of the women baking and cooking and spinning wool in the open courtyard, and hiding behind the mats used to separate the rooms. But from the day Ada's engagement became known, her husband's sister had distanced herself, staying loyal to her brother.

"Shalom," she said from a distance and stopped, waiting for an invitation.

"Shalom," Ada replied, gesturing for her to approach.

Her sister-in-law came without speaking, put the bundle down and gave her a handful of dates in a clay dish. Ada took a date, thanked her, and asked, "Has your brother sent you?"

"He asks if you are ill," her sister-in-law said directly.

"Neither ill nor well, and there have not yet been seven clean days, not even one clean day."

"We have been on the road for twenty days."

"I have not had a clean day for twenty days."

Her sister-in-law looked at her with narrowed eyes, trying to determine if this were a lie or an illness.

"And you said you were not ill?"

"I also said I was not well. Go and tell him this: when we return from the Temple, he shall have his wife back. Here, he will let her be, he will let her unite with God."

"It is in honor of God that you do not have one clean day?" Her sister-in-law bestowed upon her a look of disbelief.

"And in honor of Jerusalem," she said.

"Becoming sanctified in their honor with blood?"

"And sequestering myself."

"Is it in honor of God and Jerusalem that you sanctify and sequester yourself, or is it in honor of someone else?"

She looked serenely and confidently into her sister-in-law's eyes. "Is that what he thinks? That another has come to me?"

"He does not know what to think. For twenty days his wife has not been with him, and now he will hear that she is sanctifying and sequestering herself in honor of God and in honor of Jerusalem."

"What will he say?"

"He will say she has lost her mind or she is lying."

"Go and tell him she has not lost her mind and she is not lying, and

no other man has come to her. He will leave his wife in the hands of God, and after the Temple, he will have her back, pure and cleansed. In a year, he will be holding a child."

Her sister-in-law wrapped the clay dish without lowering her probing gaze, and rose to go.

"Whose child? Shifra, the daughter of Absalom was stoned for adultery."

"There is no adultery. Tell him that for me."

"The women say that you rise at night, walk past the ones who are sleeping, and steal silently away."

"That is true," she admitted readily, disturbed by the thought that the women had been watching her from their places on the mats, pretending to be asleep. "It is difficult to sleep because of the Jerusalem air. I go up to the hill and I am calmed. Tell him and he will believe."

"Whether he believes or does not believe, the women are already laughing. Honor is more important than what he will believe."

Her sister-in-law gave her a piercing look and began to descend, and Ada called after her with all the strength she could summon, "And you, what do you say?"

Her sister-in-law said something in reply, but she did not turn around, and her voice was carried off by the wind without reaching Ada.

*　　*　　*

For the first minute, until it entered her mind that she had to immediately pull the Autobianchi onto the side of road, Idit's eyes were drawn to the nice little jug of oil, a childish paper cut-out blazing on the car's dashboard. It evoked a memory of her class decorations committee meeting before Hanukkah, and of the smell of cut crepe paper and glue mixed with the thick, tempting aroma of steamy donuts. Arising automatically with that memory was the song "Jug of clay, jug of clay, that gave them oil for eight whole days..." In the middle of the line, she suddenly remembered that it was dangerous to keep driving when the oil indicator was on, and she called out in alarm, "Something wrong's with the car." Then she looked in her rearview mirror and signaled in the direction of the lane to her right. She heard the concern in his voice, "What happened, Diti?"

"I'm stopping," she said quickly, and it crossed her mind that his mysterious ability to read her suddenly vanished when she and her body were not involved. She merged right, looked into her mirror again, and pulled onto the rocky shoulder, the hood of her car facing the hilltop, pointing to the sign that said twenty kilometers to Jerusalem.

"Diti, Diti," his voice said, bursting through the phone as if they were in a disaster movie, "where are you?"

"I stopped the car," she said.

"You disappeared for a minute. What happened?"

"Looks like there's a problem with the oil. The indicator light is on."

"Perfect timing." She heard his petulance.

"Yes," she said, and waited for him to go on speaking. When he didn't say anything, she added, "That's probably the reason for the bad feeling I had at the airport."

"What bad feeling?"

"I felt that something would happen to me on the way to Jerusalem."

"You turned into a prophet in Hiroshima."

She ignored the teasing. "What am I supposed to do now?"

"You probably need oil. Why'd they give you a car without oil?" he said reproachfully. A feeling of disappointment rose in her as the magic of their flirtatious conversation began to wane, cut off so abruptly and replaced by a matter-of-fact tone.

"Where will I find oil now?"

"Maybe there's a can in the trunk?"

"The trunk's completely empty."

"Check it."

"There's nothing to check. I put both my suitcases in it, and it was empty. Wait a minute, something else just lit up. What's a flashing orange box on the right side?"

A truck climbing the hill passed her car, making it shake, and she sat staring at the nice little oil jug glowing red next to the persistent orange flickering that was like the winking eye of a madman.

"Hello?"

"I'm here. The whole dashboard's lit up."

"First of all, turn off the motor."

She turned off the motor and the winking square was swallowed up into the dark dashboard display.

"It's off. What now?"

"Turn on the flashing lights."

She pressed the button that turned on the flashing lights and her image appeared and vanished, appeared and vanished on the windshield in front of her.

"They're on."

"Do you have the rental company's phone number?"

"Yes."

"You have to call them. They'll send a mechanic."

"But it'll take forever."

"Right."

"Can't you come?"

"Me? I'm not really . . ."

"Why not?"

"I have a problem moving the car. I told you that Anat's brother lives across the street, and they might see . . . I think his wife's been watching me since Anat left and if they notice . . . it might look bad at the trial. But if you really want me to—" Perhaps he had picked up the coldness she was beginning to feel because he continued in a firm, amiable tone, "I can be there in twenty minutes."

"So what do you suggest?" She was put off by the thought of his brother-in-law's family peeking into the bedroom, seeing the large bed probably already saturated with the fragrance of vanilla.

"If oil's the only problem, then I'm sure I have some in my car. If there's another problem, you'll have to let them know. Where exactly are you parked?"

"Halfway up the hill, a little beyond Sha'ar Hagai."

"So maybe we'll leave the car and I'll take you here. We'll call them. They'll come by the morning."

"Are you kidding? By morning, the car won't be here."

"It might take them hours—"

"I'm not leaving the car," she said, making this a clear priority.

He was silent. The whispered, twenty-minute conversation they'd had earlier—the conversation that had slowly inflamed her body from the moment she'd passed under the bridge of the Modi'in Settlements interchange, shifting between teasing fun and daring provocation, between insinuating hints and explicit words, quickening her breath, setting free what had been icebound for nine years, preparing them for what awaited them in night's embrace, planned lustfully for months in phone conversations between Jerusalem and Hiroshima—that conversation had been interrupted and the steamy atmosphere it had created of things beginning to build up before the peak that would come in another hour, maybe two, maybe three, that atmosphere had collapsed suddenly, leaving a sense of dejection, disappointment, and shame, marked by restlessness.

"I'm going to the car to see if there's any oil," he said.

"*Arigato*," she said, unwittingly retreating from him to Japanese.

"*Ari*—what?"

"Thanks, don't bother. Let's hang up and I'll call the office."

"Wait another minute, don't hang up on me."

A fuzzy picture of them at age thirteen suddenly emerged from far away, as blurred as a worn-out video tape: the special silence of Yom Kippur, frozen and menacing, fraught with horrors and wonders, in which the world held its breath in anticipation of God's final judgment, that silence now filtered into her parents' empty apartment, into her room with its prison-cell-sized window, where they are lying on a Bedouin rug, his body pressed against hers, heavier than she thought it would be, the cold of the floor assailing her back through the thin carpet, the pungent smell of sweat rising from his skin new to her nostrils. She moans from the pain splitting her loins, and her struggle to move her face from under the strong bones of his crushing shoulder brings her ear to his whispering mouth, "Don't cry, Diti," and she looks closely at her fingers, which had probed the source of pain earlier, and she is unable to choke back her sob, "I'm bleeding."

Hours later, still enveloped by the special silence of Yom Kippur, filled with anxiety before God who, despite his preoccupation with the fate of multitudes, had seen her and Natan—even her parents' prayers in the synagogue would not atone for their evil deeds—Natan tries to convince her of the stupidity of the thought, but he stays, at her request, waiting with her until her parents return. They stand over the memorial candle flickering across the embroidered roses of the tablecloth on the dining room table, her pinkie caught in his hand, and look at the quivering flame at the end of the wick, glance at the bottom of the tin base being slowly revealed as if it were a treasure lost in the clear sea, watch the trembling cypress of flame surrounded by dripping, melting strips of wax stuck to the sides of the small box covered with a drawing of the Western Wall, and she says, "Don't you dare," and he rebels, easily blowing out the flame, which struggles against the sudden wind, feinting to the right and to the left in a meek, fruitless dance of survival, and they look in shock at the empty tin box and the suddenly darkened Western Wall. "God will definitely punish us for that," she says, breathing with pain.

"Why should he punish you? You didn't do anything."

"Yes, I did," she insisted, "I saw it happen."

"Tell me, do you think someone is punishing us?" she asked, looking outside now in quiet desperation, seeing the cars driving down from Jerusalem, rolling toward her in a straight line, then suddenly shifting aside, as if they had changed their minds, curving down the steep slope.

"Who would punish us? The god of Autobianchis?" He chuckled.

"That humor doesn't work on me."

"Should I try Japanese humor?"

"You couldn't manage it," she said unsmilingly.

"Maybe you're the one who's punishing us?"

"How? Do I have any control over the oil in a rented car?"

He suddenly understood and, apparently remembering that Yom Kippur too, said, "Diti, you still think we deserve to be punished, don't you!"

"I don't know. Coincidences scare me."

"But this isn't just a coincidence, Diti," he said. "This is Fate."

*   *   *

*She did not tell her sister-in-law—nor would she tell her or anyone else—
of her trembling desire to offer a ritual sacrifice, her yearning for the
sounds of Jerusalem, and how these had blended with her longing for a full
womb. If her husband were to hear of it, he would put an end to the alien
thing that had risen in his wife, who again and again imagined seeing
the altar of stones that had never been touched by iron, whitewashed, and
on its surface the drizzle of blood flowing, flowing like a perpetual stream,
pooling in the bottom of the stone basin. Imagining this, she would recall
her father's quavering voice describing the altar and now, as if she had
inherited from him the overwhelming desire to offer a sacrifice, she watched
her sister-in-law's back recede, while her own heart and body stirred in
excitement at the thought of the lamb giving up its blood to God, returning to Him the life it had been given.*

   *In the evening, she again saw her sister-in-law from the back. They
had all gathered around a low fire that spread warmth and had no flame,
so it would not be seen from afar. The slaves, black silhouettes, were swallowed up in the darkness behind them, moving in silence. The place for the
women was small, and they crowded together like a flock of sheep, the first
row crouching at the fire to allow the rows of people behind them to warm
themselves. Someone recounted what he had heard from a hermit he had met
on the road about the civil war being waged between the Jewish zealots and
the other Jewish citizens in Jerusalem, as if the danger posed by the Romans
had passed, and about the madmen wandering near the gates of the city
and shouting prophecies of destruction. Some three years earlier, said the
Roman who wanted to convert, his eyes burning, when Jerusalem was filled
with pilgrims, the students of Beit Shamai permitted them to fight on the
Sabbath, and they went out in droves to do battle with the Romans. And
again, as always when he spoke—about the date and persimmon groves
near Jericho, about the money that had been collected at the Dead Sea for
embalming the dead, about the trees around Jerusalem that were being cut
down every day of the siege, about the seventeen gold squares the Romans
had stolen from the Temple treasury, and about the mad prophets—Ada*

felt herself drawn to the Roman, recognizing the fire blazing in him, and she felt a holy spirit emerge from within her and blend with the light radiating from him, her eyes glowing and her body burning, burning. Jerusalem, he said, his eyes afire, all its streets are paved with pure marble, and the Temple—his voice rose, inflaming her spirit—has been standing for six hundred years and will always stand, as eternal as the sky and the earth.

Beyond the tongues of flame, she saw the face of her husband, his gaze fixed upon her questioningly, searching her eyes, suspicious, seeking to discover the secret of her transformation. It was easy to escape her husband's eyes. She looked to the hills of Jerusalem, effortlessly cutting herself off from the circle of people gathered around the fire, cutting herself off from the voices of the women encircling her. Only the ecstatic spirit of the Roman moved with her toward the aura radiating from the distant hills, one pair of legs folded under her, the other pair scaling the hill with him.

*   *   *

An army van appeared in the Autobianchi's side mirror just as an historian, whose name she didn't catch, was being interviewed on the car radio, and he said, speaking with an announcer's rolling *r* and in the sad voice of one to whom the awful future has been revealed, "The problem is how to restrain the fanatic elements. One can explain logically that Israel has the power to completely destroy the Palestinian economic infrastructure; their water and power sources are in our hands. One can warn that anyone taking radical steps must remember the price we will pay in addition to the actual cost of the destruction of tourism and personal safety. We will pay with the destruction of our moral standards. The problem is that those people do not think rationally, they act according to a different logic."

The army van passed the Autobianchi, slowed down, and stopped on the side of the road. Idit's heart rejoiced at the sight of it. Years of living in Hiroshima among people frozen in their individual bubbles had caused her to forget that heartwarming sensation of strangers volunteering, and the IDF—the IDF itself—had come to her aid even before she'd had the time to get angry and

worried, before she'd had the time to call the car rental company,
and even before the trembling of her body caused by the man waiting for her twenty minutes away had abated. And maybe, hope
kindled in her, maybe she'd be held up only briefly, no more than
a few minutes, while one of the soldiers repaired the damage. The
core of her trembling would be easily aroused again, and she'd
evade the eyes of his brother-in-law's family, sneak into the house
of the man waiting for her, into the room he had fixed up for her,
filled, undoubtedly, with vanilla sweetness and chimes.

But then the light came on inside the van parked in front of her
car and she thought she saw—her heart stopping—a man wearing
civilian clothes sitting in the driver's seat. In the turbid light, she
saw the profile of a dark face, a mustache, and all at once she remembered that a young Jewish man had been kidnapped near an Arab
village on the road leading to Jerusalem, and his savaged body had
been found tossed in a ditch at the side of the road in Abu Gosh. On
the radio, they had said that the Palestinians disguised as Israelis
were also suspected of using a stolen Israeli taxi to kidnap someone.

Had the army van also been stolen? Had the Palestinians who
stole it killed the soldier who'd been sitting in it and was she now
falling into their hands, trapped in her car like easy prey? Would
they shoot her with the Israeli soldier's gun and would the TV
news analysts report her murder and mention the last series of
murders that might indicate the modus operandi of an organized
group? And would the sad historian on a panel of intellectuals, or
maybe just some ordinary citizen on one of those radio shows
meant for ordinary citizens, say that Israel had the power to completely destroy the Palestinian economic infrastructure, but we
should keep in mind the price we'd pay for that?

Her eyes remained fixed on the unmoving van, its back to her,
like a dangerous animal contemplating its next move. She remembered the images she'd seen over and over again on Japanese TV of
the Palestinians who had lynched two Jewish men, of the body of
the victim being thrown out of the second-floor window like a rag
doll thrown to the people celebrating in the street, of the police-
men rejoicing inside the building, of the young man who appeared

momentarily in the window and showed his hands, covered with the blood of the Jews, to the cheering crowd.

Terrified, but part of her maintaining a surprising clarity, her fingers roamed over the buttons of her cell phone and she managed to dial 100, but she didn't recognize her own voice as it said to the operator, "I have . . . something happened, is happening . . . I'm on the Jerusalem road . . . there are Arabs here . . . an army van . . . and the Palestinians . . . " The last word turned into a scream.

The operator said in a sharp, efficient voice, "Wait a minute, Miss, wait on the line," and Idit immediately heard a man's voice, "You're okay, aren't you, Miss? You're not hurt?"

There was something soothing in the deep, authoritative voice, as if now, when it came to her car, he was taking care of the matter and she shouldn't worry. She said, "There are Palestinians . . . " and her voice vanished at the sight of the van rolling toward her, her eyes on the bumper as it neared the flashing headlights of the Autobianchi.

She heard the firm voice asking, "Miss, can you hear me? Are you in a car?"

He grunted and said in a calm voice, as if she had answered him, "Can you see the license number of the van? Can you give me the number?" And when she didn't reply, he continued, "We're on the way to you, Miss. Now listen carefully: lock all the doors from the inside and put on your flashing lights. Do you hear me, Miss? You have to make an effort. Lock the door next to you and all the other doors too. Look and see if the buttons are down. And if the window is open, close it. We're on the way—"

And beyond that, she heard nothing but silence and she saw nothing but the man, as heavy as the bear walking on two legs she'd once seen in the circus, approaching her car, and a metallic light, like a hidden blade, glittered momentarily in his hand.

She fell back into her seat, preparing herself for the moment when he would come and open the door easily, even though the button was down, and she would see the magnificent sunset over the hills of Jerusalem, like a huge, glorious halo, absolute perfection, shining around his head, a crimson glow, shooting dazzling arrows into the slits of her closing eyes.

*   *   *

In the chill of the clear evening, lying on the cold, rocky ground, her head split open, Ada saw a wild dog racing toward her as she watched the back of her husband, Yehuda Ben-Shaul, receding. Her husband was descending the hill in large steps, moving rapidly away from her and she imagined she heard his voice: "There is no longer a need to sanctify yourself. There is no longer a Temple. They are burning down the Temple." Her fingers reached down to feel the coins hidden in the folds of her dress along with the coral stalactite amulet, and she found the steamy tongue of the dog. Her husband's head disappeared, and now she felt the pain clutch at her eyes as if they were being ripped from their sockets. As the strong, demanding touch of the rough tongue moved toward her face and the gurgling growl came into her ear, there rose within her, faint and trembling, the priests' chant. "They are burning down the Temple... burning down the Temple..." She rose slowly, leaving behind the pain, rising from the hardness of the rocky ground, and she glided softly, slowly toward the hills.

In a last effort, she turned eastward to face the city. Through the slits of her eyes, she saw the splendid redness rising over the hills of Jerusalem, flooding, dominating, scattering over all the world, bringing with it the taste of blood—blood pushing its way into the earth—the smell of burning granaries in the distance, and the light of the flames rising from the ruins of the Temple, tall and strong, tearing at the heavens like swords of fire.

A Good Place for the Night

IN THE FOURTH YEAR, the funnel of air passed frequently over the house, teasing, descending to the garden of wooden monsters where the child used to wander. Every few days, Gila would hear the distant whistle grow shriller, like the siren on the eve of Holocaust Memorial Day or on the eve of Memorial Day for the Fallen in War, and she'd run out and pull the boy home. She was almost late once, and at the last minute, as she grabbed him from the sucking flow, she saw the opening of the funnel up close for the first time, damp and quivering, like an elephant's trunk. And once she was late. The boy's arm had been sucked in, but he struggled, flapping at the mouth of the funnel, swinging his short legs and his free arm, moving away and rising, and Gila ran under him, screaming, until he was dropped on the other side of the fence into the area of the epidemic over which birds were flying in circles. He was caught in a tree, then fell to the contaminated earth along with some branches, bruised all over. Later, frightened and exhausted, he let her isolate him in his room for three days and smear his body with an ointment she made from the bark of a tree that burned the skin and its fruit, which was shaped like cats' heads. Sometimes, when he cried and Gila was too tired, the nun would come out of her room and lovingly tend to him. But when he'd recovered from his mysterious illness and grew calm, he insisted on going out again, especially to the garden of monsters, as if he were heeding the call of his parents beckoning him to their burial place.

When the boy was outside, Gila would coax and threaten and plead with him to come in, but he, recalcitrant and rebellious, his body sturdy for a two-year-old, would slip away from the windows to the garden of warped tree trunks, and she became accustomed to straining her ears for the sound of the whistling air that heralded the coming of the funnel.

Not until he was asleep in his bed and she was secure in the refuge of the house did she stop the constant straining to hear. Then she waited for the funnel with forbidden excitement, occasionally seeing objects fly past like lightning and remembering how she had once seen a remarkable spectacle. It was as if the funnel had decided to tease her—like a naked young girl in a dark window, waiting to tease a neighbor across the way. The streams of haze rising from the ground began to move slowly, drawn in a single direction to form a clear diagonal curtain, curled at the edges and with a long, hollow space in the center, and one end of it moving lustfully, seeking prey. A large tree complete with its roots appeared suddenly at one end of the channel of clear air, flew like a shot arrow to the other end, and disappeared instantly. She stood there terrified and enthralled by the haze that was now flattening, returning to its former state, as calm as an animal whose appetite has been satisfied.

But then, the boy had already been a year old.

The first time she saw the funnel, she still hadn't known the boy existed. As soon as she walked into the house with the man, even before they saw the five dead people, before they found the boy sleeping in his bed, they suddenly heard the noise of a storm, and a tube of bright air cut through the smoke that had already begun to darken outside. Inside the illuminated tube of space, stretched parallel to the horizon and twice the height of a person, numerous objects sailed around slowly, becoming entangled in gentle circles: stools and a bookshelf, babies' clothes, frying pans, a mattress, a straw lampshade, landscape paintings, a tapestry of harem women, a bouquet of flowers and the vase that had once held them, pillows embroidered with silver and purple birds, a blue enamel kettle, a carpet, a woman's purse, newspaper pages. Gila looked in horror at the contents of the ghost house hovering in front of her: not too long ago, someone had read that newspaper and had drunk tea brewed in that kettle; a dog had lain on that carpet; a woman had worn the straps of that purse on her shoulder; babies had soiled those clothes. Where were they now?

The graying smoke had once again subdued the channel of air, but still she stood at the window, waiting, as if she had been told part of a story and wanted to know the ending. Then the man had come out of one of the rooms and said, "There are five dead adults here and one live baby."

Two of the dead people had been guests, an elegant couple of Indian descent sitting in the garden on a wrought iron bench, he smoking and she brushing her hair. The three other dead people had been employees of the inn: a very tall, thin young man doing accounts at a desk in the office; an older man with gray sideburns bent over the stove in the kitchen; and a girl wearing a frilled chambermaid's apron lying like a contortionist at the foot of a half-made bed in one of the rooms on the top floor.

Elated, Gila stood beside the sleeping baby's bed and recalled a children's story one of her little girls had liked and the other had loathed: the three bears come home after an evening stroll to find Goldilocks sleeping in the small bed.

The man scrutinized her, pondering, watching this unknown woman glow at the sight of the sleeping child, reach out and cover his exposed shoulder, take pleasure in something familiar amidst the chaos they had been thrown into, holding onto the temporary ordinariness of a child breathing peacefully in his bed.

Then they began a search of the inn together. Stepping noiselessly from room to room, they looked into the gleaming bathrooms, examined the beds, were drawn to the windows that looked out onto a landscape of thin columns of dust that covered the earth.

Once, when the child still obeyed her and didn't go out into the garden, the funnel of air stopped in front of the house and tossed a cloth-wrapped bundle onto the doorstep. From the window, Gila looked at the package of rags that had been spit out at the door and saw it begin to move. A head emerged from it, the head of a very old woman. The child, who had never seen such an old person, screamed in fright. This wasn't the first stranger he'd seen. Although he'd known the nun and the sick man from the time he was a baby, occasionally, someone would stumble upon the house, speak an incomprehensible language, look pleadingly at Gila, and wolf down the food she offered. Sometimes the stranger would fall asleep in one of the armchairs, and the man would sit beside him holding a stick, and when he woke up, the man would send him on his way. Once, three wild-looking women appeared, their hair and their nails grown long. One of them reached out to touch the child, and he drew back with a cry. Then time passed and no one came to the house until the funnel spit out the old lady. Gila went out to her and, her hand covered with cloth, looked for the signs but didn't find even one: the backs of the old lady's hands were not covered with brown spots, there was no swelling behind her ears and no pus leaking from her eyes. Gila dragged the old lady into the house, sat her down in an armchair and gave her some water, which she drank slowly. The old lady sat in that armchair for three days, sipping water, taking bites of a biscuit, relieving herself in her clothes. The child stood beside her all his waking hours, studying her from every angle, imitating the sounds of her strange language. On the fourth day, she spit up black blood and died. The child cried when the man buried her in the yard where—this he did not know—his parents were buried along with the three employees of the inn.

One time, the child had been close to discovering his parents. Driving rain had poured down all night, washing away the dirt that covered the bodies and scattering fragments of skeletons over the yard. From his room, the child saw the bones first, and the man hurried outside to bury them. Gila watched from the window, recalling the beautiful Indian woman they had found dead in the garden, wearing an orange sari edged with gold embroidery. Even if she had been preserved whole in her grave, the child would not have recognized her. Gila would sometimes wonder, and ask the man, whether a four-month-old baby had memories, whether he might know that the people raising him were not the ones who had given birth to him, whether they would tell him one day about the circumstances that had brought the three of them together, whether they should wait until he himself discovered how different his appearance was from theirs.

They agreed that, one day, they would tell him the whole truth, they would show him his parents' passports and his name and date of birth written in one of them. Meanwhile, the days passed, one following on the heels of the other according to the clock, but never revealing the secret of time. From the first day and through all the years, they were never able to unlock the secret of the changing seasons, and only the chart they kept of the days helped them mark off time. The weather seesawed from day to day like a bad-tempered person: the sun blazed not like a ball of fire, but like formless lava spreading like a puddle over half the sky; rain fell not in a downpour, but like an entire cloud being hurled down, exploding on the ground with a crash that made the tree roots quake. Sometimes it would be dark and stormy for days at a time; sometimes the primeval landscape was bathed in a blinding, phosphorous light that flooded the enormous desolation, as flat as a tray, devoid of forests, grooved with fissures that spread in straight lines to the horizon like the furrows of a plowed field, spitting jet-streams of transparent dust from its grooves—a magnificent and menacing stage set. But sometimes Gila would wake and see, as if it were an ad for a tourist site, the kind of pristine, clear, fresh world you see after the rain: bare trees exposed to the pleasant sun; and above them, a sky beautiful with baby-blue clouds, as if it had not witnessed the scenes of horror that had raged under it on that cataclysmic day; and in the distance, in a uniform shade of green, pastures as smooth as lake water; and on the horizon, a row of trees with densely tangled foliage, a kind of tree she had never seen before. Her gaze traveled over the clouds, assembled like a mountain ridge, as if they were the repository of memories from other landscapes that had sailed onward over the flat, bright countryside, and she felt suddenly calm: the sky was in its place and the earth was in its place. It was impossible that, beyond the distant trees, there were no roads or cities of living people now planning their day, which had just begun.

"Do you think the train might be working again?" she kept asking those first few months.

The man would look at her, saddened that she had once again been carried away by the deceptive landscape and that she would once again have to travel the path to the knowledge that the world she knew had vanished while she was in the train's smoking car, and he said, "The train is stuck in exactly the same place."

On evenings reminiscent of summer, the three of them would go out into the garden, or walk, or ride their bicycles far from the house until they got tired, sometimes heading toward what had been the train station and sometimes toward the corpses of the railroad cars that, before the catastrophe, had crossed Europe. Sometimes they'd pass the charcoal shepherd and his charcoal flock and see the three skeletons in the station and the skeletons of the passengers crumbling inside their tattered clothes. From the day he learned to walk, the child, used to the sight, would go into the ticket seller's booth, move the skeleton that had once been the ticket seller to the edge of its chair, squeeze in beside it and play with the equipment and the money, but Gila and the man gazed at the skeletons and remembered how they'd looked on the day of the cataclysm. Then the child, hoisted up to the windows, would look at the skeletons in the train, his glance lingering on the skeleton of the little girl holding the book he would know by heart in another year, *Alice in Wonderland,* a birthday present from her teacher, who had written in it the false prophecy, "To the talented Mary Jane, who will write books like this herself one day, when she grows up."

In her dreams, she would relive the moment the car shook suddenly, like a ghost train in an amusement park, and she opened the door of the smoking car and saw the sleeping people who, an instant before, had been awake. The brazen young couple who had been making love on the bench across from her (the girl's panting had embarrassed the other passengers, who shot glances at each other) were embracing, deeply asleep—she arched backward, her hair hanging over the seat, and he bent over her, his face buried in her neck; the frenetic young man's head was pressed against the window, as if he were kissing the cracked glass goodbye; the older man who had been flashing surreptitious glances of longing at the couple making love was tilted back, his hands crossed on his groin, his gaze fixed on the ceiling; the two strangers who had become friends during the trip, one explaining that he had come from a conference of ecology experts, the other proffering pieces of choice tropical fruit wrapped in cellophane, were sitting mummified, staring at each other; the little girl who had been engrossed in reading *Alice in Wonderland* was bent forward as if bowing deeply, her forehead touching the open book. Many of the train's windows were shattered and splinters of glass glinted on the dark floor; objects and packages that had fallen from the overhead rack were scattered in the aisle, one travel case that had not been completely closed was now open and meticulously ironed shirts were spread around it as if they'd been arranged for display. A suitcase had fallen, burying a redheaded young man so that only a clump of his hair stuck out over the handle of the suitcase and a pair of new jeans showed at the other end of it.

From where she was standing at the end of the car, Gila's eyes darted about, taking in the sight with the utmost clarity in incandescent, diamond-like brightness. She felt a momentary stirring of the hopeful suspicion that the passengers had conspired to pretend they were asleep to see how she would respond, and the whole thing—the artificial light, the unnatural positions—had been staged for a television show that tortured people for the enjoyment of other people, and in a minute, the famous director would suddenly appear and the sleeping people would open their eyes and delight in her embarrassment. But the astonishing silence in the car, broken by the strange sounds of the earth cracking and the bubbling flow of dust from outside gave her gooseflesh, and the scene visible through the windows completely ruled out the idea of a hidden camera. The flat surface of the earth was now covered with a thick veil that flowed from it and billowed up to the sky, as if the earth's belly were boiling.

She tried to get a sound out of her throat to wake up the sleeping people, and a low, unintentional croak emerged, like the sound
made by a mute trying to scream. Nothing moved in the car, and
she stood mesmerized, refusing to acknowledge what she saw,
refusing to think about what lay behind what she saw. Her legs
began to move of their own volition over the shards of glass and
articles of clothing scattered in the aisle, and she pressed her handbag, which held her passport and the pearl rings she'd bought for
her daughters in the art museum, against her body. The people in
the next car were sleeping too. The headrests, which were not covered with white doilies—she could see through the glass of the
door that was stuck halfway open in its track—gave away the fact
that it wasn't a first-class car, but it appeared that the passengers
who had bought cheaper tickets had seen a more splendid show:
feathered hats, lacy shawls, colored scarves, fur stoles, and bridal
veils that had fallen from the trunk of a troupe of actors were scattered over the people, the seats, and the aisle.

"Hello, hello," Gila shouted into the car, but nothing moved.
"Is anyone here? Is there anyone here?" she added in English, in a
braver, more desperate voice inflamed by the fear that had begun
to creep into her mind, by the knowledge that she could not ignore
for long what she was seeing, and that she was not dreaming, but
witnessing a dream-like reality.

Her ears, which had already adjusted to the sounds of the splitting earth and had accepted them as background noises, suddenly
seemed to absorb a new sound in the distance, as abrupt as a dog's
bark. She hurried to one of the broken windows, stuck her head
out between the sharp peaks of glass protruding from the window
frame, listened hard, and screamed to the smoke-filled world outside, "Hey! Hey! Hello! Hello!"

A very faint voice sounded from the depths of the thick white-
ness, "Hey, where are you?"

"Here, inside the train!" she shouted toward the human voice
and stretched her neck even further, putting it in danger of being
slit. "Where are you? Where are you?" Her throat swelled with
the effort.

"Here," a distant voice echoed.

"I'm inside the train," she shouted excitedly. There was no doubt: a man's voice. "Don't go in the wrong direction! Come this way!"

"It's okay." The voice crossed the diminishing distance, and now the owner of that voice could hear that hers was a woman's voice. "Wait for me. I'm coming in your direction."

"I'm waiting for you, I'm waiting," she called, her excitement overcoming her embarrassment. She was seized by a strange feeling, as if she were in a movie she'd seen a long time ago and now she herself was the heroine, calling to a man she didn't know, the hero of the movie, quoting lines from a script that bore some sort of insane similarity to the present situation.

"Where are you?" she asked, frantic with worry.

"I'm getting closer to you," the voice said. "Keep on talking. I'll find you through your voice."

Now she no longer doubted the reality of the voice, and as nervous as a girl about to go on a blind date, she wanted to impress the stranger and to recall a song she'd learned by heart in English class, to assure him that she was worth the effort.

"Hey, are you still there?"

"Yes. I'm waiting for you in the same place."

"Why didn't you say anything?"

"I'm trying to think of something interesting . . ."

"That doesn't matter, the important thing is to keep talking."

"I don't know . . ."

"Maybe you should sing something, that's easier."

The words of the Israeli anthem came into her mind automatically and she pulled her head back inside and started to sing, and as she did so, she straightened like the encyclopedia illustrations of the evolution of monkey into man, "Our hope is not lost, the hope of two thousand years . . ." She sang standing tall, like an instructor in a youth movement standing before his charges and singing with them, her head held high and her heart threatening to overflow. The words of the anthem suffused her with a sense of brotherhood and strength, and she heard her clear, lone voice, separate from the host of sounds around her, "To be a free people in our land, the land of Zion and Jerusalem. To be a free people . . . "

A man's head suddenly appeared under the window behind a thin covering that looked like a transparent scarf, his damp hair speckled with white dust, dark crescents under his eyes, and he asked, "What language is that?"

Panting as if she had asthma, she gave silent thanks to whoever had brought her that man, who looked robust and spoke sensibly, and said, "Hebrew."

He reached up to the window and she reached down through it, and their hands met, crushing the dust between them.

Many times afterward, she tried to recreate that moment, the first touch of their fingers, and couldn't remember anything special that might have made it one of those moments whose fateful nature is perceived only after it has passed. He turned to come onto the train, tugged at the stuck door to open it, and stopped there, stunned by what he saw. Through his eyes—like a child seeing for the first time the amazing sights of his country through the eyes of a tourist—she saw the inside of the car, and before she could ask what had happened to the people in his car, he said, "We have to get out of here right away."

"Where to?" She didn't doubt for a minute that she had to go with him.

"We passed a station a few kilometers back. I assume there's a telephone there. The cell phones are dead."

On cold nights, they'd sit in front of the fire and the boy, from the day he began to speak, always asked to hear stories. They didn't tell him about their lives before they'd come there, leaving that for when he grew up and could understand. They spoke as if life had begun the moment the train stopped, and Gila—as if she could look into his mind—understood how the fairy-tale was taking shape in his imagination, how it would be magnified as time passed and one day would be told as a creation story: the story of how the train had stopped at an unknown place between Odessa and Frankfurt; the story of reaching the inn, which was surrounded

by a network of intertwined, bare branches like a malignant tumor
entrapped by blood vessels, an inn whose frightening façade
enclosed an amazing interior, as in the fairy-tales of wanderers who
enter a lost wonderland and find a child asleep in his cradle.

After they found the boy and discovered that the telephone was
dead and the electricity cut off, they went to bury the dead. The
back garden was burned, and beyond it was a garden of misshapen,
severed tree trunks that had screaming, evil-looking faces and
grooved tongues, roaring with pain or hunger, and beyond that,
were gaping, smoking pits and earth that seethed, as if to show
that even sand could boil. Every time the man dug a hole to bury
the dead in, Gila stood guard, facing the trunks as if she feared
that malevolent spirits dwelling in the evil shapes were plotting to
leap out and tear the dead and the living to bits.

Later, they sat down to eat in candlelight that illuminated and
shadowed their faces. The bread, the cheese, the olives, the home-
made jam lent things a deceptive air of normalcy, but she couldn't
identify the sweet liquid in a pitcher whose flavor reminded her of
a Columbian spread she had bought in the neighborhood super-
market during its "South American Festival."

"Are you American?" she asked, as if now, after they'd been
saved from the catastrophe and had walked half a day together and
found the baby and buried the dead, the time had come for a personal conversation.

"Yes."

"I'm Israeli."

"You live in Israel?"

"Yes. And you?"

"Near New York. A little north."

"Where exactly?"

"Do you know the area?"

"I have a sister in New Rochelle."

"So we're neighbors. I live in Scarsdale."

"Ah—" She was speechless with surprise.

"Yes," he replied, as if he knew exactly what she meant.

"What happened today. . . " Just as she had given the signal to start their personal conversation, she now gave the signal to stop it and realized that she didn't have a name for what had happened.

"A new kind of catastrophe," he said. "Probably radiation that evaporated immediately."

"Did you see how it started, how it happened?"

"No. I was in the smoking car—"

"I was in the smoking car, too!" The coincidence excited her, the discovery that within the incomprehensible reality surrounding her so inexplicably, like a nightmare, there was suddenly a certain order, and now she was beginning to catch on to its logic.

"The walls of the smoking car must have been made of a material that stopped the radiation. The window faces upward, and that probably has something to do with it, too. The boy was in a closed room, which is probably what saved him."

"It's like what happened in Chernobyl, isn't it? I once saw a TV program."

"This seems much worse than Chernobyl. But it might also be some kind of natural disaster."

"How long do you think it'll take them to get the trains moving again?" she asked, as if she hadn't heard the terrifying things he'd said.

He gave her a sideways look of astonishment, as if at that very moment, as she was carefully spreading cheese on her slice of bread, he'd learned something important about her.

"That'll probably take some time," he said cautiously.

"They must already know in Frankfurt that something went wrong. After all, the train didn't arrive on time, and they're very precise there."

"Maybe they don't know. Maybe things went wrong there, too."

"They'll send someone to find out what happened," she promised.

"Who will they send, your army?"

She seemed to be picking up a tone of derision, and she bristled. Over the last week, she'd been hearing a lot of teasing about the Israeli army. "And why not the American army?" she shot at him, "We don't have any weapons that you don't have too."

He laughed. For the first time since they met so many hours ago, she saw him laugh. His laughter seemed strange to her, wolfish.

"Why are you laughing?"

"Because this sounds like a conversation between generals," he said. "And besides, I like to hear women talk about the army."

She fell silent. Something new, a faint hint of courtship, the feeling of tension familiar from other places, infused his voice when he specified what he liked in women.

She was so embarrassed by the subject of the conversation that she changed it. "Do you think the baby is healthy?"

"There are things we'll be able to see when he wakes up, and there are things that might appear much later on," he said, the tone of his voice now restrained, as if it were a dangerous animal rounded up to be put back in its cage.

"What will we feed him?"

"I imagine his mother must have had a supply of food for him that would last a while. We'll find something." His voice was already as soothing as it had been earlier.

That night, lying on the sofa bed in the baby's room, wearing her underpants and the Indian woman's lovely nightgown, hearing the man in his double bed in the adjoining room, Gila was free to think about her home in Israel, which seemed as imaginary as a previous life viewed from the distance of the month she had spent in Odessa and the new reality that had assailed her that morning. Maybe they already knew about the catastrophe. She tried, in her imagination, to bring a picture of the house closer. Maybe, in the early evening, they'd called the hotel in Frankfurt she was supposed to be staying in and found out that she hadn't arrived. At this very moment, her husband was probably making urgent calls to his brother, a brigadier general; his cousin, the ambassador to Switzerland; and her sister in New Rochelle, speaking in a whisper from his study, trying to keep his concern from the girls for the time being. Maybe the evening news had already reported on the train that had disappeared in an area where a mysterious catastrophe had occurred; maybe they'd listed the names of the Israelis who were on the train, her name among them. At a certain point, they would have to tell her parents. Her mother would get into bed like she had when told of the death of her son in Lebanon, pull the blanket over her head and refuse to eat or drink. How happy they'll be when they find out she was one of the survivors! What a welcome she'd get, with flowers and a banner the girls would paint, covered with hearts pierced with arrows!

The baby suddenly began crying and, thrust from the joys of the future to the nightmare of the present, she got up and groped her way to him in the dark. The touch of her hands or her smell, which were new to him, caused him to cry harder when she picked him up carefully, took him into her bed, held him close, and put into his mouth the nipple of the bottle she had prepared earlier according to the instructions on the box. And she said to the man who appeared in the rectangle of the door, "It's okay. This is how I used to calm my girls," and she didn't realize until after he'd gone, that she had mentioned her daughters to him for the first time.

Right then, before she felt the movement deep inside her, as if her body alone had recognized it first, she reached down as she had when she was pregnant, and with her fingers spread, she would draw circles, soothing the fetus that was moving toward the wall of her womb. She thought she felt a movement in her belly, and suddenly, a small limb bulged from her body like a sharp fin sent to take a quick look around and then withdraw immediately. She continued to move her hand, searching for the limb that was teasing her, scorning her efforts, urging her groping fingers in one direction, disappearing into her body in another. So she lay there in the dark, her heart pounding, and pressed the unknown baby to her body, one hand holding the bottle, the other lying in wait at the bottom of her stomach.

On the day after the catastrophe, when they went back to the train station, about an hour's walk from the inn, they met the nun who looked like a girl, and the sickly, bad-tempered man she was tending to. On the previous day, they had been too worn out to look around the station office and storeroom. As soon as they'd discovered that the phone line was dead, they had turned and walked in the direction indicated by the large sign advertising, in pictographs, a place to sleep and eat: a bed and an "X" formed by a knife and fork. On their way back to the station, they came upon a group of bronze statues: a flock of sheep, some of them pushed up against each other and some of them standing alone, and at the head of the flock, a shepherd with an army backpack slung over his shoulder. They didn't wonder what a piece of art was doing in that remote place. They knew that ten hours earlier, the man and his flock had been living creatures and now they were frozen in time in the smoky expanse. Gila stood motionless and let her eyes register the incredible sight, and she discovered that the sights she'd seen on the previous day had blunted her sense of amazement. He touched her arm and they continued walking, their eyes growing more accustomed to a new visual language.

They found the cashier sitting in his booth, squashed against the window, his eyes gaping. The woman on the bench was also sitting as she had been the day before, her face sunk into the fur of her coat, clutching her travel case to her chest the way a mother clutches her baby. Standing up, leaning against the wall as if he'd fallen asleep on duty was a railroad employee wearing an elegant uniform covered with buttons and buttonholes. A nun suddenly appeared at the door to the office looking like a child dressed up as a nun. Agitated, she hurried over to them, sentences in Italian pouring out of her mouth. She grabbed Gila's hand and pulled her inside the office, where an old man sat shrunken in a chair. He looked at them and cursed in German, and to the man's question, he replied that he spoke English, and promptly began cursing in that language.

At the beginning of the third year, when she'd stopped dreaming about her girls, Gila dreamed that the rusted cars had been removed from the tracks and a sparkling, new train was waiting in the station, all its doors open invitingly, its flickering lights signaling that it was about to move. By then, she was sleeping in the man's bed, and she awoke with a start. Once, she'd managed to slip out of the bed without waking him and left the house before dawn. She rode there on her bicycle, a part of her going over and over the news that the world had returned to its former state, a part of her already afraid of the moment she would part from the man. At the station, the woman stroking her tattered bag and the cashier's skeleton bent over, counting its treasures, were still there. On the train, two skeletons had already begun to disintegrate. The passionate girl was almost completely bald; the nose of the man who had hidden his genitals had fallen off. Gila stood at the door, opposite the skeletons, and was almost relieved: and if she did manage to leave the man, who knows what she would find at home when the trains were back in operation again. Maybe the Arabs, the former owners, had come back to reclaim the house with its turquoise shutters and open balconies where she had lived since her marriage. Seventeen years ago, her husband had carried her over the threshold as if she were a baby, and five years after that, he carried their two baby girls into the house in the same way. Maybe the house was deserted and the turquoise shutters had rotted and her beloved family was sitting motionless like the train people. Yet here, in the haze, life was beginning to stabilize: within a ten-minute walk from the inn, they'd discovered a treasure of flints, and two days ago, they'd found another well. The tree in front of the door had begun to bear sweet, fig-like fruit, and the boy had succeeded in writing another three letters in Hebrew in a handwriting similar to the one that had filled her daughters' first-grade notebooks. On her way back to the inn, like someone who had been in a coma and had regained consciousness, she scolded herself: the house in Jerusalem was still standing and her dear ones were alive and healthy and very worried about her.

Several months after the catastrophe, at night, panting into his neck after making love so passionate that it never ceased to surprise her, she would say to herself: this is real life. This is real life with the distinct feeling of a new kind of happiness, lived on the edge, as it sometimes is in childhood, with the intriguing sense of danger and the thrilling pulse of life that had been absent from her former life, the sort that stirs people to climb mountains of ice and race cars across the desert like a storm. But in the morning, those trembling moments were forgotten and she'd again ask him when the trains would start operating.

At the time, she regretted having taken the nun and the sick man to the inn. The nun secluded herself in her chosen room, rarely coming out and rarely eating, but the sick man, aggressive and quick to shout, would seek her out instead, lie in wait for her, taunt her. Later he would taunt the boy, too. He would draw her into conversations in which she found herself helpless, impelled to ask questions she hadn't intended to ask, giving answers she hadn't intended to give, as if she'd lost control over what she said; later on, he'd do the same with the boy.

"Will you miss me when they find us?" he asked her on one of the first days.

"I don't think so." She took the opportunity for revenge.

"But we'll never know!" The roaring laugh exposed his dark palate. "You'll never have the chance not to miss me!" He slapped his knees, "You know why?"

"Why?" Once again, she felt that helplessness of having fallen into an invisible trap.

"Because no one will ever rescue us. We'll be stuck here together."

"Till when?" the trap snapped shut around her.

"Till we slaughter each other." He threw his head back with the shrill laugh of an asthmatic.

"You'll slaughter each other" was also one of the things the Pole had said too, his eyes riveted on the nun, who had come out of her room for a moment.

One day, on the morning she'd seen orange water spouting from a hidden spring in the pestilent area paint a stripe of wild, orange grass on the scorched earth, Gila decided to tell the man about the limb growing in her belly. But that was the day the Pole came riding to the inn on a new bicycle, clutching a huge sack in his arms. Muscular and energetic, bubbling over with ideas and speaking broken, but understandable English, the Pole infused her with sudden hope: here was the man who would put things back the way they had been.

He'd learned English, he said reluctantly, from his dealings with tourists. On the nature of those dealings he refused to elabo-

rate, as if there was still a danger he'd be extradited to the authorities, but she guessed: speculating with foreign currency, maybe
pimping prostitutes.

They were happy to see him, gave him food and sat down to listen to him. This was their first encounter with an English speaker
who could explain to them where they were and describe what was
happening in the surrounding villages. He'd been on the road for
months, he said, going from village to village on his way to his
own village to see what had become of his family. His home was
five hundred kilometers from there. He'd covered most of the way
on foot. He'd found the bicycle at the train station and he already
knew, to his regret, that he would have to leave it behind because
of the poor condition of the roads. Meanwhile, he'd passed through
ten villages.

He got up suddenly, grabbed the sack he'd brought with him,
spread its contents on the floor and showed them a priest's robe,
statuettes of Jesus and his mother, bouquets of flowers made of
painted clay, boxes of incense, candlesticks—objects he'd found in
ruined churches.

Gila wanted to know the name of the inn and pointed to the
sign outside.

"A Good Place for the Night," the Pole said. "A very strange
name." He pointed toward the pestilent area and told them that
near a distant train station, he'd happened upon an inn called
Katarina. He'd stayed there until he'd finished the supply of food.

The man wanted to know the condition of the villages he'd
passed through, and the Pole used hand movements in place of the
words that did not exist in his vocabulary to describe what he'd
seen: one village was sunk in mud up to the roofs of the houses; in
other villages, most of the houses, made of wood, had been razed
down to their foundations; in three villages, even the church,
which was made of stone, had collapsed; in the fields and houses,
he found only dead people. On the second day after the catastrophe, he'd heard a baby crying but he couldn't get to it, and then
the crying stopped, and once he saw a young girl, who ran away
from him and disappeared among the ruins.

"No more," he spread his hands to the sides as if to encompass all the horizons, "No more people in the world."

"And animals?" the man asked.

"Animals there are." The Pole counted on his fingers: horses, dogs, cats, mice. All hungry, all dangerous.

"Where exactly are we?" the man asked.

"In Poland, near the Austrian border."

"But the people we met don't speak Polish," the man said.

"Around here, they speak a different language. The people from the village speak—"

In the middle of the sentence, the Pole froze. The nun had come out of her room and walked through the hallway on her way to the sick man's room.

"There is a nun here?" He rubbed his eyes.

"Yes."

"How many are you?"

"Five."

"And there are more women?"

"No. Only a sick man and a baby."

"I must go to my family," the Pole said, as if he were giving up the chance of a better life for the sake of his family.

They told him they hoped he would find his village still standing and his family alive, supplied him with edible leaves, a bottle of water, a jar of jam from the pantry, and they accompanied him to the path. Outside, the Pole tied the sack, his eyes roving constantly from window to window searching for the nun, and then he mounted his bicycle and rode off, waving to them until he disappeared.

The first few days, which turned into the first few weeks, Gila was still expecting to hear the sound of a car or a motorcycle: a representative of the local authorities come to inform them that the train was running again; a representative of the UN sent to the area of the catastrophe who might perhaps bring some sign that all was well at home. But in the meantime, life began to take on the form of a routine. She stayed at home to watch the baby; washed clothes in the river, a five-minute walk from the inn, whose water

was not good for drinking; sifted through the things they'd
brought from the train; boiled leaves and roots the man brought
and then checked in a laboratory of sorts he'd set up in the kitchen.
The man came back from his wanderings every evening like a man
returning to his home in the suburbs to tell his family about his
day in the city.

Despite the family pattern that was taking shape, throughout
the first few months, Gila and the man kept their previous lives to
themselves. She knew he was a chemist, married to a musician, a
harpist, and the father of a son who was also planning to be a musician; he knew that she illustrated children's books, that she was the
mother of twelve-year-old twin girls, married to a businessman.
She knew he had gone to Odessa to attend an international conference on ecology; he knew she had gone there to copy illustrations
from an ancient book of legends kept in a museum.

The horror outside bound them together; within the cramped
togetherness, they maintained their independence. He put his
shirts and pants on the pile of her clothes, which was separate from
the pile of cloth diapers cut from sheets, but his underwear and
socks he washed himself, as if he were drawing a boundary line.

Around the time the boy started to smile, Gila was once again
seized by restlessness. For a few days now, she'd seen the funnel
lower like a plane in an air force flyover, dipping and raising its
nose, then mockingly disappearing in a climb, sending out unclear,
anxiety-provoking signals.

One evening, before the nun and the sick man came down from
their rooms, as she was eating a tasty new dish and the child was
jabbering to himself in his cradle (which had probably been a gift
to celebrate his birth from a relative he would never know), she
suddenly asked the man, "Is it possible that the world's been
destroyed? That we're the last people left?" And she herself was
shocked at the question.

The man raised inquisitive eyes from the calendar he was making on a wooden tablet, as if he were assessing her ability to face
the truth. But even before he replied, she understood—for the
first time since she came out of the smoking car—that she might

never again see her daughters or her husband or her mother or her childhood friends or the other people who had populated her life, from the woman who cleaned the stairwells to the elderly lady with the girlish braid who sold her flowers on the street corner every Friday, and for the first time, she was struck with the profound awareness that her girls and her husband and all the other people in her life probably no longer existed, and she burst into tears, immediately smothered them with her hands, and lowered her head to her knees, her hands still covering her eyes. A picture flashed through her mind of her daughters standing shoulder to shoulder, waiting to be photographed, then switched rapidly into a picture of the girls sitting opposite each other at the dining room table, illustrating the invitations to their bat mitzvah party.

Feeling the man's warm hand sending currents of calmness along her back, she straightened up, and even though she knew that her eyelids tended to swell and redden when she cried, making her face ugly, she raised her head.

"It's because of my daughters."

"I can imagine," he said.

"I have no idea how this will sound to you," she dared to say, completely vulnerable, "but I'm so glad you were in the smoking car."

"It's mutual," he said.

And she thought that this was probably the new, flexible vocabulary that adapted itself to the time and the place and although what they'd said entailed no commitment, it nonetheless signaled a potential alliance.

"So what does it mean—the world has been destroyed?"—she repeated the incredible words—"That no one is looking for us, that there is no place to go back to, that we'll stay here forever without electricity, without water..." Her voice emerged in a childish singsong, an intonation appropriate to the words, "without home, or books, or paintings..."

He suddenly hugged her tightly, pulling her out of her chair and pressing her to him, burying her head in his chest, shielding her like a parent protecting his child from all the dangers lying in wait for her, dangers she cannot imagine, as if he were trying to compensate her for the things she would not have—the loss of which was only now beginning to seep into her awareness—a list of things that she had only just begun to enumerate and that would grow longer. She sank into the consoling embrace, trying to subdue her renewed sobbing—about the electricity and the water and the terror of the funnel of air and the fact that she would probably never know the fate of her daughters.

Suddenly she felt his hand resting inquiringly on her stomach, and she understood immediately that this was not the touch of a lover, but the pressure of a doctor's hand feeling some worrying symptoms in the body of a patient, and like an obedient patient, she let him lift her blouse and run his expert hand, pleasant to the touch, over her belly. The tips of his fingers felt the edge of the limb slightly above her navel, and in the momentary battle between the lump in her belly and his fingers searching for it from outside, she felt a digging movement as the limb flipped over and slipped away into the depths of her stomach like an agile diver.

She expected him to recoil from her, from her strange body in which growths were sprouting, but he did not pull his hand away, he simply held it there as if to soothe the troubled spot and said, "I have two of them."

Without a word spoken, she went to his bed that night and found him waiting. As she approached in the darkness, he lifted the blanket over the place he had made for her, and when she slipped in next to him, she was immediately trapped in his embrace, her face close to his. She stopped breathing, waiting for the first movement that would dictate the movements to follow, but he remained quiet and tensed, locking her in his embrace and still waiting. She reached up to his face, trying to learn the features she knew by sight but not by touch, which was strange and new, a treasure of surprises, and she ran her fingertips over his chin, stubbly because of the blunted razor; over his jaws, his cheeks, his eyes, which closed under her touch; over the side of his nose, his lips, which opened like a trap in the darkness and caught her thumb in his teeth. She drew back in alarm and he, as if his plan had succeeded, laughed gently and reached down to the backs of her thighs and raised her nightgown over her shoulders, her arms and her hair pouring out of the neck opening. Then he bent over and pulled her under him, and they both stopped for a moment, his stomach lying against hers, before he began to move. The memory of the limbs wandering about in their bodies flickered through her mind and though she pushed it away immediately, it left behind a faint, persistent fear. Her movements became suffused with despair when, from beneath him, as if she were verifying their existence, she moved her caressing fingers over each part of his body: his nape, his shoulders, the long back, the line of his spine swallowed up by the rise of his buttocks, the muscles of his thigh down to the back of his knee at the farthest reach of her fingertips, all of which swayed together until the movement of their bodies took on a life of its own, absorbing currents from the ground that turned it into a timeless rocking, a reminder of the soothing rocking of an earlier life, until the sweeping, protracted moment of climax that sent ripples to the edges of the body, subduing the storm, also calming the untouched place where the quivering source dwelled, and she wondered as she always did about the mysterious riddle of the body's ability to forget and its ability to remember. And within that remembering—like everything that had happened from the moment she'd walked out of the smoking car—the echo of distant sensations rose inside her, reminiscent of the maelstrom that had begun in her body when the man entered her, and she fell backward like someone collapsing into an abyss, knowing that his body too had memories of other places that were stirring now and filling him with longing, knowing too that as long as there was the promise of this moment, always surprising in its generosity, it would be possible to bear the horror outside that bed.

Many days passed and their life was channeled into a routine, somewhat reminiscent of the routine of the life she had left in the previous world, and yet, it did not resemble it at all.

Sometimes she heard distant voices that aroused a faint memory of a house bordered by pitango bushes, a guava tree that bore so much fruit in the spring that its heavy fragrance spread to the inner rooms, and an almond tree at the edge of the garden that dotted the earth with its fallen fruit; of a little girl building a Lego tower in her room, the walls covered with pictures of parents and two little girls, a host of parents and girls, and in another room, another little girl seen from the back, giving milk to a cat, and a man sitting in his room leafing through his papers. Sometimes, the images vanished suddenly, like in a magic show, and sometimes the picture became so clear that she could dive inside it and see up close the fabric of the girl's blouse, the cat's whiskers twitching in the milk. The reincarnation of her previous life would alternately awaken in her and then become dormant. Sometimes a familiar smell would arouse it, sometimes a touch. Sometimes it was aroused by the light of dusk that would appear at a random moment, a faint, expectant light that even in her former life had stirred in her a mysterious longing for something unclear, a feeling of certainty that she had missed out on something, and she felt burdened by an oppressive helplessness. If only she knew what that feeling referred to, she would rally and act to change it, but her inaction and the knowledge of missed opportunity saddened her so deeply that she cried now, as she had then.

At the beginning of the second year, turbid water fell from the sky day and night, and Gila was filled with restlessness. Now that they had a roof over their heads, a constant supply of food, a clear picture of the near future, and her feelings for the man were growing stronger, nightmares assailed her. She woke at night in a bloodbath, her two girls had drowned right before her eyes and she herself, handless, had tried to get them out by pushing and poking at them with her head, then had dived in after them, kicking her feet to raise them up, but they sank into the dark water, and she watched with desperate eyes as their hips, their shoulders, their faces, the ribbons in their long hair vanished. Dripping blood, she went into her bedroom and saw the large light fixture fall from the ceiling onto her husband sleeping in the double bed, the copper prong of the fixture directed at his head like a spear, and to the sound of bones being crushed, she woke with a shriek and found the man leaning over her, brushing her hair away from her face, whispering, "Sshh..." the way she once had whispered to her daughters.

"Don't you dream about them?" she dared to ask him one peaceful night.

"I don't have to dream; I think about them all the time."

"All the time?" she asked, almost insulted.

"Yes. And I know that I'll never see them again. I hope that if they survived, they'll find good people the way I found you."

Astonished, she rebelled, refusing to accept his brand of mourning, and she kept having nightmares filled with feelings of rage and helplessness for many more days. But in the end, she surrendered, and a short while before the Pole returned, she could already think of the man as if he were her husband, even though the two were different in appearance and character, in their thoughts and actions, in the way they made love to her, and she taught herself to believe that everything she told him, she could have told her husband if he had been beside her. Months later, she'd stopped dreaming about her girls and imagined them part of a large group of children their own age, studying and spending their days as if they were in the camp they used to go to every summer from the time they were eight, and becoming teenagers and young women and finding husbands as much like their father as possible. One day, she noted with astonishment that her nightmares had become rare and all of her strength was invested in worrying about the man's safe return from his searches and about the child wandering in the garden of wooden monsters, exposed to the ravenous funnel of air. She was amazed at how old forces continued to operate like a well-oiled machine forever, and how the senses were now turned toward new people, remembering their old movements, like ancient springs forging their way along a map of channels that had altered, struggling in the depths of the earth, bearing the memory of that earlier flow, directing it toward a place that had suddenly changed. And how, after a period of paralysis when certain functions of the body had stopped, they awaken like a tree sprouting buds and continue along their path, blind to what is going on outside the shell of the body, assailed by stirrings of desire as often as in the past, causing people to grope their way to each other to find refuge, shelter, and repose; to seek affection and grace in a child, the heart opening to him when he smiled or learned something new; taking pleasure in the warmth that rose at the sight of the nun, in the sweet friendship.

In the midst of this newly forming serenity, the Pole came back long after he had left, waving his arms in the distance like a voyager returning home, and brought turmoil with him. His wild eyes in constant search of the nun, his hands flapping every which way, he told them about the destruction he'd found in his village. In the direction of the sunrise, on the ridge, several buildings were still standing, probably a military base, strewn with rifles and equipment and soldiers' uniforms, but everything else was in ruins. The village was located high on the mountain—he waved his hand upward—chasms and a valley below. In the place where the church used to stand only blackened stones remained. And everything was shrouded in fog. He hadn't met another living soul on the road, only hungry animals. He'd stopped in other villages on his way back. In one of them, he'd found an undamaged house, but he didn't take anything from it, "Except for this," he said and pulled an antique ring inlaid with stones from his pocket and put it on the table in front of Gila, then returned his hand to his pocket, took out a plainer ring and put it down next to the first, "And this is for the other woman."

The church—he continued speaking as if he hadn't noticed that his gifts were not received with thank-you's—the church had collapsed and the wind had blown everything away, leaving only the foundation stones. His house and his brothers' houses had been swept away, trees had been uprooted, even corpses of people and animals had been carried off. He'd seen some of the dead lying on the mountain slope, unidentifiable. Those, he'd buried. The bodies that had been swept into the chasm, he was unable to reach.

Silence fell after the Pole stopped speaking, as tired as if he'd just made the journey again. Even the sick man didn't snigger. Then the Pole asked, his eyes blazing, whether anyone had come to the inn in his absence. The man told him about the old woman who'd been tossed out onto their doorstep and asked if the funnel of air had also reached the distant villages. The light in the Pole's eyes died when he heard the reply. Several times, he said, he'd seen the funnel. Once, it had almost thrown him into the abyss; another time, it almost snatched him up, but he flattened himself on the ground and held onto rocks; and three times he'd seen it from far, twice completely empty and once sucking up a pretty, live girl, he said, fixing mesmerized eyes on the nun, who pressed her shoulders closer together, shrinking under his gaze.

The nun refused to touch the ring the Pole had put on the table in front of her. The next day, he blocked her way on the stairs and tried to kiss her, but her shouts summoned Gila, who came running and managed to push him down the steps.

Frightened that the Pole might attack her, too, Gila begged the man to send him away, but the man claimed that the Pole had apologized to the nun and that they really needed the help of another man. And in fact, the intrepid Pole, with his highly developed senses and knowledge of the secrets of the place, would sometimes discover treasures, and in the end, his presence in the room he chose for himself, next to the child's room, was accepted as permanent. Again and again, he'd offer the ring to the nun, which she refused, and because of that, or perhaps despite it, he would lie in wait for her, trap her in the pantry, where one day, he managed to rip her dress, and one night, he sneaked into her room and stroked her breast as she slept. The nun was terrified of him. For days after that night, she trailed after Gila like her shadow, barricaded the door to her room with heavy furniture, prayed out loud, murmuring the name Mary over and over again, and sought the nearness of the child, who would soon be three, sitting beside him as he studied Hebrew, writing square words on pieces of flat leaves that were as strong as cloth with a pipe stuffed with the peel of a black fruit, as hard as lead.

On clear mornings, the two men would go out together, and whatever they brought back was received with cries of joy: wild chickens, edible fruit, a kitten they gave to the child as a gift that made him glow with happiness. Those days brought with them an

awakening of new life, and Gila discovered in herself hidden
desires she hadn't known before. They further helped to delineate
the borders of her new world, and just as, in the past, she used to
long for new clothes she saw in shop windows, she now longed for
a hat she'd seen in the passenger car of the train lying in the aisle
among the theatrical clothes strewn there.

One day, a golden-tailed bird appeared and built a nest in one
of the trees, and a few days later, two more birds arrived, one white
with a crown that resembled a bridal veil and the other covered
with blue spots. On mornings when there were wind storms, Gila
stayed under the covers beside the man, luxuriating in the ordinariness and the tranquility of the birds' chirping, and she would feel
her stomach and find the limb that had sprouted overnight, then
shift her hand to the man's stomach and hear him say, "It's still
there." Sometimes the child would squeeze in between them, and
the three of them would lie together in a tangle of arms and legs.
One day, the Pole succeeded in igniting a large flame by rubbing
two bits of metal together, and they immediately replaced the rare
flints, which required expertise to kindle. When the wild wheat
ripened, they refrained from touching it because it reminded the
man of a poisonous plant, but the Pole explained that it was edible and they went out into the fields the way people did in Biblical
times, and Gila had a memory from her previous life, the story of
Ruth and Naomi and a play in her elementary school in which she
played the part of Ruth for which her cousin had lent her an
expensive white nightgown she'd bought in Paris. That memory,
like so many others, no longer caused her severe pain or longing,
but merely tugged gently at her heart, as if she'd received regards
from a distant lover. And there was a joyous day when the man
found a bush whose leaves were excellent for making cigarettes.
He kept the process a secret, but allotted a generous number of
cigarettes to the others, and in the evening, they sat together and
smoked, all except the nun, filling the air with yellowish smoke
that smelled as sharp as eucalyptus. And one day, Gila and the nun
walked as far as the strange trees at the edge of the plain, and saw
that they had turquoise orbs, like amulets against the evil eye,

hanging from the tips of their branches, and they found wild berries. The nun taught Gila a children's song in Italian about children picking wild berries. The whole way they spoke in the new language they had created, a mixture of English and Italian, and before they reached home, the nun had gotten Gila to swear twice that she would protect her from the Pole.

When the boy turned three, the sick man's condition worsened. Now it was difficult for him to climb the stairs, so they emptied out the office for him and he slept there. The nun brought a tub of water there every morning and helped him wash and dress, as devoted as a daughter. The sick man spent most days sitting and looking at the back garden. On cold days, he looked out at it from inside the house, and during warmer hours, he sat in the garden with his eyes closed or else he stared at the mounds of earth that marked the graves of the dead. Gila would occasionally go out and sit down beside him, fearing conversation with him, and fascinated by it. And he, aware of this, openly amused himself with her.

"What do you look at all the time?" she asked.

"The question is not what we look at, but what we see. You, for example, look but you don't see."

She knew he was talking about the man, whom both of them had once seen staring at the nun.

"What do you see?" She would not allow him to drag her where he wanted.

"The question is not what I see, but whether what I see actually exists."

"And how can we know?" She was still thinking about those looks.

"We can't. Kant asked whether our consciousness has the tools to decipher the reality outside of us. And what, in your opinion, did he think?"

"What?"

"That we don't!" He celebrated his victory over her lack of knowledge. "But Heidegger, yes, Heidegger thought that the question was irrelevant, that we are inside reality, we know it. Oh, Heidegger, I would love to know what he'd say about the reality

here." He closed his eyes and cut himself off from Gila with deliberate cruelty, leaving her determined not to think about the man
looking at the nun.

Later on, as if the Pole had infected everyone with his own delir-
ium, came a time that was as feverish and overwrought, as strident
and unpredictable as adolescence. Something in the air signaled
calamity, and even the child felt it, never leaving the woman's side
throughout that time. The Pole tried again to attack the nun, and
she managed to escape to Gila's room. The old man, overtaken by
rage, destroyed the fence in the back garden before he calmed
down. The man, Gila knew without his saying a word about it,
thought constantly about the woman who played the harp and
about the son who was planning to be a musician. Restlessness permeated the air, as if the era of unexpected disasters had passed and
dozens of signs were heralding the arrival of the next disaster.

During one of their nocturnal conversations, her head on his
shoulder and her eyes on the moon that linked the worlds of time,
the man suggested setting up a place for prayer in one of the empty
rooms because it was now — after they had a place to sleep and bread
to eat and they knew of the treasures and traps the world around
them held — now that they might begin to ask themselves the questions the ancients had asked after natural disasters had occurred,
about good and evil, about crime and punishment, and it seemed
right to prepare a place where they could draw strength from God.

"But you don't believe in God," she said in astonishment. "And
besides, what kind of God could we create that would be good for
me and for the nun, too?"

"As a nonbeliever, it's clear to me what isn't clear to believers:
that they all believe in the same thing. But we won't make a rev-
olution, we'll split Him up. We have at least two Catholics and
one Jew, and the child's parents were probably Buddhists."

She chuckled in the darkness, "Look, you've created a new
religion."

The next day, the two women emptied out the small room with
tiny windows, took down many of the paintings from the walls of
the house and hung them in the room as crowded together as if

they were stamps in an album, next to each other and above each other, wall to wall and floor to the ceiling. They put small tables in the corners and assigned a different religion to each. The nun, radiating an aura of light, put a picture of Jesus and the small wooden cross the boy had made for her on one of the tables and decorated it with flowers and leaves. Gila took off the chain and Star of David she had bought for herself on Rosh Hashana and put it on the table across from the Christian corner. The child put on his table one of the cars from his toy train, which had once belonged to a child who himself had been a passenger on a train. The old man, ridiculing the entire idea, put on the fourth table an empty pillbox and a cane that he hadn't used in months, and the Pole put the ring the nun had refused to accept beside them. Then chairs were brought to the room, and the child dragged them this way and that to form a circle.

After supper, everyone went up to the prayer room. Gila was excited by the smell of the boiled apple leaves and the special tranquility that reminded her of the synagogue on Rosh Hashana eve, permeated with holiness and splendor and the fear of God, who was looking into people's souls. And that spirit, she imagined, had wandered from the synagogue on the shores of the Mediterranean Sea to the inn whose owners had given it its name in a moment of prophetic inspiration, and the spirit pervaded the room with its two small windows, enveloping the random, everyday objects as if they were holy vessels. Gila looked at the cane and remembered the watercolor that had hung next to the blackboard in her first-grade classroom: a group of people and a flock of sheep led by Abraham, his expression determined, walking toward the Promised Land, and the walking stick in his hand was the cane lying on the table in front of her.

The nun began praying in a hushed voice. They joined her until she whispered "Hallelujah," to which they responded like a practiced, many-voiced choir, and all the while a splintered, striped light filtered in through the small windows, softening their features. Gila looked at the Pole, wondering if he was sorry for what he'd done to the nun, then shifted her gaze to the man and saw that he was looking at her. A flood of feelings rose in her, and for some reason, she recalled the excitement that had made her knees weak on the day of her bat-mitzvah, and she reached out to put her hand in his, which she found waiting and welcoming.

The old man watched them from the side, his malicious gaze fixed on their joined hands. For a moment, she caught his glance and he did not hide from her the laughter in his eyes.

"Why did you come to the room yesterday?" she asked him the next day.

"I couldn't pass up the entertainment."

"So you came to laugh at us?"

"I like to watch people. I'm interested in their need to look for a reason for something that has no reason."

"So what is all this," she waved her hand around at the evidence that stretched as far as the eye could see, "Isn't there a reason for it?"

"That is the external manifestation, not the reason."

"What's the reason?"

"No one knows, not even a scientist who studies it for a million years."

"But there has to be reason!" She fought for the last remaining bit of logic.

"No."

"So what is it the result of?" she persisted.

"A whim."

"Whose whim?"

"That's the whole point: no one's whim."

Once again, she was annoyed after the conversation with him, but she could see clearly that something had changed in the group from the minute they'd begun praying, joining them to each other with the force of destiny, as she had been joined to the man in that miraculous moment she'd met him on the train of the dead. The man, like someone with a detailed plan who bases his actions on intelligent logic, said later, "The time has come to start thinking about the future."

"What do you mean, the future?" she asked, remembering how, in another world, she had been proposed to.

"I mean the next generation."

She looked at him in surprise. She had mentioned her infertility problems to him many times and had told him about the many years of treatment she had endured before she became pregnant with the twins. "And who will give birth to it?"

"Not you," he said as if it were a promise.

"But she's a nun!" she said, horrified.

"She's the only one who can do it. She'll have to understand."

"And who will the father be?"

"Whoever she chooses."

She needed a long minute to digest this new situation, and also to absorb the fact that he had made his plan secretly, without including her, and the seed of suspicion planted in her by the sick man began to sprout.

"And if she chooses you?"

"Then it'll be me," he said like a soldier volunteering for a mission.

"Have a good time," she said, anger rising in her at his plot, his pretense. "And who's going to tell her about this interesting plan?"

"You, of course."

"Not me, and not of course," she said, revealing how offended she was.

But the idea insinuated itself into her until it gained a foothold and would not let go, and the thing she was supposed to be fighting ambushed her, and against her own wishes, Gila set out to fight a new war—to convince the nun to have a child—a war that was lost before it began, where her victory would also be her downfall, where she might lose more than she possessed. But she didn't give in to logic, and in a short time, she had thrown herself into her mission as if she were obsessed. Again and again, the image of a baby girl flashed through her mind, the image of her daughters when they were babies, a baby that was crawling on all fours around the furniture in the room, holding onto the back of the armchair and rising up onto her feet, rocking in her cradle, sleeping between her and the man in their bed; sleeping between the nun and the man in the very same bed, and Gila was shocked at the sight.

On one of their fruit-gathering walks, after scrutinizing her constantly from every angle, Gila asked the nun if she liked babies, and the young woman nodded happily. Gila asked if she wanted a baby of her own, and the nun looked at her inquisitively. Gila pointed wildly at the nun's stomach, and the nun looked at the feverish eyes in front of her, embarrassed and blushing deeply. Gila did not mention the idea again for several days; she let herself calm down, let the possibility sink into the young woman's awareness. One day, while they were preparing a meal in the kitchen, Gila looked at her and, as if the matter had been settled, asked which man she'd choose to make a baby with. The nun gave her a penetrating look, suspecting that her only ally was about to betray her, and Gila, as if the name Judas Iscariot had not passed through her mind, spoke the name of the man as if it were a question. The nun shook her head firmly, her eyes terrified, perhaps recognizing the signs of an evil spirit that had taken possession of the woman who had sworn to protect her, perhaps frightened by the menacing persistence and by what lay beyond the menacing persistence.

But the thought of the nun's pregnancy—sometimes separate from the man—gave Gila no rest, and a few weeks after the idea had first been raised, as if she were thinking logically, she convinced herself that there was no choice: the child was already three years old. In another fifteen years, he'd be ready to be a father himself. Who could guarantee that he'd find a bride then? Now, now was the time to arrange for a wife for him with whom he could continue the next generation.

She schemed for hours about how to convince the nun how imperative the act was, to describe to her in simple words, in her basic Italian, that there was no choice and she had to choose one of the men because she was the only one who could guarantee that life would continue, and there was no doubt that both Jesus and his mother would understand and permit it, because after all, Jesus too was born in an unusual way. Over and over again, with growing excitement, she told the man of her musings and imagined she saw a look of amazement in his eyes. His look, like a mirror, made it clear to her that he had been a part of her life for only a few years, and that she would never know whether it was his desire for the nun that had spawned the idea. She pursued the relentlessly intractable young woman the whole month, kept the child away from her, punished her with prolonged silences, and did not soften even when she heard the sounds of weeping coming in from the nun's room at night. Every morning, in a voice that grew colder and colder, she asked again which man she would choose, and the nun again burst into tears that made Gila feel relief and also an unfamiliar wrath.

She would never remember who came up with the idea of giving her to the Pole. During moments of self-awareness or when she was on the verge of sleep and less able to keep secrets, she suspected that the idea had been born in her own brain, imagined that she remembered some hesitation on the part of the man, but she wouldn't allow the memory to come. She did remember—but perhaps it was only after he brought up the idea and she objected— that the man had suggested waiting until the nun matured and maternal feelings developed naturally in her, and maybe, in the meantime, a man would appear who didn't frighten her; or maybe another young woman would come in another few years who could be the child's bride. Gila remembered herself becoming furious— but perhaps that was only after he had planted the idea in her brain —no man the nun might want, would suddenly appear, she had said heatedly. The girls who survived after the cataclysm had probably been devoured by animals or sucked up into the funnel of air. Finally, she told him angrily of her suspicion that he hoped the nun would choose him in the end, and that he wasn't trying to protect the young woman, but to keep her from the Pole. Several weeks afterward, he grew tired and surrendered to the madness that had gripped her and he agreed to her idea, not so he could implement his plan but to put an end to her suspicions. But she took as a good sign the fact that he agreed on that particular day, because that very morning, it had occurred to her that the funnel of air hadn't been seen for quite a while. On the calendar they had marked, she counted forty days. A good rain was falling outside, the sign of a blessing, not a lashing rain and not a rain that uprooted bushes, but one that fell generously and quietly, fertilizing the earth.

Gila also began to prepare the Pole with hints, with movements he was quick to grasp, with a quick, conspiratorial smile he understood well, and inflamed by the fire burning in her, the passion that had already begun to wane in him ignited into a surprising blaze. One night, as if by chance, after she had quieted the child and the sick man with a fruit extract that would keep them asleep for half a day, she and the man went out to the wrought iron bench at the far end of the garden.

The distant slam of a door came first and they fell silent, stunned, the way it sometimes happens when events are expected. The man withdrew into himself and dropped his chin down to his chest, a sign that she was familiar with. Then they both tried unsuccessfully to shut out the sounds that assailed their ears, sounds that seemed to be shattering bone and penetrating veins and poisoning the body from within; spreading over house, the back garden, the garden of monsters, and the pestilent area to beyond the row of trees in the east and beyond the low mountain ridges in the west; echoing to the edges of the horizon: first the shrill, surprised cries of fear, and then the determined attempts to regain composure, the wild, courageous but futile rebellion; then the horrifying, despairing comprehension and the beginning of the body's surrender, the shift to a stream of explaining, scolding, pleading words; and suddenly the sobbing, the screaming that shook the blood vessels, the persistent pounding that sought to break through the imprisoning wall, the continual weeping like a siren, the harsh sounds of scraping like iron combs plowing the walls, the animal groans coming not from her throat but from the depths of her loins, the desperate sobs and then the wailing, slashing shrieks, the choking roars that make the throat swell; then the sudden silence of choked breathing and the submissive, sinking whimpering, feeble grunting, the squeaking of the door to the Pole's room as it opened and closed when he went to his bed.

And then silence prevailed: deep, dark, full of fear and guilt.

They did not go up to their room that night. From the moment they heard the sounds blaring from the house and restrained themselves for the sake of the future, they sat in silence, cut off from one another, looking inward, trying to formulate for themselves their individual stories about what had taken place. Even after the long, mournful sobbing subsided, they did not go to their bed but continued to sit silently until the sun, surprising in its splendor, rose over the heavy treetops and so generously illuminated the wide sky and the fields— made them gleam in the first light—that she suddenly remembered a school trip and the breathtaking sunrise that had turned the Judean Hills pink.

In the morning, wrapped in the sweetness of slumber, silent and sleepy, the child slipped between them, and they made room for him.

"I dreamed that the nun was screaming," the child said.

"In dreams, everyone is always screaming," the man said and wrapped the child's small, bare feet in the edge of his shirt.

Gila stroked his disheveled hair and said, "Look, sweetie. Look at what a beautiful sunrise we have today."